NAUGHTY & NICE

TRACY LORRAINE

Have you been a good girl this year?

Of course you haven't, you opened this smut filled why choose book...

But which twin do you want to take you over his knee...

Or do you want both?

NOELLE

"Are you nearly ready?" Hendrix bellows up the stairs.

We agreed to leave ten minutes ago, but I'm still rushing around my room, throwing things into my small suitcase.

I stayed up late last night reading, something that I'm now regretting.

"Yeah, I'm right there," I lie, stuffing a handful of panties into my bag.

A deep chuckle comes from downstairs.

I've no doubt that he predicted this. My best friend knows me better than to expect me to be organized and ready on time.

I scan my closet, trying to decide what I should take. It's easy, really. We're staying in a log cabin for five days to celebrate the holiday away from all the stresses of real life. All I need is sweatpants, hoodies, my most comfortable underwear, and a whole heap of books.

Heaven.

It's another ten minutes before I'm zipping up my

suitcase and hauling it from the bed. It thumps against the floor and not a second later, Hendrix races up the stairs.

"Done?" he asks, poking his head into my room.

"Yes, we can go now," I laugh as he grabs my luggage and turns his back on me.

"Knew we should have booked for seven days," he mutters flashing a grin over his shoulder.

"Dude, we're like ten minutes behind schedule. We'll make it up on the drive."

Oh man, and is it going to be a drive.

Thirteen hours on the road with my best friend. Honestly, I'm almost as excited about the road trip up to Canada as I am the cabin itself.

The snow... I can't wait for the snow.

"Not with your driving," he quips.

"Good thing you're taking the first leg, isn't it?" I tease, already feeling the stresses of college slipping away.

This break is exactly what we need.

We started at Trinity Royal College three months ago after a childhood of not believing it would be possible for either of us.

Sure, we may have had to swallow a little bit of our pride and accept some help—the biggest of which being the house we currently live in. But Hendrix's big sister Lorelei and her husband wouldn't have it any other way.

We couldn't have achieved any of this without their help. I owe them everything.

A cool breeze whips around me as I step out of the house, but I shake it off. It's got nothing on the place we're heading.

I drop into the passenger seat of Hendrix's Audi, something else that's courtesy of Lorelei, and wait for him to join me.

"How confident are you that you've got everything you need?" he asks the second he drops into the driver's seat.

"Uh…"

"We're leaving," he says with a laugh, starting the engine, ready to floor the gas and speed away.

"Rude," I mutter.

"You've already packed more than you used to own," he points out.

I think it's meant to be a joke, and it is. But also… reminders of our pasts always hurt a little.

It's not that I miss it. I don't. I love my new life at Trinity Royal; it's everything, and more than I thought it would be. It's just… sometimes it can be hard, being the girl from the trailer park and trying to fit into a world that is vastly different from everything we experienced in our early lives.

Life here is… easy. We don't walk around looking over our shoulder. Street corners aren't littered with used needles. There aren't gunshots and shootouts every few days. And the best part… we have actual food in our refrigerator, heat, and electricity. I hope they're things I never get used to and take for granted. I always want to feel this grateful for the life we've fallen into here.

"Yeah," I agree sadly.

"Shit, sorry. I didn't mean—"

"It's cool. It's… true."

"All talk of the past is banned from this trip," Hendrix suddenly announces.

"Sounds perfect." The less I have to think about it, the better. And it's not like my family will call over the holidays to check in on their eldest daughter. As far as they're concerned, I've left their lives and that's it. It hurts, of course it does, but also… it's a relief. It wasn't until they were no longer a part of my life that I understood what a drain they were. I feel like a whole new person now, and I love myself so much more for it.

"Ready?" Hendrix asks with an excited twinkle in his eye.

My best friend is my savior. He was always the one good thing in my life from our hometown. I don't think he understands just how much he's saved me over the years. No matter what happened, he was always there. I hope it's something I never lose.

"So ready. Take me to paradise, baby," I sing happily, images of the cute log cabin we've rented filling my mind.

Hendrix presses his foot to the gas and the car pulls out of the driveway, but we barely move an inch before the back door is yanked open.

"Hey, vacationers. Room for another one?" A familiar voice fills the air and the interior of the car instantly feels smaller.

"The fuck, Wild?" Hendrix barks as he glares at his twin brother in the rearview mirror.

"I thought I was going to miss you," Wilder pants as if he's run all the way here.

"Sadly not," I mutter under my breath, although I ensure it's loud enough for everyone to hear.

He sucks in a breath like he's about to bark out a retort, but Hendrix cuts him off.

"Why are you here, Wilder? You're meant to be heading for the airport."

"Flights were canceled due to the weather."

Silence fills the car.

"So do something else with the team," Hendrix suggests.

"Most of them are going home instead." He doesn't say the words, but they're not necessary. There is no chance of Wilder doing the same. None of us ever want to go back to our hometown to spend the holidays with our parents. It's just not an option. "A couple are staying. But fuck that. Especially when my little brother is heading for a vacation right this second."

"A vacation you weren't invited on," Hendrix points out, stealing the words right from my lips.

"Well, I'm here now, so let's go."

Without instruction from my brain, I spin around and glare at Wilder, but the second our eyes connect and my stomach knots with guilt, I regret the move.

I don't keep secrets from Hendrix. He knows every single thing there is to know about me. Hell, he was even the one I called the day I first got my period. But this…

Fuck. This is one thing that I can't tell my best friend.

Ever.

Wilder's eyes wrinkle as he smirks back at me.

Asshole.

He sits back and pulls the seatbelt around his stupidly big body.

Hendrix and Wilder are identical twins, but in only a few months of training with the Trinity Royal Titans, his already ripped body has only grown, becoming more powerful, and more… sinful.

My cheeks heat and I twist back around, wishing I could extract myself from this situation.

Hendrix can't say no to Wilder. Not that I think he should. Deep down, I know that we can't leave him here to spend the holidays alone. Wilder isn't a bad person, he's just… a lot.

If I thought leaving him here wouldn't mean him being alone, then I might push for it. But with Lori and Kian away, he doesn't have any other options.

"Wilder," Hendrix sighs, predictably coming to the same conclusion that I have.

"It's fine," he says dejectedly.

The click of the seat belt unlocking rips through the air before it rolls back into place.

"I'll go. A couple of the guys are staying. I'm sure they'll have me. Can't cook for shit, though," Wilder mutters, making a show out of shoving the car door back open. "It's not like we have any childhood traditions to uphold or anything."

My heart aches as memories from our former years hit me upside the head once again.

"Get back in." My voice rings out around the car and for a couple of seconds, it's met with nothing but silence.

I don't look back to see Wilder's reaction. I can't.

Whether he's rocking a smug smirk or an expression of disbelief that I've caved, I don't want to know. I'm too busy mourning the loss of what I had hoped the next few days would be like.

I guess our plans really were too good to be true.

"Are you sure?" Hendrix asks in shock.

"We can't leave him here alone. It's the holidays," I say, cringing because he's listening to every word I'm saying.

Why can't I be more cutthroat?

We should leave him behind. This is our vacation. Our plans.

But... he's family.

With or without the colossal mistake I made a few weeks ago, he's still one of the closest people I have in my life, even if it isn't really by choice.

"She's right and you know it, Bro," Wilder says when Hendrix pauses as if he's about to argue.

Wilder's arrogance makes my teeth clench, but I guess it's something I need to get used to, because now we're stuck together for the next seven days.

On two thirteen-hour road trips, there and back, and in a small, remote log cabin.

My stomach flips.

This is a disaster.

"This is going to be so much fun," Wilder says, wrapping his arms around the front seats and sticking his head between them.

His fingers brush my shoulder, and despite the fact I'm wearing a thick hoodie, I can't catch the sharp intake of breath that turns two sets of identical eyes on me.

"Everything okay?" Hendrix asks. There's nothing but concern in his, whereas, when I glance at his twin brother's, all I find is mirth and excitement.

I really should just get out of the car and spend the holiday lost in books. It would be the most sensible thing to do.

But being alone...

No, thank you.

"Yeah," I say, plastering a fake smile on my face—one which I pray my best friend falls for. "I'm just excited to hit the road."

"Same," Hendrix sighs, falling back into his seat. "I am so ready for it."

"You know," Wilder says, also getting comfortable in the back for the first leg of our trip, "when you first told me about your plans, I thought it sounded pretty dull. But I think you're right. This vacation is going to be epic." Unable to stop myself, I glance back and my stomach twists at the smirk playing on his lips. It's full of promises of things I don't want...

2

———

WILDER

I rest my head back and slump lower in the seat.

Hanging out with my twin brother and his bestie in a remote cabin in Canada was not a part of my holiday plans.

I was supposed to be heading toward the ocean for ten days of sun, sex, and relaxation. I wanted to fuck a different girl every night, drink my body weight in alcohol, and sleep until sunset.

No, it's not a very festive way to spend the holidays, but fuck it. It was going to be perfect for me.

I've never been a huge fan of the holidays. They always sucked sweaty balls when we were kids.

I remember watching the commercials of happy families enjoying spending time together as a kid. The decorations, the roaring fires, the gifts...

It was nothing but a tragic reminder of the life we didn't get to live.

Sure, we always had gifts. But only because our big sister ensured there was something for us to open.

It rips me apart inside if I think too hard about what she experienced before we were old enough to return the favor.

I've tried talking to her about it a time or two, but she just shuts it down, telling me it's unnecessary to dwell on those times. I've no idea if she does that to protect herself or me. Or maybe a little of both.

Our childhoods were horrific. I can't really argue with her not wanting to talk about it. If I had my way, I wouldn't even think about it.

Losing myself in thoughts of Christmases gone by, the darkness I try to keep banished to the peripheral threatens.

Just when I don't think I'm going to be able to drag myself back, the song playing through the car changes and a soft female voice floats through my ears.

My skin pricks with goosebumps as I latch onto the words she's singing.

"Mariah Carey, really?" I ask.

"What?" Noelle says, breaking the tune. "It's the holidays. It's like... tradition."

"One I could do without," I mutter, keeping my eyes locked on the back of her head, waiting to see if she's going to risk looking back at me again.

The last time she did, I swear it was almost like getting shot at point blank, the way the chemistry crackled between us.

It takes a couple of seconds, but eventually, she turns.

Her entire body flinches when she finds me waiting for her.

"I get that it's the holidays, but can we cancel all the festive shit?"

Her eyes narrow, anger flickering through her green orbs.

"Just because your vacation has been ruined," my

brother snaps from the driver's seat, "it doesn't mean you need to fuck ours up as well."

Noelle smirks and turns back around, happy that I've been put in my place by my very slightly older brother.

Asshole.

"Then maybe you should have planned something a little more fun. A cabin in the woods... So cliche."

"Would you like me to pull over?" Hendrix threatens. "It's not too late to change your mind and stay home alone."

I roll my eyes hard. "Keep your lace panties on, Bro."

His grip on the wheel tightens and his neck pulsates with tension.

"We're going to have fun together." I lean forward, once again hooking my arms around both of their chairs. "Right?" I ask as I shamelessly graze my knuckles down Noelle's neck.

She reacts to my touch just like she did earlier.

Fire burns through my veins as I remember the last time I had my hands on her.

Halloween.

I didn't even realize it was her... until it was too late.

I should have stopped immediately.

I should have regretted it.

Hell, there are a lot of fucking things that I should have done both that night and after, but here I am instead, taunting her with what we discovered that night.

We've barely seen each other since.

Sure, she's been at my games with Hendrix. She's been at the house when I've swung by for a visit... or to raid their kitchen for food. But she's always made an excuse to disappear to her room.

As far as I can tell, Hendrix hasn't noticed. Or if he has, he hasn't cared enough to question it.

No. He hasn't noticed. Noelle is far too important to

him not to say anything if he thinks something is up with her.

He is usually much more in sync with her than this. She must be putting a hell of an effort into hiding what happened.

Mischief stirs within me.

I might tease them, but something tells me that there's going to be nothing boring about us being on this vacation together.

Noelle doesn't continue with her singing. In fact, she says absolutely nothing as we continue on what feels like an endless road.

"Your snacks are shit," I complain, having eaten my way through the good stuff. "Who brings fruit as a road trip treat? What the—" I gasp when a small, feminine hand reaches into the back of the car, snatching the container of fruit from my grasp.

"As an athlete, you should understand why it's important not to fill your body with crap."

"Road trips don't count," I mutter, rummaging at the bottom of the bag for any lingering candy.

Not finding anything, I fall back into the seat and look out. There is nothing but fields surrounding us.

"Can you pull over? I need to piss."

"We're not stopping yet," Hendrix states.

"Bro," I warn.

"You can wait," he counters.

"Can't."

Noelle mutters something to herself that sounds suspiciously like, 'Give me strength,' before combing her fingers through her auburn hair.

With a groan, Hendrix signals and then pulls off the road at the next opportunity.

I throw the door out and stumble a few feet away, not bothering to hide what I'm doing from passers-by. Who am I to stop them from the thrill of seeing me?

"It's like traveling with a toddler," Noelle complains not quite quietly enough from inside the car.

"Noelle," Hendrix warns, attempting to fight my corner, although if I'm being honest, it's weak at best.

"What? He's your brother, Rix. I get it. On some weird level, I love him too. But ugh... this was not the trip we planned."

I get it too. I just barged in on their cute, non-couple romantic holiday vacation. Neither of them expected to 'babysit' me.

I shake my head as I finish what I'm doing. I don't want to ruin their vacation, but also... I need to have some fucking fun.

If I don't, then...

Fuck.

I have to have something to keep my mind and body active. If I don't, I'll be forced to really think about my life. I'll have to feel... and that is not fucking happening.

There will hot girls where we're going... right?

"I'm pulling over," Noelle says when we're only three hours out from our destination. The sun has set, plunging us into darkness, and a gas station glows ahead.

Both of them have taken a turn at driving now, and I have eaten my way through the snacks they brought with them, plus the ones I picked up at an earlier stop.

"Great. I'm starving," I announce, sitting forward, ready to go and find more food.

Noelle shakes her head. I can't see Hendrix's response, but something tells me that he rolls his eyes.

The second she pulls the car to a stop, I fly out and make a beeline for the store, leaving Hendrix and Noelle to deal with the gas situation. Their vacation. His car. Not my problem.

I walk up and down every aisle, filling a basket with everything and anything that should help to make the final few hours of this trip bearable.

So far, I've had to endure their endless chatter and shitty taste in music. I need something to help get me through.

I'm walking toward the checkout when a familiar figure emerges from the end of the aisle and darts into the bathroom.

Abandoning my goodies, I slip around the corner that's hiding the bathrooms and wait.

I rest back against the wall opposite the ladies' with my foot propped up casually.

With every second that passes, my heart rate picks up and excitement bubbles up in my stomach.

This... this adrenaline shot is what the car journey was missing. The only fun bit was experiencing Noelle's reaction to my touch. But unless I wanted to out her and her lies on day one, I needed to hold back.

The lock disengages and my heart jumps into my throat.

She doesn't look up immediately, and I can't help but smirk in anticipation.

I clear my throat and her gaze lifts.

Her eyes widen in shock as a small gasp escapes from her lips.

"What are you doing?" she hisses, quickly recovering and giving me a hard glare.

"Just making sure you're safe," I say, pushing from the wall and stopping in front of her.

"Totally unnecessary and unneeded," she says through gritted teeth. "Could you please get out of my way?" she demands, staring up at me with nothing but irritation in her eyes.

"Maybe I don't want to," I tease, cocking my head to the side.

She lets out a massive sigh, and I can't help but wonder if she's been holding her breath since I climbed into the car all those hours ago.

"Wilder."

I take a step closer.

"Mmm... I love it when you say my name like that," I whisper, dropping my lips to her ear so only she can hear.

Her entire body tenses as my breath rushes down her neck.

"You need to stop this," she demands, although her voice isn't as strong as I think she'd probably like. It's raspy and full of need.

She remembers...

"I'm not sure you mean that, Rebel."

I can sense her confusion long before I pull back and see it written all over her face.

Her brow is wrinkled and her lips are pursed. She looks cute. The exact opposite of the nickname she didn't know I've given her.

I understand why she's confused. She is the furthest thing possible from a rebel.

She has every reason to be wild. To drown out her past and her issues with outlandish behavior. But she's gone in the opposite direction.

She'd be happier spending her nights in her room

reading a book than being out partying. Or at least, she was until that night not so long ago…

"You're still thinking about it, aren't you?"

She holds her head higher and lifts her chin in defiance. It might work if I didn't know her so well.

She's been a part of my life for years. A part of our little fucked-up family for as long as I can remember.

But that night… I saw her in a whole different light.

"I've no idea what you're talking about," she argues firmly.

Reaching out, I wrap my hand around her hip and tug her forward, eliminating the space between us.

"Wilder," she snaps, attempting to fight me.

But I'm stronger. So much stronger.

"Do you want to know a secret, little rebel?"

"No," she cries a little too loudly. "No," she repeats. "I don't want to know anything."

"Well, that's a real shame, because I'm going to tell you anyway."

Her nostrils flare as she sucks in a deep breath through her nose, although much to my delight, she's no longer fighting to get away.

Leaning closer again, crushing our bodies together, I let my lips brush her ear, loving the way she shudders.

"I can't stop thinking about it."

I finish filling up the car and wander over to an empty picnic bench on a little patch of grass to the side of the store.

It's dark and cold, but I'm not ready to be enclosed in the car again quite yet.

I love driving, always have, and I was excited to embark on this road trip with Noelle. Hell, I am excited to be on this trip with her. But it's not exactly what we had planned.

I love my brother. I do. But... as much as we might look the same, we're very, very different people.

He's... a player in every sense of the word. He's always been the joker, the one who's up for a laugh, who's willing to do something wild just for kicks. He's the one who's always getting into trouble.

He used to skip class to hang out with his friends or hook up with girls, and I was in class soaking up everything I could.

He spends his weekends partying as hard as possible, and I'm at home studying.

We're like chalk and cheese. And as much as I love him, I find his constant need to be busy exhausting.

I'm pretty sure if we went to a decent school, he'd have been diagnosed with ADHD a long time ago. But seeing as we went to arguably one of the shittest schools in the entire country, no one gave a crap. He was labelled as badly behaved, and because he was good at football, everyone gave him a free pass for everything else.

Thankfully, he's also clever, so when it came to exams, despite not doing any work for them—unlike me, who worked my ass off—he passed with flying colors.

It really is a good job I love him.

I sit in the dark, lost in my thoughts and watching cars pass on the road before me as I wait for Wilder and Noelle to emerge from the store.

I'm hardly surprised he's taking forever. He went for more food. I've more than enough experience to know how long that takes. And not just because he can't decide what he wants, but because of the sheer amount of food he consumes. Sure, he's a hell of a lot more active than me, but where the hell he puts it, I don't know. But Noelle was only going to the bathroom; she should have emerged by now.

Wilder has probably collared her to help carry his goodies to the checkout.

Irritation rolls through me. It shouldn't and I feel guilty as hell for it.

Yes, there is a part of me that's thrilled about spending the holiday with family. When Lori first announced that she and Kian were going away this year, I was pretty disappointed. Lori has always been the best thing about Christmas. She's the one who's made it special for the two of us. Sure, we had a few years with Dad that were half decent, but no one ever cared like she did. It's going to be weird celebrating without her this year.

That's why Noelle and I decided to also take a trip. She didn't want to go home, and I certainly have no desire to see if our mom is still alive or not. If I never return to our hometown ever again, it'll be too soon.

I'm done with that place. I just wish the memories would disappear with it.

I'm considering going in search of them when finally, voices hit my ears and two dark figures move toward my car.

"Where the hell have you two been?"

They both pause halfway across the gas station and spin around.

"One of us got locked in the bathroom. Had to be rescued. Don't worry, though, her knight in shining armor was there to save her," Wilder states proudly.

"Of course you were," I mutter, making a beeline for the driver's door.

Noelle took the last leg as planned, so I'm up again for the final part of our road trip.

She pulls open the passenger door and drops in, and just before I get there, Wilder dives in front of me, shouting, "Shotgun," and drops into the driver's seat.

"That's not how shotgun works," I complain.

"Don't care," he says with a shrug before starting the engine and pulling his seatbelt on.

"You're an asshole."

"Just get in the back and relax. You've had plenty of opportunity to touch Noelle up so far; it's not my fault you haven't made the best of it."

My chin drops as I glare daggers at him.

"You fucking touch her and I'll—" My words are cut off when he throws his head back and barks out a laugh.

"You'll what? Fight me?" My lips open and close, but no words escape. "Just get in the back, Rix, and stop being such a pussy. If anyone's getting any action up here, it'll be her sucking my—"

"Don't you dare finish that sentence," Noelle warns before I get a chance.

His suggestion alone makes my blood boil.

"You two are so fucking uptight. You know, getting laid once in a while would do good things for both of you."

Choosing to ignore my jerk of a brother and his bullshit opinions about our lives, I rip the back door open and drop onto the seat.

"Go on then," I mutter once I'm settled.

"I need a snack first. Noelle, can you grab the cookies?"

"I'm not your slave," Noelle hisses.

"No, you're my passenger princess, and you have duties to your prince."

"Give me strength," I mutter as Noelle digs into the bag.

"Thank you," he says smugly as she shoves the bag with the rest of his snacks to the floor.

"Can we go now?" I ask tersely.

"Of course, little brother. Boring log cabin in the middle of nowhere, here we come."

"Holy shit," Noelle squeals when Wilder floors the gas and we fly out onto the road. Thankfully, we don't hit anything. Or not yet at least.

"We'd like to arrive on our boring vacation in one piece," I point out.

"Hey," Noelle argues, "our vacation isn't going to be boring. It's relaxing."

"Same fucking thing," Wilder mutters.

We both ignore him, and Noelle turns the music up loudly enough to drown out his complaining.

The sound of the latest Taylor Swift song fills the car,

and I can't help but smirk. This really is Wilder's version of hell.

Oh well, it was his bright idea to jump into the back of the car with us.

The next three hours of the journey seem to take longer than all the others.

Thankfully, at no point does Wilder even attempt to follow through with his plan of getting Noelle to suck on anything. Well, nothing more than some of the candy that was in his massive snack bag.

Even him suggesting she suck on that sent a shot of jealousy burning through me.

Noelle is... Noelle is my best friend. Always has been, always will be. But also... I'm pretty sure I've been in love with her since long before I knew what the word meant.

She's everything. Literally my perfect woman wrapped up in one tiny, hot package.

As much as I love that she is. I also hate it.

If I ever did anything to ruin our relationship, I would never, ever forgive myself.

It might sound pathetic—I'm sure Wilder would point out that it is—but I'm willing to forgo what I want to ensure our friendship continues. Even if that means one day she meets someone.

It'll hurt. It'll hurt so fucking bad. But a part of her would still be mine.

If I were to do something and lose her...

No.

Fear cuts through me like a knife.

I might have Wilder and Lori in my life. But Noelle...

Fuck. Noelle.

I watch her through the gap in the front seats as she pulls the sun visor down and flips the little mirror open.

She wipes the stray makeup from under her eyes and then coats her lips with her favorite strawberry lip balm.

I don't need to be closer to her to know exactly how that smells. I have it committed to memory.

As if she can sense me watching, she looks up and her eyes catch mine in the small mirror.

I can't see her mouth now, but her eyes tell me that she's smiling.

'You okay?' I mouth.

She gives a simple nod before the GPS speaks up, letting us know that our destination is up ahead.

Despite our current situation and the guy sitting in the driver's seat of my car who is no doubt going to spend the next five days complaining like a petulant toddler, excitement bubbles up.

I've been waiting for this trip for weeks, and nothing Wilder can do is going to ruin it.

"This place is so freaking cute," Noelle says as Wilder pulls the car to a stop out the front of our cabin.

It looks just like the photograph online, which is a relief. Neither of us has a lot of experience with booking vacations, and while I know that I could have asked Lori to help, we wanted to do this ourselves. And I've got to say, I'm impressed with what we've achieved.

"It's small," Wilder complains.

"It's perfect. I hope it's decorated," Noelle exclaims, her voice all light and whimsical. It makes my heart sing hearing her so happy.

We climb out of the car, shivering. While Noelle scrolls through her cell to find the instructions to get inside, I grab our bags from the trunk, leaving Wilder's backpack for him to get himself.

"Ready?" Noelle asks once I join her at the front door.

"Ready," I agree.

She pushes the door open, and the scent of Christmas immediately hits my nose.

"Oh my god," Noelle gasps happily before rushing inside.

I follow her, unable to believe what I'm seeing. The entire place has been decorated like a winter wonderland. It's incredible.

Lights twinkle everywhere. There's even soft Christmas music playing.

We nailed it. Totally fucking nailed it.

"There's mulled wine warming on the stove. Rix, this is incredible," she says excitedly, turning to me with wide, glittering eyes.

Seeing her so happy melts my heart. It's all I've ever wanted for her.

Heavy footsteps out on the front deck clue us into Wilder's arrival—not that we need it.

"What the fuck?" he barks as he steps into the cabin. "It looks like a bunch of elves threw up in here."

"I know. Isn't it awesome," Noelle says, clapping her hands together.

Despite having experienced shitty Christmases to rival ours in the past, somehow, Noelle hasn't lost the excitement for the holidays. She believes in the magic, and I can't lie, it's pretty infectious.

"Err..." Wilder says, watching her as if she's grown a second head. "Is that alcohol?" he asks, changing tack.

"Yep. Mulled wine," Noelle says excitedly before opening and closing the cupboard until she's located the glasses. She pulls three out and then pours a ladleful of wine into each. She passes them out before lowering her nose to hers, breathing it in and letting out a contented sigh.

"Smells gross," Wilder whines before lifting it to his lips and hesitantly taking a sip. "Ew, it tastes it too." Although despite his complaint, it doesn't stop him from swallowing the lot down. "What?" he asks when we both just stare at him blankly. "I need something to get me through the next few days."

"Lovely," Noelle mutters before taking a sip of her wine. Her eyes close as she savors the taste. "Shall we go and check out the bedrooms?" she asks, ignoring Wilder's presence.

She takes off and I can't do anything but follow, and it soon becomes clear that Wilder is just as willing to explore when his footsteps follow behind me.

"Oh my god, look at the size of that bathtub," Noelle says after discovering the bathroom first. "What if it snows? We could lie in that tub and look out over the snow-covered hills."

"Could we?" Wilder asks.

"I," she corrects. "I could. Alone."

"Lame."

She spins around and moves toward the next door.

Just like the rest of the cabin, the master bedroom is a replica of the photos we've seen, only with the addition of more decorations.

Noelle squeals in excitement and rushes inside.

Placing Noelle's small case inside the door, I stand back as she checks it out and then continues to the final door.

But when she throws it open, it's not the second bedroom.

It's a closet.

"But... there aren't any other doors," Noelle exclaims with a frown marring her brow. "We booked a two-bed cabin."

4

NOELLE

"Maybe they gave us the wrong one," Hendrix suggests. "It's probably just a mistake. Call them."

Turning my back on the one and only bedroom, I locate my purse on the kitchen counter and dig my cell out.

The call connects and a voice tells me that the company I booked with is closed for the holidays, but gives me an emergency number.

Holding my hand out for Hendrix's cell, I quickly tap the number in and call that.

I wander off with his cell to my ear, my eyes scanning the cabin.

It's perfect. Everything I could have asked for for a festive few days away with my best friend.

If it were just the two of us, having one bed wouldn't have been an issue. We've slept together many times in the past.

But having Wilder here too...

That changes everything.

My stomach knots with a mixture of regret and guilt as the ringing continues in my ear.

After a minute or so, the inevitable happens, and the call cuts.

"No answer," I confess without looking back.

They're both watching me, the heat of their stares burning into my back.

"It's fine. The bed looked pretty big. Noelle can take the middle, and we'll go either side of her."

"Absolutely not," Hendrix barks. You can take the couch or the floor. They're your only options."

"And you're going to sleep where, exactly?" Wilder asks, wiggling his brows.

"Fuck off, Bro. This isn't even your vacation."

"So you get to sleep with Noelle, get all cozy in that romantic bedroom, and I get to attempt to sleep out here on that?" he mocks, pointing at the couch. It looks pretty comfortable to me, but then I'm not a six-foot-two football player.

"Yep. If you don't like it, you could always…" He throws his hand out, gesturing toward the front door.

"That's not very festive, is it?" Wilder complains before stalking forward and dropping onto the couch that has just been allocated as his bed.

He bounces a couple of times before announcing, "I've slept with worse."

I just manage to catch my laugh before Hendrix groans and drags his hand down his face.

"I need more mulled wine for this," he mutters before disappearing into the kitchen.

I take off after him but am slowed down when Wilder speaks.

"I know you're thinking about what it would be like to

be snuggled between the two of us." My teeth grind and my lips purse, holding in the words I don't need to say out loud.

"You're lucky he didn't kick you out before we left," I seethe.

"I think you mean, you're lucky he didn't. Just think of the fun we can have over the next few days."

Instantly, I'm taken back to the bathroom that night where he...

I slam that thought down. Nothing good can come from me thinking about it.

It was a mistake. A massive fucking mistake that I need to forget about.

If only that were possible...

My entire body is on fire as I step into the kitchen.

"I'm so sorry," Hendrix says.

He's resting back against the counter with a full glass of mulled wine in his hand. His brows are pinched in frustration, and he looks tense as hell.

"It's okay," I breathe, forcing myself to let go of my own irritation over the situation. "Things could be worse." I walk closer to him and pick up the glass I assume he poured for me. "It's Christmas, and we're here just like we planned." Hendrix snorts. "Okay, so not exactly like we planned. But we can still make the best of it."

Hopping up on the counter beside him, I take a sip of my wine and groan in delight.

"This is our trip. It's Christmas, and I refuse to let him ruin it," I announce firmly.

"This is Wilder we're talking about. He always gets what he wants."

"Trust me, I know." I know more than he could ever understand. "But we don't have to let him. Not this time."

Hendrix lets out a huge sigh before downing the rest of his wine.

Unease washes through me. I'm really not sure alcohol is the best answer in this situation.

"What time are the groceries arriving?"

"About thirty minutes," I say after checking the time. "Are we still ordering takeout?"

We had planned all this out, but our wildcard out in the living room might not agree.

"This is our trip," Hendrix says, stealing my words from earlier. "We do it how we want to do it. He either toes the line, or he can leave."

I suck in a breath, shocked to hear such firm words leaving his lips.

Hendrix might often feel exasperated by his twin brother, but it's not very often he voices it. Generally speaking, he's happier just following along instead of being the one making the rules.

"Okay, then," I agree, taking another sip of my wine. "Despite the obvious issue, this place is perfect."

A small smile plays on Hendrix's lips and butterflies take flight in my stomach. I love that smile on him, the happiness in his eyes.

Yes, this trip might have taken an unexpected turn, but we're still going to make the best of it.

Leaning over, I press a kiss to his cheek before hopping down and announcing, "I'm going to unpack."

"I can take the floor if you don't want—"

"Rix," I snap, cutting him off. "I'd never make you sleep on the floor, and you know it."

I shoot him a smile over my shoulder before rushing through the living room where Wilder is on his cell and shutting myself in the bedroom.

Dropping onto the end of the bed, I lower my head into my hands and let out a long sigh.

How is this happening?

I've done everything I can to avoid Wilder since that Halloween party. How am I now stuck here with him for the next five days?

It's got disaster written all over it.

Hendrix can't find out what happened. He'd never forgive me.

The delivery person knocks on the door a while later, and Hendrix calls that he's got it. Trusting him to put the groceries away, I continue hanging my up clothes.

I'm so lost in my thoughts that I don't realize that someone has joined me until a rush of hot air tickles over my neck.

"What the hell are you doing?" I whisper-hiss as I attempt to put some distance between us.

In doing so, I collide with the freestanding wardrobe, causing it to bang against the wall.

"You okay, Elle?" Hendrix bellows through the cabin.

My heart jumps into my throat as I glare pure death at Wilder.

All he does is smirk.

It's like he doesn't care about getting caught.

Maybe he doesn't.

I've known him almost all my life, and I can count on one hand the number of times he's second-guessed his actions.

He's more of a dive-in-and-deal-with-the-consequences-later kind of guy.

The total opposite to me and Hendrix.

"Yeah, I'm good. I'll be out in a second," I call back.

I take a step, ready to remove myself from this situation, but Wilder isn't having any of it.

His hand wraps around my hip, and he pushes me back against the wall.

"You need to stop this," I demand, although it doesn't come out as strong as I was hoping for.

"You're lying," he whispers, leaning in close enough for his nose to brush mine. "Every time you look at me, all you can picture is that night."

My breathing becomes more and more erratic, and my body burns red hot.

Damn him.

"You don't need to agree. I can read it in your body. It's calling to me. You remember how good it felt. You want more."

"No," I argue, for all the good it'll do.

His smirk turns wild, his eyes glittering with excitement.

"You're a really shitty liar, Rebel. But do you know what I'm good at?"

I don't respond. I can't. I'm locked in his stare and totally under his spell again.

This is bad. Really fucking bad.

"Following through on promises. And I promise that before this trip is over, I'll have you screaming my name."

He disappears almost as suddenly as he arrived, leaving me slumped against the wall with my chest heaving and my head spinning.

Oh my god.

This is a disaster of epic proportions.

Grabbing my pajamas, I dart into the bathroom and have a very fast, very cold shower in the hope of banishing the lingering feelings Wilder dragged up with his little impromptu visit.

Sadly, it does very little, and I'm still a riot of emotions as I return to the kitchen, where Hendrix has finished putting everything away.

"Hey, have you seen Wilder?"

"N-no. He was on the couch."

Hendrix shrugs. "He must have gone exploring," he says nonchalantly. He's more than aware of what his brother is like. Wilder wandering off isn't anything out of the ordinary. "I've ordered dinner; it's twenty minutes away."

"Then I guess we know when he's going to return," I deadpan, accepting a glass of chilled white wine from Hendrix.

The second I step out of the kitchen, I release the breath I didn't know I was holding.

I was hoping that this vacation would be the epitome of relaxation, but only an hour in and I'm tenser than I remember being in a long time.

I slow to a stop as I step into the open-plan living and dining area of the cabin, debating my options.

It might be ridiculous, but I don't want to sit where Wilder is going to be sleeping. In the end, I opt for the chair that allows me to take in both the lights twinkling outside and the open fire that someone has already started.

I want to say it was Hendrix, but I know better. He was too busy with the shopping. Wilder did this, and I hate that it makes me soften a little toward him.

Hendrix joins me with a bottle of beer and doesn't hesitate to drop himself onto the couch.

"Ahhh," he sighs as he picks his feet up and stretches his long legs out. They'd reach well over the end of the rest if he were to fully lie down. "At least he'll be uncomfortable as fuck out here," Hendrix mutters with a smirk before taking a pull on his beer.

"You're mean."

His eyes find mine. "You know the alternative," he warns.

"Like sleeping out on the deck?" I ask with a smirk, making my best friend laugh.

"I want to say I'm surprised, but really, we should have seen something like this coming. Our plans were too perfect not to be ruined."

The fire crackles, the scent of Christmas fills the air, and twinkling lights surround us.

Warmth and happiness spread through me, even if they are tainted with a little bit of apprehension for what the next few days might hold.

"I'd agree if we'd had a flat on the way up or run out of gas. But adding an extra person to the trip was not on my radar."

"It'll be fine. He'll probably spend most of the time out looking for trouble, like he is now."

"Is there any to find?" I ask. "The closest store is almost an hour away."

"It's Wilder. If anyone can find trouble, it's him."

Unease twists me up inside.

Wilder doesn't need to go anywhere to find trouble. It's right here. Right under this roof.

Hendrix studies me and I wince, hating what he might see in my expression.

"Is everything okay? You seem a little on edge."

I force a smile onto my face. "It's just not what I was expecting. I was prepared for it just to be me and you."

Hendrix and I live together. Sure, our house has a room for Wilder too, but he's usually at the football house living his best life. Most of the time, it's just the two of us.. Being with him... it's when I'm at my happiest. He's always been my savior, my solace. My person.

What happened with Wilder all those weeks ago, it... it woke something up inside of me, I guess.

Sure, I've always had feelings for Hendrix. What red-blooded female wouldn't? He's hot and sweet. The most loyal and trustworthy friend that exists.

Almost to the point of being too good to be true.

But I've never really considered acting on my feelings.

How could I when doing something about it could ruin everything?

But those few minutes with Wilder made something shift...

What if it can be that good with Hendrix?

What if we've been withholding something from each other that we could have been indulging in all this time?

What if—

"There's nothing we can't do just because Wilder is here," Hendrix promises me, making my brain momentarily misfire.

5

WILDER

I stand outside, shrouded in darkness, watching the two of them in the living room.

I'll never admit it out loud, but I'm jealous.

Their friendship, their connection... it's incredible.

Sure, Hendrix and I are close. We share the kind of bond that most people could never understand.

But what they have is special in a whole other way.

I've never had a friend who's understood me in the way they understand each other.

I've been telling Hendrix for years that he literally has his perfect woman right in the palm of his hands, yet he's never done anything about it.

He's so in love with her. It's obvious from the way he watches her. He's completely smitten, but he won't make the move.

I get it. He's scared.

He's not like me. He doesn't dive into things purely for the thrill of it. He worries about the outcome. I just want the high.

It's why I never stopped that night after discovering the

identity of the dead bride who'd stolen my attention at the Halloween party.

I should have. The second I lifted her veil, I should have taken a massive step back and sent her home to him.

But I didn't.

I couldn't.

Instead, I…

Fuck. I swallow thickly, attempting to dislodge the messy ball of emotion in my throat.

I betrayed him that night. And I know that Noelle is right. If he were to find out, it would rip him apart. But also… would it be the push he needs to finally take what he really wants?

Quite honestly, the poor guy deserves to give his hand a rest. I can only imagine how fucking sore it is after all these years of jerking off over his best friend instead of letting her sit on his dick.

I stand there in the shadows, watching them talk and laugh. It hurts, but in a good kind of way.

They're both incredible people. Kind-hearted, caring, selfless. I mean, hell, they allowed me to gatecrash this party with very little complaint. Most would have told me where to go.

I lose track of time as I stand there like a creep in the night, but eventually, a car pulls up behind me, the door slamming and making me jump before footsteps trudge toward the front door.

It's cold out here. Way too cold considering my suitcase is packed for the warmth of Austin, Texas. Fucking airline. I could be off-my-ass drunk right now with a girl in each arm.

My eyes drop to Noelle as a weird tightness wraps around my chest.

That short time with her in the bathroom that night wasn't enough. I've never wanted more time with a girl before. I keep trying to tell myself that it's because we were cut short, and that I didn't get the full experience of her. But it's never bothered me before with anyone else.

Maybe it's just because I know I can't have her...

Whatever it is, this incessant desperation for her needs to stop. It's going to get me into trouble. And while that doesn't usually bother me, I know that this time I'd drag her down with me.

I wait until the delivery driver has arrived and returned to his car before I make my presence known.

"I told you he'd be back for dinner," Hendrix shouts to Noelle as I step into the kitchen to grab a beer.

"Aw, you ordered my favorite," I tease as I scan the containers littering the counter.

"Not that you deserve it. Here, take this to Noelle," he says, passing a plate over.

"I'd love to," I say, spinning on my heels and walking over to the chair in front of the fire.

She tenses the second I approach and refuses to look up at me.

"Someone's hungry," I tease.

"Someone ate all the car snacks," she counters.

"Not this snack, you didn't."

Her eyes jump to mine as she sucks in a sharp breath.

"You need to stop," she warns.

"And you need to relax."

"I would if you'd quit," she argues, having little choice but to accept the plate of food I'm offering her.

The second she rests it on her lap, I fall over her, catching myself on the back of the armchair.

"He's going to notice that you're uptight, and something tells me he won't be the one who can fuck it out of you."

She looks up, her eyes holding mine. "And you'd know that how?"

"Trust me. There might be a lot of similarities between me and Rix, but only one of us has had a taste of you." As she gasps, I push to stand and take two steps back. "Isn't that right, Noelle?"

"Isn't what right?" Rix asks, joining us with two plates in his hands.

I shake my head, refusing to respond, and dart back into the kitchen for the drink I initially went in search of.

When I return, Noelle is fully focused on her dinner, and Rix is scrolling through the TV for something to watch.

Oh, this trip is going to be fun...

"Hey, how is your cabin?" Lori asks once the call connects.

Noelle and Rix are sitting on the couch side by side with big smiles on their faces. We've been drinking for a few hours now, and thankfully, the air is a little more relaxed.

"It's so cute," Noelle says with a slight slur to her voice. "They've decorated the entire place. It's a Christmas paradise."

"Aw, that's awesome."

"What about your actual paradise?" Rix asks.

I can't remember exactly where Kian was whisking our big sister off to. I do remember the photos, though, and it looks like heaven with blue sea and white sand.

I guess that's the kind of life you're able to live when you marry a billionaire.

It's sure a long way from the life we all just about survived growing up.

I'm happy for her. Really fucking happy. Kian is a good guy, too.

"Oh my god. I swear, it's even better than the photos. I miss you guys, though. It still doesn't feel right, being apart on the holidays. Have you heard from Wilder? He should have landed by now."

Hendrix looks up and shakes his head.

'What?' I mouth.

"He didn't go," Noelle explains. "The flight was canceled."

"Oh. Is he still at college?"

"Nope," I say, hopping up from the chair and diving between them on the couch. "He's right here."

Lori's eyes widen in shock before she bursts out laughing.

"What?" I ask. "Why is me being here so funny?"

"Many, many reasons. But mostly the look on their faces."

"He invited himself," Hendrix explains.

"Yeah," Lori muses, "I can see that. Not really your type of holiday, huh, Wild Child?"

"A one-bedroom cabin in the ass crack of nowhere? Totally my thing."

Lori narrows her eyes, a smirk playing on her lips. "One bedroom?"

"It was meant to be a two bed, but..." Noelle sighs. "We can't get a hold of the company we booked it with. Their office is closed, and the emergency number just rings out, so..."

"So the three of you are stuck in a cabin with one bed," she says.

"What was that?" a deep voice asks before her husband joins her on the screen.

"It's fine; we've got it sorted," Hendrix says in a rush, not wanting to go into it.

"What are your plans for the next few days?" Noelle asks, attempting to change the subject.

It might work on Lori and Kian, but with the heat of her body burning down the side of mine, I can't say my mind drifts very far away from her as Lori explains their plans.

We chat for almost thirty minutes before they have to go for a dinner reservation and we cut the call.

"Well, this is cozy," I say, throwing my arms out and pulling them both in closer.

"Don't you have anything else to do than annoy us?" Hendrix mutters.

"Dude, look around. There is literally nothing to do here."

"That was exactly the idea," Noelle scoffs before attempting to get up.

The second she's on her feet, I wrap my arm around her waist and pull her back down, forcing her to lie across both of us.

She wriggles in her attempt to gain control, but it's futile.

She screams as I grab one of her feet and begin tickling her.

It's been the same since she was a little girl. The two of us would have her fighting for breath when we launched an attack.

"Get off," she cries, thrashing around, attempting to kick us away. "Get off."

Unable to ignore the opportunity, Hendrix dives for her waist as her tank rides up.

My fire has worked wonders in this little cabin. I'd be tempted to say that it's actually hotter in here than it is on whatever tropical island Lori just called us from. Not that I'm complaining, because Noelle shed her oversized hoodie a while ago, letting us both enjoy the vision of her braless in a thin tank top and short shorts. Definitely the highlight of this trip so far.

Her screams continue to ring out through the air, but they're laced with laughter as she attempts, and fails, to fight back. She twists and turns, her face red with exertion and her limbs flailing around uselessly. The three of us are like kids again and totally lost in the immaturity of the whole thing when Noelle suddenly shrieks, "Oh fuck," as she falls from our laps. Hendrix tries to catch her but only manages to grab her tank. She lands on her back on the floor with her tits out.

"Shit," Hendrix barks, the first to react as he reaches down to help her. Only, reality hits her at the same time. She shifts quickly to cover up but instead of helping Hendrix manages to grab a handful instead.

I can't help but bark out a laugh as the two of them freeze for a beat before freaking the fuck out.

Noelle jumps to her feet and all but flees to the bedroom while Hendrix throws himself back on the couch and covers his bright red face with his arm.

He sinks lower as if he's praying the couch will swallow him whole.

"Did they feel as good as they looked?" I ask. In hindsight, it's probably not the best leading question, but so what? "Ow," I complain when he punches me hard on the arm. "What? She's got good tits."

"Fuck's sake," he mutters.

"I'm sorry, I'm not seeing the issue here." Hendrix pushes to his feet and begins pacing. "Okay, no, wait, I do. You want more of them."

"Wilder," he warns.

"Dude, just grow a pair and go and tell her that you want to suck on them. I bet she'd let you. She might even return the favor and suck on your—"

"ENOUGH," he bellows, his voice echoing around the small cabin.

"Just think how good it could be if you told her how you really feel," I say quietly once he's stopped with his back to me.

He runs his hands through his hair before blowing out a long breath.

He stands there for long minutes, just breathing. I've no idea what's going through his head. I wouldn't even know where to begin, seeing as our thoughts are usually so vastly different. I'd never be in the position he is now.

Probably because I'm a selfish asshole and always take what I want without considering the consequences.

"You never know; maybe she wants you for Christmas."

I have no idea if it's what I say, or if he's just trying to get away from me, but no sooner are those words past my lips than he spins on his heels and marches toward the bedroom.

6

NOELLE

ll I can see as I stare out of the window is my own reflection. I need a distraction, but my own face isn't it.

Night one of our vacation and everything is already going wrong. And it's all my fault.

I never should have gone out that night. I should have stuck to what I told Hendrix I was going to do before he left for his study session.

I don't even know why I thought going to a party would help. It never has in the past.

I just... I didn't want to be alone, despite me convincing Hendrix that I was okay and that he should go.

Biggest mistake I ever made.

If I'd just stayed home, I wouldn't have found myself in the toilets of that party with my best friend's twin brother, and this vacation wouldn't be so freaking awkward.

The sound of the door opening behind me startles me.

I know who it is, but I don't turn around. I can't. I'm too embarrassed.

I flashed them. Both of them.

God, could this trip get any worse?

He walks across the room, staying as silent as I am before he steps up behind me, wraps his arms around me, and rests his chin on the top of my head.

"It's okay, Elle," he says softly, instantly making me feel better, his arms tightening around me. "You've got really nice tits."

"Hendrix," I shriek.

"What?" he asks as I spin around in his hold and stare up at him. "And if it helps, it's not the first time I've seen them."

I see the moment he hears what he's saying. His eyes widen and uncertainty washes through his expression before his cheeks turn crimson.

"When have you seen them before?" I ask, unaware that this event has ever occurred.

"U-umm," he stutters. "It was an accident."

I quirk a brow.

"I accidentally walked in on you in the shower once."

"And you accidentally stayed and watched?" I ask in horror.

"I never said that," he argues.

"Rix," I laugh, suddenly feeling better about the whole thing.

"I was a horny teenage boy. I couldn't help myself."

"You're still a horny teenage boy," I point out with a laugh.

"Yeah," he muses. "And you're hot."

He reaches out, tucking a stray lock of hair behind my ear, his eyes bouncing between mine.

My heart jumps into my throat as the hand he's wrapped around my hip tightens as if he wants to pull me to him just like his brother did not so long ago.

"Hendrix?" I whisper, feeling both completely out of

my depth and exactly where I'm meant to be at the same time.

His eyes drop to my lips for the briefest moment, and for less than a second, I think he's going to do it.

I think he's finally going to kiss me. But then…

Suddenly, he steps back, removing his hold and allowing a rush of cool air to billow between us.

A shiver rips through me and my nipples harden against the soft fabric of my tank, something he doesn't miss.

"Fuck, Elle. I think I've had too much to drink," he mutters absently as he spins around and combs his fingers through his hair.

He hasn't, though. Out of the two of us, I've had much more.

"I'll leave you to get ready for bed," he says before marching toward the door.

His fingers are wrapped around the handle when I call out his name.

"Yeah?" he says in a rush. He looks back over his shoulder, and I swear there's hope in his eyes.

Does he want me to—

"I-I'm sorry," I blurt, making him frown. "I didn't mean to freak out and make it awkward. They're just tits, right?"

His eyes drop again at the mention of them. My skin burns under his attention and my arms twitch, threatening to come up to cover myself.

"Yeah, it's not like I haven't seen any before," he says, forcing a smile.

The thing is, though, Hendrix and I don't have any secrets. Or at least, we didn't until Halloween. I know exactly what his experience is with women, and let's just say, seeing my tits is up there with the best of it.

Sadness washes over him, but before I can respond, he's gone, leaving me alone once again.

"Shit," I hiss, regretting every second of that interaction.

I know what he wants. I'm not that naive. I just wish... sometimes I wish that he could be a little more like... Wilder. Hendrix is so concerned about me and the future that he holds himself back.

I can't really say anything, though. I'm not exactly pushing things beyond what we've always had. I'm just as scared as he is.

If we fuck this up, what do we have left?

Sure, Hendrix will have Wilder. But I'll have nothing.

Every good thing in my life is because of Hendrix.

I have a family because of him. I have a big sister in the form of Lori. I have college, a life, a future.

Without him...

A sob threatens to erupt, but I catch it before it can.

It's Christmas. I'm with my best friend. Nothing should be making me sad right now. That's why we booked this trip —to leave all the heartache and drama behind. We're supposed to be enjoying ourselves.

I don't remember Hendrix coming to bed last night, but the second I wake up, I'm more than aware that he did.

His heavy arm is wrapped around me, and the length of his body is pressed against my back.

I love it.

He makes me feel so safe, secure, wanted, needed... loved.

Sucking in a deep breath, I hold onto those feelings.

There were so many years when I was a kid when I

didn't experience a single one of them. Now, I never want to lose them.

With Hendrix, I belong, and it would kill me if that ever changed.

But as much as I love being in his embrace, now I'm awake, I need to pee and get up. It's one habit that I haven't been able to break.

If I didn't get up for my little brother, no one would. And he was always awake with the sun. No matter how sick or exhausted he was, he would always wake up.

It was our time. The house would be in silence, no one shouting or screaming. No one hurting each other. It was just the two of us playing silly little games, trying to make the best out of the shit hand we'd been dealt.

Now, it's just peaceful, only instead of enjoying my time with him, I'm forced to remember him.

Pain cuts through my chest just like I'm sure it always will.

There's a part of me that can understand why my parents completely fell apart after his death. But I will never, ever understand why they couldn't have been there for either of us before the worst happened.

I'll never forgive them. Ever.

It takes some serious ninja skills, but I manage to slip out from Hendrix's arm without waking him. I might be an early riser, but he is not.

I pad to the door, swiping a hoodie he abandoned yesterday before silently slipping from the room.

I sneak into the bathroom to pee and freshen up before tiptoeing through the cabin. The last thing I need right now is to wake up Wilder. I require at least an hour and some good, strong coffee before I can deal with him. But the second I step into the living room, I discover that being quiet isn't necessary.

The couch is empty.

Startled, I look around, expecting him to be hiding in the shadows, waiting to pounce on me when I least expect it.

But there isn't any sign of him.

The sun has barely risen above the horizon, so it's not that which has woken him. Maybe he... I press my hand to my stomach when it knots up at my thought. Maybe he didn't sleep here at all. Maybe he managed to find someone to hook up with and left.

That thought affects me way more than it should, and I force myself to forget it as I walk into the kitchen to make myself a large mug of coffee.

Thankfully, there's a decent coffee machine and generous-sized mugs in the cupboard. I make myself a hazelnut cappuccino with a double shot of espresso before collecting my book from the coffee table and the blanket from the back of the couch and heading outside.

It's cold. Freezing, actually. But it doesn't stop me.

There are heaters out here, it was one of the things that excited me about this place.

I turn them on and just get settled on the swing seat that faces the mountains in the distance when I discover things are even better than I thought.

It's snowing.

It's actually freaking snowing. And as the sun rises, I discover that the mountains are already covered.

The view is the thing Christmas dreams are made of.

With the seat rocking gently back and forth, a blanket wrapped around me, my coffee and my book, I fall into the kind of relaxation I was craving when we booked this place.

Silence continues to fill the air around me as I lose myself in my book.

I've been reading romance for as long as I can

remember. The first ones I found were sweet, teenage puppy-love ones. But then I grabbed one, completely innocently, from a thrift store. It had this cute cover that pulled me in, but the inside... whoa... that got my innocent twelve-year-old heart racing.

Since then, I've tried every and any romance book I can get my hands on. I love it. And I guess, it helps to make up for the lack of romance and spice in my own life.

Up until very recently, my only personal experience was courtesy of my own fingers or a toy or two I've branched out with in recent years.

I was fairly satisfied. But then Wilder...

I want more. I do.

The way his touch lit me up... The way he made me feel... it was a million times better than I have ever made myself feel, highly rated vibrator or not.

The scene I'm reading begins to heat up, and I fall deeper under its spell, losing all sense of my surroundings. My heart races and I devour the words faster, needing to reach the climax.

The description of the setting, the feelings, everything... I'm right with them, my blood boiling as it courses through my veins.

If it weren't for the mug, right now would be a fantastic one-handed reading situation.

I'm debating losing the coffee and taking advantage of just that when a shadow falls over me.

"Oh my god," I gasp, dropping my book and just about saving the mug from shattering all over the deck.

Wilder leans down and picks up the book, his eyes roaming over the cover.

"Whatcha reading?" he asks before lifting the blanket and dropping down beside me.

"Where the hell have you been?" I ask, reaching out and attempting to snatch my book back.

I'm not ashamed of what I read, but I really don't need it to become a hot topic right now.

He lets me get my fingers on it before he tugs it away and tucks it under his thigh, forcing me to either let it go or climb over him to get it back. The latter is certainly not happening.

"Couldn't sleep; went for a run."

His words give me pause, and I look at him properly for the first time since he appeared.

Snowflakes dust his dark hair and stick to the scruff covering his face, and his shirt is soaked through. "You're wet," I point out.

"Yep, running in the snow will do that," he mutters before reaching behind him to pull his long-sleeved shirt off, letting it drop to the deck with a wet slap. "Question is though, are you?"

7

WILDER

Credit where credit is due—despite blatantly wanting to, Noelle's gaze doesn't drop to the skin I've just exposed.

Her eyes narrow and her lips purse in frustration. It's cute. Hot, actually.

Poor Noelle. She has no idea that she has guys everywhere—none more than my sexually frustrated brother—walking around with semis for her.

"Can you go shower or something?" she mutters, ripping her attention from me in favor of the view. "I was enjoying a quiet morning."

"So I saw. I thought you'd still be in bed with my brother."

"He's sleeping."

"Fucking idiot," I muse. "Bet he's dreaming about your tits."

"Wilder," Noelle snaps, sounding utterly exasperated with me.

"What? I'm just stating facts. You've got a good rack. But then, you already knew I thought that, didn't you."

"Can we please not? That night... it was a massive mistake. One that I never want to think about, let alone discuss, again."

"I never regret making a girl feel good," I explain.

"Jesus," she mutters under my breath.

"And you shouldn't be ashamed."

She sits up a little straighter. "I'm not—do you know what, I'm not letting you drag me into this. It happened. It's over. It won't be happening again."

"If you say so."

"If I... fucking hell, Wilder. What exactly am I saying that you don't understand?"

"I understand everything perfectly well. But the thing is, your head and your body are on a totally different page. You might think you don't want a repeat, but let me tell you... your body? It's begging for it."

"I'm not sitting here listening to this."

She pushes from the seat, but I'm faster. My hand wraps around her thigh and I easily pull her back down.

"Stay. Hang out with me for a bit."

A frustrated growl rumbles in her throat and I can't help but laugh.

"You know, I think you're on to something here. This is the perfect spot to read."

"Wilder, no," she cries when I retrieve her book from beneath my leg.

I've no idea where she got to, but there is a page with the corner bent down, so I go for that.

"Please don't," she begs.

When I picked it up, the cover looked innocent enough. But something tells me the inside is going to be anything but.

I know the kinds of books she loves, and I also know that

dark, heated look in her eye. I may have only seen it once before, but I know.

"Okay," I muse, scanning the page. The moment I get the gist of what's happening, my eyes widen and my smile grows. "Well, this is an interesting subject matter."

"Oh, Jesus."

She tries to get up again, but I quickly slide my palm down her thigh and pin her in place as I begin reading.

"He crawls on the bed, forcing you to fall back. Your chest heaves and your skin burns knowing that he's not the only one watching you."

"Wilder," she complains.

The book is written in first person, but switching it up is an opportunity I just can't miss.

"On the other side of the bed, still fully dressed, he watches with his hands in his pants pocket. The fabric pulls tight across his crotch, letting you know how much he's enjoying this moment.

"Your eyes meet as your back finally hits the mattress.

"Your mouth waters, desperate for a taste of him.

"Reaching out one arm, you gesture for him. But he holds firm, waiting, watching.

"Frustrated, you look back down, watching as another set of hands slide up your thighs."

I do the same, easing my palm down the soft skin of her inner thigh. I figure that she's still wearing her pajamas under this blanket. Those tiny shorts are perfect for what I have in mind.

"Oh my god," she gasps as my little finger hits the juncture between her leg and her pussy.

The heat from her burns, and it only makes me more desperate to continue.

"Hooking his fingers into the sides of your panties, he

begins dragging them down your legs, exposing you to both of them.

"The second the fabric is free of your feet, he grabs your ankles and spreads your legs wide, letting both of us see what we really want."

Moving, I ghost my fingers over her wet panties, gently grazing her clit.

"Your pussy is wet, swollen and desperate."

I might read the words from the book, but they couldn't be any truer as her juices coat my fingers through the fabric and her breathing becomes even more erratic.

She shifts in the chair, spreading her legs wider for me and making the entire thing rock.

"'Undo your bra,' the man between your legs demands, and you waste no time in following orders, letting your heavy breasts fall free.

"'Now tell us what you want,' the man watching asks.

"'I... I...' you stutter, unable to voice your needs. 'I want your mouths on me,' you finally gasp.

"The man between your thighs drops to his stomach as the other finally crawls on the bed.

"'Yes,' you cry as he blows a stream of air across your sensitive pussy. 'Yes.'"

"Touch me," Noelle suddenly begs.

I still for a moment, shocked by her brazen demand. But if I learned anything that night, it was that once she's in the zone, she's anything but the shy and innocent girl I know her to be.

"Thought you'd never ask," I muse, lowering the book and looking at her instead. I need to see the moment we connect. I need to see her reaction.

Tucking my fingers under the sodden fabric, I brush my fingertips over her clit.

She gasps, her body slumping lower in the chair as she squeezes her eyes closed.

"Oh no," I warn. "Eyes on me, little rebel. You watch me as I do this to you."

Reluctantly, her eyes open and they find mine.

Internally, I can hear her screaming "I shouldn't be doing this" at the top of her voice. But her body is too far gone, she can't hear it.

I work her just like I did that night in the bathroom, and she's just as desperate for the release as she was then.

I tease her clit, making her moan and mewl before dropping lower and pushing a finger inside her.

She's tight. But then I guess she should be, seeing as no man has been inside her before.

My cock aches with the need to be her first, to know exactly how tightly she'd squeeze me.

Before I know what I'm doing, I reach over with my free hand, wrap my fingers around her wrist, and guide her to me. With the blanket hiding her movements, I encourage her to stroke me over my sweats as I work her closer to her release.

I feel like a schoolboy getting his kicks at the back of the classroom. It shouldn't be enough to get me anywhere close to coming. But only a few seconds in, and I fear it is.

"Oh god," she gasps as I shift my position so I can push a second finger inside her and rub her clit with the heel of my hand.

"That's it, I want you to come for me."

"Wilder." I've no idea if it's meant to be a warning; all I hear is a moan, a plea for more.

"Are you picturing him watching? Is he joining in too? You could put him out of his misery and let him suck on your nipples as you come all over my fingers."

Unwilling to let this be over quite yet, I keep her riding

the edge of her release. Just when she gets close, I change up my pace, dragging her away from the edge.

"Is that why you were so hot when I sat next to you? Were you reading that and imagining us? Thinking about where last night could have gone?"

"Yes, yes," she whimpers.

"Maybe Rix and I can make all your Christmas wishes come true this week, huh? Would you like that? Do you want to be a dirty girl for us?"

"Oh my god. Please," she begs. It could be for her orgasm or for the picture I just painted, or it could be both; it doesn't matter, it still has me on the verge of coming in my pants.

The closer she gets, the faster she rubs and the tighter she squeezes.

Echoing her desperation to be touched, I lift my hips and awkwardly shove my sweats down over my ass.

"Oh my god," she pants, her eyes wide as her slender fingers wrap around my shaft.

Her movements slow to almost nothing, but embarrassingly, her touch alone is almost enough.

"Keep going. It feels so good."

Spurred on by my praise, she does as she's told.

"That's it. Fuck."

Silence falls between us as we lose ourselves in pleasure.

It's wrong. So wrong. Rix is right inside the cabin.

But also... it's so fucking good.

"Need you to come for me, Elle. Be a good girl and come all over my fingers."

I fuck her harder, making her whimpers get louder and louder as my own release surges forward.

"Come. Come now."

And she does, her pussy clamping down on my fingers,

pulling me in deeper as I pulse in her hand, coming hard and making a mess on the blanket shielding what we're doing from the rest of the world.

"Holy shit," I gasp once I've come down and pull my fingers from inside her.

She's sated and sleepy, her body limp and exhausted.

But that doesn't stop her from tensing the second I lift my fingers to my lips and lick them clean.

Her taste floods my mouth and I groan in delight.

"So sweet," I muse.

There's a bang from somewhere behind us, and we both move as fast as humanly possible to cover ourselves up under the blanket.

Her cheeks burn bright red, and I'm not sure if it's from the release, embarrassment, or unfiltered shame over what we just did. The thought that it could be the latter makes my stomach knot up.

How could something that feels so right cause shame?

A door opens and footsteps pad on the deck.

"Hey," Rix says, appearing just a beat after I've handed Noelle her book back.

Hendrix's eyes drop to it and his brow wrinkles. I follow his attention and discover that she's holding it upside down.

He is going to fucking kill me.

"Everything okay?"

Noelle swallows nervously.

"Yeah, of course. Did you sleep well?" she asks, her voice calm despite how I'm sure she's feeling on the inside.

"I did. Missed you when I woke up, though. Did you want another coffee?" he asks, eyeing her empty mug.

"Yes, please."

He takes off with her mug, more than happy to get her a refill.

"I'll take one too, if you're making them."

Rix stops just before he leaves our sight and mutters, "What did your last slave die of?" before disappearing.

"Lovely," I muse as he disappears. "I'm sure he wouldn't be making yours either if he knew what we just did."

"Don't, Wilder. Just... don't."

Throwing the blanket off, I push to my feet. I might have come, but my dick is already half-mast again just from the memory.

"Okay. I won't say any more," I announce making a show of pushing my hand into my pants, giving her very little choice but to see what I've got going on. "But know this..." I state, leaning forward so I can whisper in her ear. "It doesn't end there. This is only the beginning."

8

HENDRIX

Passing one mug to Noelle, I keep the other in my hand and lift the blanket, slipping under.

Noelle gasps as I get comfortable beside her. And when I look over, I find her tense as hell.

"What's wrong?"

"N-Nothing." It takes a couple of seconds, but she finally looks up at me.

Her cheeks are red from the cold air making her look cuter than normal.

"You sure?" I ask.

"Of course. Look," she says gesturing to our surroundings. "What could possibly be wrong?"

It's so peaceful out here.

I stare out at the falling snow as I get settled.

Nothing more is said between us as we enjoy the view and the company.

With my feet on the deck, I gently rock us back and forth.

Noelle's book is closed on the blanket between us as she

hugs her mug and blows across the surface of the hot coffee, sending steam floating off into the cold air around us.

I watch her, not liking the slight frown marring her brow.

"Are you sure everything is okay?" I ask, unable to stop myself.

She startles at the sound of my voice as if she isn't even aware that I'm here. It only makes my concern grow.

"Y-Yeah," she says, very briefly glancing over at me before her eyes focus on the tree-covered mountains once more.

"Noelle," I sigh, regrets from last night bubbling up inside me.

I knew it was inevitable that I'd wake up alone this morning. The only time Noelle ever sleeps in is if she's sick. But I hated not knowing if she was okay.

I wanted to wake her when I crawled into bed last night and apologize again, but I didn't want to disturb her. She looked so peaceful.

But everything that had happened, the stupid things I said...

I don't know what came over me. I'm usually good at keeping my feelings for her locked down. I'm not sure whether it's the freedom of being away from normality, or the 'jokes' Wilder keeps making, but the words just blurted from my lips.

I told her that I once crept on her when she was topless. *Fucking great friend you are.*

"I'm so sorry. Last night... things got a little—"

"Stop apologizing; you didn't do anything wrong," she says, reaching for my hand and squeezing in support. "It's me. I—"

"You're perfect," I say, cutting her off. "I know you had an image in your head for what this trip was going to be like, and it hasn't turned out quite as you hoped. But it's still going to be awesome."

"I know," she whispers.

Silence falls again. I get the feeling she wants to say more, but I don't push her. She'll open up when she's ready.

So instead, we sit and swing gently as we drink our coffee and watch the snow fall.

I haven't been up all that long, but the thickness of it on the ground has already doubled.

Eventually, Noelle picks up her book and twists around to get comfortable.

Our legs entwine under the blanket and she smiles softly at me before losing herself in whatever story she's reading.

As always, jealousy rushes through me.

I'd love to be able to read as effortlessly as she does. She always looks so relaxed, like the realities of life no longer weigh down on her.

Reading will never be like that for me. It's been hard since day one, and I know that'll never change. It doesn't matter what diagnosis or support I get, I'll always have to put loads more effort in than the average person.

It used to get me down. Used to make me feel stupid and weak. But I know better than that now, and Noelle is one of the biggest reasons for it.

She's proven to me how one struggle isn't enough to hold you back from your dreams. She's worked with me, supported me, tutored me. And together, we've made it to where we are now.

Once upon a time, I didn't think college was going to be on the cards for me. For any of us really, but mostly me. I never believed I'd get the kind of grades that anyone would be interested in. Hell, there was a time I wasn't even sure I'd graduate, if I'm being honest.

But here we are. Sure, it helped that Lori managed to snag herself a billionaire husband who's eradicated any money worries we once had. But that's only a part of the reason why we were all accepted into Trinity Royal.

It was Wilder's choice. Some might say we were weak for following him, but then some don't know the kind of lives we've lived.

Family. It means everything to us. There was no way that we were being split up across the country.

Wilder might drive me crazy, and I might not be that much of a football fan, but there was no way I was missing him playing college football. I've supported his career all the way from Little League. I don't plan on stopping now.

I might not tell him often enough, but I'm so fucking proud of him.

Of Noelle, too. She might not know what path she wants her life to take right now, but whatever she decides to do, I know she's going to kill it. It's just the kind of person she is.

And as for me... honestly, as long as the most important people in my life are happy, then I'll take it as a win.

Pulling my cell from my pocket, I open up my gaming app and lose myself the best way I know how.

Time passes and the snow around us gets deeper and deeper. Wilder makes himself scarce for once, and Noelle and I get to hang out exactly as we'd planned.

"Did you want more coffee?" I ask when I lose the level I'm currently on.

Noelle thinks for a moment.

"No, I'm okay. I think I might go and have a bath though," she explains as she closes her book and throws the blanket off.

Standing up, my hoodie that she's borrowed falls to just above her knees, leaving her legs bare.

Her skin is flawless, beautiful, and so soft. I just wish I had a reason to indulge.

"I'll make breakfast," I blurt as she walks toward the cabin, completely oblivious that I'm sitting here checking her out, silently praying for things I know I can't have.

It's been years. I should be used to it by now. I guess, in a way I am. It doesn't stop my need for her growing, though.

She pauses and looks back, not expecting me to have followed and been so closely behind her.

"You don't have to do that," she says softly.

There's a sadness on her face that makes my chest ache.

I want to give her the world, every single thing that she deserves, but I've no idea how.

An ice-cool breeze blows between us now we're away from the warmth of the heaters, and I can't help but take a step closer.

Her cheeks are rosy from the cold, making her look even cuter in my massive hoodie.

Reaching out, I cup her jaw and brush my thumb over her cheek.

My heart jumps into my throat when she leans into my touch.

"Noelle," I breathe.

She sucks her bottom lip into her mouth, her skin turning white where her teeth sink into the soft flesh.

Time stands still as my head and heart war.

Kiss her.

Back down. She deserves better.

Kiss her.

You'll never know how good it could be if you don't grow a pair and try.

I lean forward, almost convinced that I could do it. That I could show my best friend just how much I really do love her. But just a beat before I get close enough to give her a clue as to where my head is at, a loud alarm blares from behind her.

She jumps a mile and my hand drops from her face.

"What the hell?" she blurts, throwing the door open and racing inside.

Smoke billows from the kitchen, and the scent of burned fuck-knows-what fills the air.

"What are you doing?" I bark when we find Wilder standing in the middle of the disaster zone that is the kitchen.

"Cooking," Wilder states, rolling his eyes like it's obvious.

"I beg to differ," I mutter, throwing the windows open in the hope of losing some smoke.

"Okay, well, I was trying."

And right here is another reason why Wilder and I couldn't live on opposite sides of the country. The asshole can't cook to save his life. If it weren't for me and Noelle, he'd live on a diet of takeout and donuts. Not the best idea for an athlete who dreams of going pro.

"Jesus Christ," I mutter when I get a proper look at him and find his t-shirt covered in... "Is that tomato sauce?"

"Maybe," he mumbles.

"Fucking hell. Just go and get changed, I'll sort this out."

"I am capable, you know," Wilder scoffs.

"Are you, though?" Noelle quips from the doorway.

An irritated growl rumbles in Wilder's throat as he turns to glare at Noelle.

He takes a step toward her, but she knows him well enough not to be scared. He might be big and intimidating, but not to someone who's known him since he was in diapers.

She holds her head high and waits for his next move.

Although, it soon becomes clear that neither of us correctly predicts that.

He moves with the speed of a kick-ass football player as he swipes the tomato ketchup from the counter and squirts it in Noelle's direction.

It lands on her cheek.

"You absolute—" Her curse is cut short when Wilder suddenly dives forward.

I'm frozen in place as he grabs her by the throat and pins her back against the wall.

My chin drops, although no words leave my mouth as he leans forward and slowly licks the sauce from her cheek.

All the air rushes from my lungs as if someone just took a baseball bat to my back.

"The fuck are you doing?" I whisper in utter disbelief.

I have never, ever seen him manhandle her in any way before. Okay, that's not true. There have been times where she's got wasted and he's carried her home and put her to bed, but that is very, very different from what I'm currently witnessing.

He stares down at her as she remains motionless against the wall.

Her lips are parted, her eyes wide, her cheeks stained pink, and her chest is heaving.

I want to say it's with shock. But... I know the kinds of books she reads, the kinds of things the guys do in them.

Is she... is she... enjoying this?

Suddenly, it's as if someone hits the fast-forward button because in a flash, Noelle comes to her senses and her hands lift, pushing against Wilder's chest as if she's strong enough to move him.

"Get the fuck off me," she shouts.

"Shit," he hisses before shooting me a guilty-looking sideways glance.

My eyes narrow, trying to read what I can see dancing in his eyes, but it's impossible.

Movement to his right catches my attention, and I look down just in time to see my best friend dart deeper into the cabin before the sound of a door slamming rips through the air.

"What the hell was that?" I demand, moving closer to my brother.

It takes him a beat longer than it usually would to shake off whatever that was, and he shrugs his shoulders. "What? Just messing around."

I shake my head, unable to believe that was just him acting the fool.

I know Wilder. I know him better than anyone, and that was not him messing about.

It was serious. Intense.

The air between them as they stared at each other... it was charged.

Charged with something I do not want to identify.

"No." I shake my head as my warning hangs in the air. "Not Noelle. You can have any other girl out there. Treat them as your playthings and leave them sobbing in your wake, if you must. But do not go after Noelle."

He throws his head back and laughs, but the sound that erupts from him isn't as light as I'd like.

"What the hell, Bro. Noelle? Your Noelle?" He tsks as he combs his fingers through his hair. "I'd never take her from you, man." My lips purse and my teeth grind. Why don't I believe him?

Without another word, he disappears in the direction

Noelle did, leaving me standing in the middle of the mess he made that started all this, a million and one questions spinning through my mind.

65

9

———

NOELLE

"**F**uck," I breathe, wrapping my hands around the sink as I hang my head in shame.

It wasn't my fault.

I didn't do anything.

Well... not that time, I didn't.

This is a mess. A ticking bomb just waiting to go bang.

I can practically see the fuse getting shorter and shorter in my mind.

"Fuck," I hiss a little louder this time as I spin around and rest back against the wall. My hand lifts and my fingers dance over the delicate skin of my throat where his calloused hand just was.

My eyes flutter closed as I remember how it felt.

No one has ever touched me like Wilder has.

Something inside me burns red hot as I remember each time we've collided.

I need to put a stop to it. But...

"Fucking hell, Noelle. You need to get a grip," I mutter to myself.

A shriek passes my lips when there's a knock at the door.

Sucking in a deep breath, I try to force down the feelings that Wilder has ignited within me.

It's not going to be him on the other side.

It'll be Hendrix coming to check that I'm okay. Every time he looks at me, I fear he's going to be able to see the truth written as clear as day in my eyes.

I count to three with my eyes closed and then reach for the door, pulling it open before I have a chance to talk myself out of it.

A loud gasp rips from my throat when I discover I'm wrong.

To many others, Hendrix and Wilder will look completely identical. But to me, they're totally different people in every way.

Yes, there was a time when they were able to pull the wool over my eyes and trick me with some twin-switching. But that hasn't happened for many years.

"What?" I snap.

It's not often that Wilder looks bothered by anything, but as he stares back at me, guilt and concern are more than obvious in his expression. The sight makes my breath catch. He looks so much more like Hendrix right now.

"I'm sorry. I wasn't thinking."

"We're going to hurt him," I state, knowing without doubt that I'm right. "And I—"

"We won't," Wilder says firmly, cutting me off.

"How? How won't we? This," I say, gesturing between us. "It never should have happened. It shouldn't still be happening. That out there," I say, throwing my hand out in the direction of the kitchen. "It was... it was—"

"Hot?" Wilder asks with his signature smirk appearing on his lips.

"That is not what I was going to say," I say firmly.

"You know it was," he says, ignoring everything I just said.

"What do you want?" I ask, holding the door as tight as I can in fear he's going to force his way inside and make this whole situation even worse.

"He wants you. You know that, right?"

"Wilder," I warn.

"I'm not playing games. My brother is so madly in love with you that he can barely see straight. I might have fucked up back there, but did you see that look in his eyes? He wouldn't hesitate to hurt me if it meant protecting you.

"You are the most important person in his world. And something tells me that you feel exactly the same."

My eyes bounce between his as my heart rate picks up.

"You two are fucking idiots."

"But—"

"There are no buts, Noelle. You two are it. Fucking happily-ever-after shit."

I stare at him, unable to believe what I'm hearing.

"Sometimes, you've got to live on the wild side and just take a chance," he says before taking a step back. "Think about it, yeah?"

Slowly, I close the door behind him, my head spinning as I struggle to match up the advice I was just given with the man who delivered it.

I work on autopilot as I fill the tub and pour a generous amount of bubble bath into it.

Stripping off Hendrix's hoodie, I can't help myself, and before I drop it, I gather up the fabric and hold it to my nose.

Wilder is right. Hendrix is the most important person in my world. Has been for a long time, and I'm pretty sure there is no one else on the planet with the power to overtake him.

But does that mean I could risk it and take our relationship to the next level?

I want to. Holy hell do I want to.

But could I?

Unable to answer my unspoken questions, I lower Hendrix's hoodie to the floor and shed the rest of my clothing before stepping into the bathtub.

A contented sigh slips from my lips as I sink into the just-too-hot water.

My skin prickles as it burns, but I figure after what I've done this morning, I deserve it.

I lose myself in my thoughts, and another knock on the door startles me.

Refusing to guess which Kemp twin is standing on the other side this time, I call out and hope for the best. Although, if I'm being honest, I've no idea which option is preferable right now.

"Is it safe to enter?" my best friend asks through the crack in the door.

"Don't even pretend like you're hoping it's not," I tease.

He's wearing a knowing smirk when he enters, holding a mug in his hands.

"You're never going to forget that confession, are you?"

"Unlikely."

"I know you said you didn't want one, but I made you another anyway."

He places the mug on the side and then lowers his ass to the closed toilet and rests his elbows on his knees.

My heart begins to pound, and it only gets worse when he looks up at me through his lashes.

Hendrix is hot.

Both of the Kemp twins are.

Hendrix is a little softer around the edges, both with his body and his personality. He's still fit, he works out with Wilder a couple of times a week, but he doesn't quite have the muscle definition of his slightly younger brother. His hair is a little longer and he doesn't bother styling it like Wilder.

Where Wilder appears to give no shits about anything but having fun and being... well... wild, Hendrix overthinks everything.

I know hands down that I am safe with him. He would never do anything to put me in danger.

Wilder has shown me how easy it is to cross the line that Hendrix and I have always teetered on the edge of. Would it be so easy with us, too?

"Thank you," I whisper, the weight of my secrets pressing down on my shoulders, threatening to push me under.

His eyes bore into mine. He has so many things he wants to ask me right now, but he's holding back.

He's too scared.

He saw the familiarity between me and Wilder almost as clearly as I felt it.

"Are you... are you okay?" he finally asks, silently begging me to say yes and tell him that what he witnessed out there wasn't anything to be concerned about.

I mean, it's not. Not really.

My heart has always belonged to Hendrix Kemp, and I'm confident that it always will.

But what happened on Halloween shifted things.

It opened my eyes and allowed me to think outside the box.

Is Wilder right? Is it just my crazy romance novels that are giving me unrealistic ideas? Or...

My blood heats and my cheeks burn.

"Yeah, of course," I lie, forcing a smile onto my face.

"I-is there—" My heart jumps into my throat as he cuts himself off. "I'll leave you to it."

Pushing from his seat, he stands tall. He makes me feel tiny, but not as tiny when I'm with both of them.

My stomach knots and my mouth runs dry.

Get your head out of the gutter, Noelle.

You have yet to experience things properly with one guy, let alone two.

Brothers.

Twins...

He's at the door before I find my voice.

"Are you okay?"

He stills, sucking in a deep breath that makes his chest expand and his shoulders rise.

Dread seeps through my veins, and then he makes it worse by looking back over his shoulder.

The sadness in his eyes hurts.

You did this, Noelle. You put that look there.

He sucks in another breath before letting his eyes drop to the floor. He mutters, "I have no idea," before pulling the door open and disappearing.

My heart plummets as silence rings out around me.

I've got to fix this.

But... how?

"Where's Rix?" I ask when I step into the living room a while later and only find Wilder laid out on the couch, watching ESPN.

"He went out," he replies absently.

"Out?" I ask, my eyes darting toward the window.

There's nothing but white, fluffy snow as far as the eye can see.

Jesus. How long was I in the bath for?

"But it's—"

"He'll be fine," Wilder assures me, finally pushing himself up and turning around to look at me.

I'm dressed much like I was earlier in one of Hendrix's hoodies and a set of pajamas. I don't have much other choice, seeing as I packed with never leaving the cabin in mind.

"Where?"

"Nowhere. Just wanted to clear his head."

All the air rushes from my lungs and I look up at the ceiling.

"This is our fault," I whisper.

"He'll be fine," Wilder repeats in that uncaring Wilder way of his.

"He's hurting. *We* hurt him."

"Did you tell him?" Wilder asks, watching me as I move to the armchair opposite him.

"No. Did you?"

He shakes his head.

"We need to."

One of his brows lifts. "Do we, though?"

"Wilder," I groan. "This isn't a joke. I'm not just some girl you had some fun with and turned your back on. This is different. We fucked up. We fucked up big, and now we need to fix it."

When he doesn't respond, my eyes widen to urge him to say something.

But he just slumps back on the couch like he doesn't have a care in the world.

"Actions speak louder than words," he finally says.

My brows pinch. "What the hell is that supposed to mean?"

He shrugs one shoulder.

"He wants you, Noelle. Give it to him. It is Christmas, after all."

HENDRIX

The snow falls heavily around me. But it's too soft. Too peaceful.

I need the anger of the lashing rain, not the gentle flakes.

Unlike Wilder, I actually packed for this trip and have some winter clothes, but that doesn't mean I'm currently warm. Quite the opposite, in fact.

I'm pretty sure it's worse than it actually is as well. I'm numb.

The past hour... well, to say I didn't see it coming would be an exaggeration.

Sure, Noelle hasn't been quite like herself since we left our house in South Carolina yesterday morning. But while I suspected that Wilder's sudden appearance on our little trip might have had something to do with it, I never could have predicted what I now fear to be the reason.

Was running away the best reaction? N

If I were more like Wilder, I probably would have stayed and had it out with them both.

But I'm not him. And isn't that the whole fucking issue with my life?

I. Am. Not. Wilder.

I've learned to deal with not being the fun one, the smart one, the athletic one, the popular one. I could because I had her.

Noelle never looked at me like the second-best twin. From day one, our connection always made me her favorite, and that meant everything to me.

If that's no longer the case, then...

I stop in the middle of the deserted street and look up.

The falling snow makes my head spin like I'm in a wintery vortex, but I welcome the sensation. It's a hell of a lot better than focusing on the pain in my chest.

I've no idea what to do.

I know what I should do. I should confront them and demand the truth.

But that's going to hurt. I don't want that.

It's Christmas.

It's supposed to be the time for happiness and miracles, not pain and heartbreak.

This should have been the trip that dreams are made of for us, but day one and it's already turning into a nightmare.

The snow is settling faster than I've ever seen, and not two seconds after I've taken a step has my mark been eradicated.

It's a sight that doesn't make me feel any better about the current situation.

Could I be forgotten about just as easily?

I have no idea how long passes by the time I convince myself that I need to return to the cabin and deal with the situation.

The sun is already sinking in the sky, teasing me with the fact that I've wasted the first day of our vacation.

I can barely see anything in front of me as I close in on our cabin, the snow is so heavy. The wind is also picking up, bitter and painful against the exposed skin of my face.

With my head down, I trudge through the snow and up onto our deck.

The lights glowing through the windows taunt me, and I can't help but slow my pace and look into the living room.

Wilder is on the couch on his cell and Noelle is reading. It's a sight I've seen many, many times over the years. But this time, despite the fact they're sitting feet apart and totally innocently, my heart picks up speed.

What would I have done if I'd discovered a very different scene?

If Wilder was touching her the way he had earlier? His hand around her delicate throat, her breath catching, betraying her feelings?

Would she lean into him? Beg for more in the way I want more from her?

Heat surges through my body as my imagination runs away with me. Watching them together shouldn't affect me like this. But it does.

Shaking my head, I rip my gaze away from them and continue toward the front door.

Unease trickles through my veins. I want to ignore everything, bury my head in the sand and just continue as usual. That's the easiest, least stressful and painful way to deal with this. But it's also wrong.

For once, I need to poke my head above the parapet and find out the truth, consequences be damned.

"Rix," Noelle cries the second she hears my return.

Her quiet footsteps race through the cabin and in a heartbeat, she's right there in front of me.

Her hair is piled on top of her head and she's still wearing my hoodie. The sight of her in my clothes gives me the warm and fuzzies just like it always does. When she's in my things, it's easy to lie to myself and pretend that she's mine.

I just manage to shrug my coat off when we collide.

"Shit," I grunt, taking a step back as the force of her small body hits me.

"Oh my god, you're soaking," Noelle points out, releasing me in a flash.

The loss of her body heat causes a violent shiver to rip through me.

"Come on," she says, taking my hand and leading me through to the bedroom.

Wilder's gaze burns into me, but I don't look at him.

I can't.

If I do, I fear that all I'll see is my worst nightmare playing out in my mind like a high-definition movie.

"Where have you been?" Noelle demands as the door closes behind us.

"Walking," I mutter.

"In the snow?"

I shrug. It's a Wilder move, and I hate that I've been reduced to that now.

"Take your clothes off," she instructs as she rummages through my case to find warm replacements.

It's something we've done a million times for each other in the past, but suddenly, everything feels different, and the prospect of stripping down to my underwear is suddenly very, very daunting.

When she spins around with a pair of sweats and a t-shirt in her hand, I'm still standing in exactly the same place.

I had no idea that my coat was doing fuck all to protect

me from the snow. It just goes to prove how numb I was out there.

Right now, though, everything is coming back with the power of a tsunami.

"Rix, you need to—"

"I need to know everything," I blurt, cutting her off.

Her brow creases with concern. "W-what?" she stutters.

"Something has happened with you and Wilder, and I need to know what that is," I state, my voice steadier than I was expecting.

"Rix," she warns.

"No," I bark. "Don't try to protect me. It's too late. I've got all these images and ideas floating around my head, and I need to know if they're right or not."

"There's nothing going on with us," she says firmly.

"Something has happened though, hasn't it? That out there," I say, throwing my arm out in the general direction of the kitchen, "wasn't the first time he's been that close to you."

Her eyes hold mine for a few seconds, and I hate what I can see in them.

Fear.

Pure. Unfiltered. Fear.

I know because I feel it too. Right down to my fucking toes.

Ripping her eyes from mine, she stares up at the ceiling for a beat before wrapping her arms around herself as if they'll help keep her together before she turns around.

"I went out on the night of Nick's anniversary," she starts, her voice weak.

Nick was her brother. He was the most incredible kid. Sweet, funny, smart. A lot like Wilder in many ways. He was destined to break hearts and do incredible things. Or at least, he was until he got sick.

Watching him suffer, and in turn, watching Noelle fight to stay strong for him was the hardest thing I've ever experienced.

Their parents couldn't cope. Hell, they'd checked out long before he was ill. But it got worse once he was diagnosed with Leukemia.

Noelle became his parent even more than she already was. But she couldn't give him what he really needed.

Sure, he had all the love and support he could ever want, but as far as medical attention went…

Not being able to get him the treatment he required is something that's going to haunt her for the rest of her life. She was only a child herself; it wasn't her responsibility, but that doesn't mean she doesn't feel the weight of it in the way her parents should.

"Noelle," I breathe, taking a step closer, although coming nowhere close to touching her.

"I know," she confesses. "I know."

I'd told her I wasn't going to go out that night. I'd told her that I'd stay with her, do whatever she wanted to do, be whatever she needed me to be, just like the other years I've supported her through the worst day of her life.

But she persuaded me to go.

I had an assignment due and I needed all the support I could get. I didn't want to go, but she convinced me.

She fucking convinced me, and I wasn't there when she needed me.

Wilder was.

Fuck. Pain lashes at my chest knowing that I had a part in whatever is going to happen next.

"There was a frat Halloween party I saw posted online about an hour after you left. I don't even know why I thought it would be a good idea. Hell, I knew it would be a really bad idea. But once it took hold of me, I was powerless to stop it.

"I pulled together a questionable costume and left the house without second-guessing my decision. The party was in full flow when I got there, and I slipped in unnoticed.

"One drink led to a few more. I was dragged out onto the dancefloor by someone in a werewolf costume, and I let go.

"For a while, it was great, and I started to wonder why I hadn't done it before.

"My dance partners came and went, but I didn't really notice. Not until one guy grabbed my hips.

"Admittedly, I was pretty drunk by this point, but it was different."

My stomach knots, knowing exactly who it was, and terrified of what happened next.

"We danced. It was..." She trails off, clearly uneasy about confessing how it really felt. "It was everything I didn't know I needed.

"His touch burned. Lit me up inside in a way I kinda always thought it might do but was never curious enough to find out."

I close my eyes as pain slices through me.

I should have given her that.

Not him.

"We danced and danced. Things got... a lot."

A growl fills the room, and it takes a few seconds to realize that the noise actually comes from me.

Noelle spins around, facing me for the first time since she started this little story, and my chest tightens at the sight of her tears.

"Did you sleep with him?" I force out.

She hiccups but thankfully shakes her head.

"No, Rix. I haven't—we haven't."

The breath I didn't realize I was holding comes rushing out of me.

"So..."

"He..." She swallows thickly. "He touched me. Made me feel good. Made me forget."

An image very similar to earlier with him pinning her back against the wall fills my head, but his hand isn't only around her throat...

Silence falls, the air between us charged with a million and one emotions we're battling with.

"I'm sorry," she whispers, her eyes locked on the floor.

My chest heaves as I stand there staring at my best friend curled in on herself as her regrets get the better of her.

Anger pulses through my veins, but there is more than just that. My feelings for Noelle have never been that simple. They don't fit neatly into any box.

I've tried to keep her contained in the best friend zone, but she's never managed to stay there.

"Noelle," I breathe, needing to see her eyes.

It takes her a couple of seconds, but she finally lifts her gaze.

Something crackles between us, and for the first time ever, the barrier that's always stopped me from crossing the line with her has gone.

Not just gone.

Obliterated.

11

NOELLE

Something changes in Hendrix's expression. His eyes darken and pure determination flashes across his face.

I was expecting to see nothing but anger and betrayal.

Both of them are there, sure. But they're not the overriding emotions. Something else is, and it makes my stomach twist and my chest contract.

"Rix, what are you—" My words are cut off as he lurches toward me.

His hands grip the sides of my face and his lips slam down on mine.

Holy shit.

I'm so shocked, I'm frozen in place as he kisses me.

I've dreamed about this over and over, tried to imagine what it might feel like, but I never thought it would be like this.

His tongue drags across my bottom lip and I'm powerless but to fall into it with him.

My lips part, granting him the permission he's seeking,

and the second our tongues collide, my body sags against his.

Releasing one side of my face, his hand drops. It starts innocently on my back before it slides lower. My entire body erupts with tingles as he drops it to my ass, squeezing gently and pressing me harder against him.

Oh my god.

Hendrix is kissing me.

My tongue is twisting with my best friend's.

And...

And he is hard as hell between us.

He should be hating me. I just confessed to being with his twin brother. And yet...

"Rix," I groan when he drags his lips from mine and kisses along my jaw toward my throat.

My fingers twist in his still damp and cold shirt, and I remember why we were in here in the first place.

Pushing the fabric up, I try to force him to take it off. I'm too short to do it all myself. The second he takes over, I start on his sweats, unaware of what I'm really doing and how it looks. That is, until I've pushed the fabric over his hips and he takes a step back.

My eyes drop and—

Oh my god.

I've seen Rix in his underwear a million times over the years, but I have never seen Rix in his underwear like this...

His hair is wild as it dries, his cheeks still red from the cold. His body is exactly how I know it to be, but the way his boxers are bulging...

Holy hell, my best friend is packing something I was not expecting. Hoping for, sure, but not expecting.

Time stands still as we stare at each other, me fully covered in one of his massive hoodies, and him on the verge of baring all.

We've hit a crossroads.

He might have been the one to finally take the leap we've both been too scared of making, but now it's on both of us.

We have a choice to make.

Stick or twist.

I know what I want.

Reaching for the bottom of his hoodie, I peel it up my body before throwing it to the floor. My skin prickles with awareness. I may not have bared as much to him, but it's enough for now.

I take a step closer to him and turn so my back is to the bed. As predicted, he follows, his eyes locked on mine.

'Noelle,' he mouths silently.

A small smile pulls at my lips as I lower myself onto the bed and crawl back until I'm right in the middle, resting back on my palms.

Lifting my chin, I wordlessly tell him that I'm his, if he wants me, and wait.

My heart is like a runaway train in my chest, and it only gets worse when Rix runs his eyes down my body as if I'm lying here naked.

"Rix?" I whisper, my patience running out.

He swallows, his hand coming up so he can drag his fingers through his hair.

"I hate that—"

"I'm sorry," I breathe.

"No, let me finish." My fingers twist in the sheets beneath me as I wait for him to find his words. "I hate that he was the one to push me into this, but also..." He reaches out and wraps his hand around my ankle, dragging me down the bed so I've no choice but to fall onto my back. He crawls over me, the heat of his skin burning into me as his eyes bore into mine. "I'll probably be forever grateful for him forcing me into action."

"Hend—" He cuts me off with his lips, kissing me as thoroughly and as deeply as he did before, only this time, the weight of his body presses me into the mattress.

I love it, and it also makes me realize—

"He never kissed me," I blurt, pressing my hand to the center of his chest, forcing him to lift up a little.

His eyes bounce between mine as he registers what I just said.

"That's because you're mine."

Any response I might have is stolen by his kisses.

I'm aware of time moving on as we make out like teenagers, but I don't care about anything other than this moment.

Our hands are everywhere as we learn each other in a whole new way, but neither of us makes a move to push it any further.

I might have been waiting for this for a long time, but I don't want to rush it.

Rix rolls onto his back, taking me with him and settling me over his waist.

The thickness of his erection presses against me, making me gasp.

My eyes pop open and I instantly find his dark blue orbs staring back at me.

Desire unfurls through my body, making everything south of my waist clench.

Needing more, I risk rolling my hips.

"Oh shit," I breathe at the same time he grunts, "Fuck."

Sitting up straight, I do it again, loving the way his jaw pops as his teeth grind.

"Rix," I moan when I do it again.

I'm never going to need my little vibrator again.

"Keep going," he encourages. "Use me."

"Fuck, that's hot," I confess, my hips picking up speed.

Every muscle in his body is pulled tight as I rock over him.

It's so innocent compared to what we could be doing, but also, it's perfect.

"You're hot," he counters. "Jesus. Just look at you." His eyes drop to my chest. My nipples are hard, pressing against the soft fabric of my tank. My breasts are heavy, craving his touch, but I don't do anything about it. There will be time for that, I hope.

This is only the beginning.

Wilder's promise rings so loudly in my ear that I still.

"What's wrong?" Hendrix asks, his grip on my hips tightening with concern.

His eyes hold mine, begging me to share.

Shame burns me up inside.

I know the outcome has been more pleasurable than I was expecting, but I'm aware that it could switch at any point.

I betrayed him that night at the party, and I betrayed him this morning out on the swing.

"Noelle," he warns.

I desperately want to grip onto what we've found here and never let go. But I can't. This little bit of heaven is already slipping through my fingers like grains of sand.

"It wasn't just the Halloween party."

He stills at my confession. In fact, I'm pretty sure he actually stops breathing.

Dropping my gaze, I focus on his abs.

"This morning. On the swing."

Hendrix sucks in a deep breath as those words settle around us.

"I see. And are you planning on doing it again?"

A bitter laugh tumbles from my throat.

"Nothing about this has been planned, Rix."

"So you don't want this?" he asks, hurt clear in his voice.

My eyes jump to his.

"This?" I ask, gesturing between us. "Yes, I want this. I've always wanted this."

His face drops, hurt darkening his eyes.

"Then why him first?"

I let out a heavy sigh. "I didn't go out looking for him or for anyone that night. He wasn't looking for me either; we both had masks on. It wasn't until he followed me to the bathroom and pulled his mask off that I discovered his identity."

"You could have stopped."

And isn't that the crux of the issue?

"Yeah, I could. I should have. But... I can give you all the excuses about being drunk and swept away by it all. But the truth is I could have stopped and I didn't."

"You knew I'd find out and it would hurt."

"Yeah," I agree because I can't do anything else. "But maybe there was a part of me that thought it might help." My confession is quiet, almost inaudible, but he hears it. "And it has."

"That's a dirty, risky play."

"I never said it was rational," I argue.

Dropping over him, I plant a hand on either side of his head and brush my lips over his.

Butterflies flutter in my stomach.

I'm kissing Hendrix Kemp. Finally.

"Noelle," he warns, although there's no strength behind it as his hands slide to my ass, forcing me to begin grinding again.

"You feel so good," I whisper in our kiss.

"So good," he agrees. "Can we forget how old we are so you don't forever tease me about coming in my pants as an adult?"

Laughter bubbles up faster than I can stop.

"Consider it forgotten. But if you want, we could just take your pants off."

His grip on my ass tightens.

"No," he says, shocking the hell out of me. "This is how it needs to be. For now. I'm not rushing anything with you."

"Hendrix," I gasp when he suddenly flips us again and takes control.

Wrapping my legs around his waist, I twist my fingers in his hair and hold him to me as tightly as I can, not that I think for a second he's going anywhere.

Our kiss is filthy and all-consuming. His hands alternate between my thighs, holding my hips, and sliding up my sides toward my breasts. But despite now knowing that he might be a bit of a boob man, he doesn't indulge.

"Please," I moan, my back arching as he thrusts against me, building me higher and higher. He watches me with fire burning in his eyes. Knowing I'm causing it makes me feel like the most beautiful woman in the world.

It's a heady feeling that I never want to lose.

Releasing him, I take the bull by the horns and drag my tank down, exposing myself to him.

His eyes drop immediately and his lips part.

Wrapping my hand around the back of his neck, I tug him down.

"Please," I whimper again. "Let me feel you."

He hesitates, but not for very long.

Leaning forward, his lips surround one of my nipples before he sucks and flicks the tip with his tongue.

"Oh shit, yes," I cry, probably a little too loudly seeing as we're in a tiny cabin with his twin brother somewhere in the vicinity.

The thought of him listening to us does weird things to my insides. And the second I consider the possibility of him watching, I explode.

Pleasure shoots from my core and doesn't end until every single one of my nerve endings are tingling.

"Hendrix," I cry as my body takes on a life of its own, twitching and convulsing beneath him.

"Fuck, Noelle. Fuck. Fuck," he grunts before his face falls lax as his release claims him.

And fuck, is it a sight to behold.

I watch him, utterly mesmerized as he rides the waves of pleasure.

"Christ. Why haven't we always been doing this?" he asks before surging toward my lips again, only we don't get to lose ourselves in this one because there's a noise at the other side of the room.

Rix twists around as I look over, and we both still simultaneously.

"What the fuck, Bro?" Hendrix barks as my hands lift to cover my bare breasts.

"Just wanted to know if either of you had seen the weather warning," he states as if this is fucking normal.

"Does it look like we're watching the fucking weather?"

"I dunno, something tells me it's pretty fucking wet in here."

12

WILDER

I didn't get up with the intention of listening at the door like a creep. I was going to get a drink, but then I heard a moan and my feet took me in a different direction from what I was expecting.

I couldn't complain, though. It sounded hot. And it wasn't my fault that they'd left the door ajar. Although, it might have been mine when I pressed my palm against the door and pushed it open a little wider.

Watching two people go at it isn't anything new to me. I've done all the wild parties and watched my teammates get up to all sorts with an audience.

But watching Hendrix with Noelle hit differently.

I was hard long before I laid eyes on them, just from the sounds they were making alone. But as I stepped into the doorway and started watching them grind against each other... Shit.

And they weren't even naked.

"You need to get the fuck out," Rix growls as he glares over his shoulder at me.

It's hard to take his anger seriously after watching him get off on his best friend.

"Sorry," I say, holding my hands up like I actually am.

I'm not. I couldn't give a fuck.

"I couldn't help it. She's hot when she comes, right?"

Hendrix's expression flips in a heartbeat, and before I can blink, he's off the bed and flying toward me.

"Rix, no," Noelle cries a beat before my twin brother's fist collides with my eye.

I stumble back, allowing the wall to catch me as my hands lift to cover my face.

"Dude, the fuck?"

He comes at me again, this time hitting my jaw. It's not the first time we've fought, and I highly doubt that it'll be the last, but unlike usual, I don't even attempt to retaliate. Why would I when I deserve the pain and everything he can throw at me?

I won't deny that I fucked up both that first night at the party and then again this morning.

I just... I can't help myself.

"That's enough," Noelle snaps, stepping between us and pressing her tiny palms to each of our chests.

Hendrix's bare one heaves with a mixture of anger, frustration, and lingering desire. I'm much more relaxed, although still very turned on.

"I should kill you for touching her," Hendrix seethes.

I can't help myself; a smirk pulls at my lips. "And why would you do that? Have you already forgotten what just happened right there?" I say, pointing at the bed.

"You're an asshole," Rix points out.

"That isn't news to anyone, Bro. I do think you should probably be thanking me, though."

Rix shakes his head while Noelle breathes, "Leave it."

"I am disappointed, though. You're both wearing way

too many clothes. What's the problem, man? Worried she'll discover mine is bigger?"

"You fucking—"

"Hendrix," Noelle shouts, turning toward him and shoving him back.

"Why are you protecting him?" Rix barks back.

"I'm not. I'm stopping both of you. Fighting isn't going to solve anything," she states firmly.

"Wilder and I fucked up. It was reckless and selfish, and we're sorry. Right?" she shoots over her shoulder.

"Sorry for hurting you, yeah. I don't regret it, though."

"Wilder," Noelle hisses.

"What? It was hot. And if it ultimately leads to this," I say, gesturing between them, "then it was more than worth it. I want you happy, Bro, and I'm sorry for saying it but you needed a kick up the ass. You've been in love with Noelle for forever; you were just too pussy to do anything about it. So now... you're welcome."

Rix looks down at Noelle, and all his fight leaves him. Instead, his eyes go all soft and sappy. He really is hopelessly in love with her.

"You okay?" she whispers, stepping up to him and cupping his cheek.

I watch them, feeling totally out of place as they gaze into each other's eyes. I should slip back out and leave them to figure this out together, but I can't. My feet are rooted to the floor.

"Yes. No. I have no idea," Hendrix confesses before lowering his forehead to rest on hers.

No more words are said, at least not out loud. I might not be a part of it, but they have quite an in-depth silent conversation.

"I'm going to go and clean up," Hendrix finally says.

"I would," I pipe up. "Coming in your pants is all good fun until it goes cold and starts to dry."

"Fucking hell," Hendrix mutters as he takes a step back from Noelle. His eyes lift to mine, and I read his warning long before he says the words. "Can I trust you with her?"

It hurts that he has to question it, but also, I totally understand. I haven't exactly proven myself to be trustworthy or respectful recently.

"Of course," I agree.

"I fucking hope you're right. If you touch her again—"

"I won't," I agree. "Not without your permission, at least."

Hendrix's eyes widen, his chin dropping. "W-what?"

I can't help but laugh as my eyes meet Noelle's.

"You should get your girl to read you a bedtime story tonight. I think you'd enjoy it," I say before twisting around and walking out of the room.

Forcing myself to walk away, I stop in the kitchen for the drink I wanted earlier before dropping back onto the couch as the news continues to report the incoming storm.

It was a bullshit question to blurt out when they first found me standing there, but it was for good reason. We're about to get hit with something we weren't expecting.

"What the hell?" Noelle gasps when she joins me a few minutes later, once again dressed in Hendrix's hoodie.

Looking over, I find her staring at the TV with wide eyes.

"You said you wanted snow," I mutter.

"Y-yeah but—shit," she breathes as she lowers herself into the chair and watches the report. "That's a lot."

"I hope you brought a couple of extra books. I don't think we're going to be going anywhere for a while."

It takes her a second to look over, but when I do, I find a

mixture of anticipation and excitement dancing in her eyes. Not only that, I feel it too.

Things might be a bit weird right now, but the three of us trapped in a small cabin opens up a whole world of possibilities.

Maybe this trip isn't going to be so dull after all.

It takes another thirty minutes for Hendrix to appear, and when he does, he looks a little more put together and like himself again.

Predictably, his eyes find Noelle first, and I'm pretty sure his chest compresses the second he sees that we're sitting apart.

I might be reckless, but I'm not fucking stupid.

"Hey," Noelle says softly.

"Hey."

Christ, he looks like a love-sick puppy. I thought it was bad before, but one round of dry humping and he's completely fucking gone for her.

Suddenly, he rips his eyes away from her and turns to me.

"Get up," he demands.

My brows lift. "I'm sorry?"

"You heard me. Get up."

"But I'm watching—"

"I don't care. Get the fuck up."

Rolling my eyes, I do as I'm told and get to my feet.

"Perfect, now go and get us all a drink and some snacks. We're watching a movie. Noelle's choice."

"Obviously," I mutter under my breath.

"If you don't like it, you can go out."

"Fuck off, have you seen how hard it's snowing?"

"No, I've been kinda busy," he points out, glancing at Noelle, his cheeks heating in a way I'm sure she'd describe as adorable.

"Fine," I hiss as I continue toward the kitchen to do my big brother's bidding so he can snuggle with his girl.

"We're getting hit with a storm. They're predicting it's going to be really bad," Noelle explains. "We're probably going to be stuck here."

"Sounds awful," Hendrix quips. "Whatever will we do?"

Noelle's happy squeal rips through the cabin. Something weird twists up my stomach as I listen to them laugh.

I'm not ashamed to admit that I'm usually the focus of attention, so it feels weird to be the one on the sidelines.

I don't like it.

Jealousy...

"Get a fucking grip," I mutter to myself as I rip open a bag of chips and pour them into two bowls. Something tells me that I'm going to be kicked off the couch now.

Their laughter continues as I grab beers and head back out with the bowls precariously balanced on my hand and arm.

Unsurprisingly, they're cuddled up on the couch. It's not an unusual position for them to be in, but if it's possible, they look even closer than ever now.

Hendrix spots me the second I walk into the room, and his eyes follow me as I place everything on the coffee table in front of him.

"Good enough for you, Sir?" I mock.

"It's great," Noelle says, leaning forward to grab two of the beers.

She passes one to Hendrix, but he's too busy glaring at me to notice.

"I get that you're pissed with me, Rix. I'm sorry. I fucked up. But can you blame me? You've seen her; she's hot."

"She is sitting right here." Noelle scoffs.

"Yeah, and you're hot. But seriously, we're going to be stuck here for a few days at least by the looks of it, you can't stay pissed all that time."

"You wanna bet?"

"But it's Christmas," I state. "And we're family."

"You were meant to be in a different country right now," Hendrix mutters.

"Yeah, well, aren't you lucky that I'm not? You might not have come in your pants just now if I were elsewhere."

"Will you just shut the hell up?"

I shrug before dropping into the chair with my bottle of beer and bowl of chips.

"What are we watching?" I ask, although I already have a very good idea.

"Christmas movie," Noelle says.

"Wonderful. I hope there's a good car chase and gunfight."

I feel the heat of her stare when she turns it on me, but I don't look back. I don't need to give Hendrix another reason to hate me right now.

"You'd be so lucky. Pretty sure it's Hallmark," my brother mutters.

"Even better. I fucking love Christmas," I say before throwing a handful of chips into my mouth.

We fall into a comfortable silence as the movie begins. As predicted, it's cheesy as fuck and possibly the most cringeworthy thing I've ever seen. But Noelle seems to enjoy it, and I guess that's the main thing here.

It's only about twenty minutes in when my cell buzzes in my pocket and I find a message from Benny, one of my teammates, in our group chat.

I lose myself messaging the guys, trying to ignore the presence of the couple in front of me.

They look cute. Too fucking cute, and I can't help but find myself wondering what it would be like to find a girl I actually wanted to spend time with outside of the bedroom, or the back of my car, or the locker room...

It's a bizarre concept, but it soon hits me that Noelle is the only girl I've ever really spent any time with. All the others... they've never interested me enough to give me a reason to keep them around.

I tell myself that it's because she's Hendrix's best friend, that I haven't had a choice in having her in my life. But I can't help wondering if it's more than that.

There's a break in the group chat, and I risk looking up. I want to say I'm surprised that neither of them is watching the movie and they're instead having a hot and heavy make-out session, but I'm not. They've both been waiting for this for years; I guess it's only right they try and make up for lost time.

I just wish I had somewhere to go, but other than chilling out on their bed, or lazing in the bathtub, I'm pretty fucking stuck.

Closing our group chat, I scroll through the messages from girls I've got in my inbox. I could message one of them and I've no doubt they'd happily reply, maybe even video call, but unlike usual, the idea isn't all that tempting. Instead, I find my eyes lifting once again.

13

HENDRIX

All my life I've battled with my emotions, with who I am, who I want to be and what's expected of me.

But it's never felt more confusing than it does right now.

My right hand aches from the punches I threw into Wilder's face, but it has nothing on my heart. That is totally battered.

On one hand, I'm happier than I've ever been. I'm lying on the couch with yet another cheesy Christmas movie playing and my arms around Noelle. It's perfect. Everything I've always dreamed of.

We missed most of the last movie because we were too busy making out. Again, something I could only dream of before now.

I knew that kissing her would be mind blowing, but I never could have imagined just how good it would be.

Having her lips on mine, her hands on my body, lights me up in a way I never thought possible.

But that's only the half of it. Right alongside my happiness is my anger.

It's not so much that Wilder did what he did. Weirdly, that doesn't bother me too much. If I'm being honest with myself, then I think I prefer that it was him than some random guy she met at a party. Wilder might be a bit of an idiot, but I trust him with Noelle in a way I wouldn't trust anyone else in the world.

He would never hurt her, because he knows that in turn, it'll hurt me.

But they covered it up. Were they ever going to tell me?

What if this trip had gone to plan and Wilder had gone away with his teammates? Would Noelle have confessed?

I'm pretty sure we wouldn't be where we are now.

One thing I know for a fact is Wilder was right. If it weren't for him and what happened at that party, then we wouldn't be here.

I close my eyes as the movie continues, vividly remembering how it felt earlier. How her body felt under my hands, how she sounded as she used me to get off.

Fuck, it was hot.

With her body pinned tightly against mine, there's no chance of her missing what my thoughts of her do to me.

Honestly, I've been rocking a semi ever since she made me come. Memories of us together, her presence, the anticipation of what's still to come has me in a constant state of horny.

Letting me know that she can feel it, Elle grinds her ass back against me.

"Noelle," I groan quietly so that only she can hear.

Wilder might be distracted by his cell now, but I've seen him looking over at us, watching us.

I can't figure out what he's thinking as he does, though.

We haven't spoken about it all yet, not really anyway,

and I can't help but wonder if he's not feeling as confident with it all as he usually is.

He's been with loads of girls. I should know; I've heard the sordid details about most of them. He lost his virginity when we were thirteen. At the time, I was a bit jealous. But that was nothing new. He was the popular one with all the friends, and I was just the quiet twin brother who spent all his time following Wilder around and hanging out with Noelle.

Other than the two of them, no one paid me any attention, so there was no way I'd get the chance to get down and dirty with a girl. Not that I saw anyone other than Noelle, and she wasn't in a place back then to really see me.

But as he started spending time with more girls, he'd return with tales, that yes, sounded fun, but also exhausting. I didn't want to be messing around with a different girl every night. I just wanted one. I still do.

"What?" she asks innocently as she does it again.

Sliding my hand from her hip, I slip it under both my hoodie she's still wearing and her tank.

There's a part of me that fears she's going to stop me. Us cuddling while watching a movie might not be all that unusual; being this close and intimate certainly is.

But she doesn't, and as my fingers hit her ribs, the breath I didn't know I was holding rushes out of me.

I move higher, but my confidence wanes when I brush the underside of her braless breast.

Oh my god. Am I actually doing this?

My stomach flutters and my dick aches.

Sensing that I'm second-guessing myself, Noelle's palm skims up my forearm before resting it over the back of my hand as she guides me higher.

"Fuck," I breathe as I take the fullness of her breast in

my hand. I almost come in my pants for the second time in a day.

Gently, I squeeze, and a smile pulls at my lips when a moan rumbles quietly in her throat.

She likes it.

Pushing myself up, I roll over her slightly, needing to see her reaction to my touch as well as feel it.

With my confidence growing, I pull my hand back a little and brush my thumb over her peaked nipple.

Her eyelids lower and a small gasp passes her lips.

I did that.

Pride and the need for more flood through me.

I want to hear her moaning like she was earlier.

I want to watch her lose control.

"Will you two just go to bed and let me watch this shit without getting turned on?"

I still before my eyes lift to my brother. But much to my surprise, he isn't watching us. Instead, he's still staring at his cell—not the shitty movie. He does have his hand inside his shorts, though. It's not an unusual position for him to sit in, but I can't help but wonder if he's teasing us or...

Does he still want her?

Fuck. Of course he does. She's Noelle. And just like he pointed out earlier, she's hot. Not his usual type, but still hella hot. And if he does still want her, does she want him? Would she choose him?

My concern only grows when she tugs my hand from beneath her tank and rolls off the couch.

In my head, I picture her walking over to him, holding her hand out and then leading him to the bedroom, leaving me here alone.

I'm so lost in my fear of being second best that I totally miss what actually happens.

"Rix?" she asks, staring down at me with concern in her eyes.

She hasn't gone to him.

She's with me.

Waiting for me.

"Shit," I hiss, my fear and anxiety giving out to a huge rush of nerves.

I have no idea what I'm doing here.

She may have got herself off on me earlier, but I didn't exactly have any input.

She's going to expect me to do something this time, but I have no idea how—

She leans down, her lips brushing my ear as her warm breath rushes down my neck.

"It's just me, Rix. You've got nothing to worry about. I've got you. I've always got you."

I close my eyes, hating that she can see me spiraling.

I've been so shit at so much in my life, I can't help that my go-to is that I'll be shit at anything new I try.

After all this, I'd hate to be a disappointment. Especially when she already knows how skilled Wilder is.

Slipping her hand into mine, she takes another step back and attempts to pull me up.

She doesn't stand a chance, so I help her out and get to my feet a beat before she takes off for the bedroom, our hands locked together.

I glance back just before we disappear around the corner and find Wilder watching us with a wretched expression on his face.

"Wild?" Concern for my brother forces his name to bubble up, and at the sound of my voice, he pulls himself from wherever he'd gone, his expression brightening.

"Go have fun," he says, forcing a smile onto his lips. "I'll be okay out here. Got my trusty right hand." He winks, but I don't feel the joke in his comment like I usually would.

A sharp tug on my hand brings me back to reality, and I remember why I shouldn't be feeling sorry for him. Turning back toward Noelle, I follow her into the only bedroom in the cabin and firmly close the door behind me.

We're not going to have any witnesses this time. If I am bad at this, at least the only other person who will know will be Noelle. I trust her completely.

"Are you okay?" Noelle asks when I don't move any farther into the room.

I look up and relax the second our eyes collide.

"I-I'm… scared," I confess, tugging on her arm so she has no choice but to step closer. Her heat sears my skin, making me desperate to continue what we started on the couch.

Her hand slides up my chest until she wraps it around the side of my throat.

"So am I, Rix. But I'm also excited."

My heart thumps so hard against my ribs I'm sure it's going to burst right out.

"Are we really doing this?"

Her head tilts to the side. "Assuming we're thinking of the same thing, then, yeah, I think we're really doing this. You want it, right?"

"So much," I confess, dropping my head to hers.

"Me too," she agrees before pushing up on her toes and brushing her lips against mine.

My heart jumps into my throat as my arms band around her, dragging her even closer into my body.

Our kiss deepens and I push from the wall, walking her backward until her legs hit the bed.

Pulling back, I gaze down into her eyes. They're blown with desire.

Desire for me.

It's mind blowing.

I dive for her lips again as I reach for the bottom of my hoodie. I drag it up and then discover my mistake when I need to pull back to let the fabric pass.

It's worth it, though. So fucking worth it.

After dropping the hoodie to the floor, I slide my hands up her sides and brazenly cup her breasts.

She lets out a loud moan that spurs me on, and before I know what I'm doing, her tank has hit the floor too.

"Fuck. You're beautiful," I breathe before picking her up and placing her on the bed.

She rests back on her palms, baring herself to me.

It's... everything.

Reaching back, I drag my own shirt off, shove my sweats down my legs, and kick them away before crawling onto the bed in only my boxers.

As I lean over her, her legs wrap around my waist, dragging me closer.

"You are so perfect," I whisper before kissing her again.

I'm addicted. So fucking addicted.

"Rix," she moans, her hands roaming over my back.

Her touch lights me up in a way I'm not sure I'll ever get used to.

Everything I've ever heard about being with a woman, about sex, about intimacy, pales in comparison to this. And we've barely even started.

14

NOELLE

"Oh god," I moan as Rix's lips leave my throat and brush over my chest.

My nipples are so hard they hurt. I need…

I need…

"Yes," I hiss when he flicks one of them with his tongue.

My eyes hold his as he does it again, and then again.

I can see his nerves, they're clear as day for me to read in his eyes, but they're not holding him back. Thank God. I'm not sure I could cope right now if they did.

My fingers twist tighter in his hair, forcing him to stay where he is and silently letting him know that he's doing all the right things.

Arching my back slightly, I encourage him on.

He ducks lower before wrapping his lips around one of my nipples.

"Oh shit," I gasp as a strong shot of lust hits me right between the legs. "More."

I might not be able to see his mouth, but I can tell from the way his eyes crinkle that he's smiling.

As he switches to the other side, I get a quick glimpse of

that smile, and it makes my chest ache to know that he's proud of himself right now.

I know he's struggling with self-confidence and standing beside Wilder, who seems to be good at everything. I love that I can give him this.

He builds me higher and higher just from his mouth on my breasts alone, but all too soon, it's not enough.

Tugging on his soft locks, I drag his head up so he's hovering right over my face.

"Take my panties off, Rix. I want to feel you."

His eyes widen and his pupils dilate.

"Noe—"

"Stop overthinking it," I whisper, slipping my hand to his jaw. "I want you. I need you. We were always meant to be each other's firsts."

"Oh my god," he breathes, dropping his head to mine as if he can't hold it up. "I never thought I'd hear you say that."

"It's always been you, Rix."

"Not him?" he blurts, unable to stop himself.

"No, Hendrix. Not him. You."

All the air rushes out of his lungs and his eyes close as he absorbs my words.

"It's always been you too," he says as his hands descend.

They tremble as they go, and I kinda love that this moment means just as much to him as it does me.

It's been a long time coming, that's for sure.

I gasp as he curls his fingers around my panties, but I'm not the only one.

"It's okay," I whisper.

He hooks them over my ass before sitting up.

There's nothing but awe and fascination as he watches himself bare me to him.

After untangling one foot from the lace, he throws them on the end of the bed and stares at me.

My heart slams against my chest.

I haven't been naked in front of anyone since I was a kid.

This is... this is nerve-wracking as fuck.

I startle when Hendrix's hands land on my ankles before hesitantly sliding up to my knees.

He pauses and then shocks the hell out of me when he spreads my knees wider, giving him a better view of my pussy.

"So beautiful," he muses.

His warm breath tickling over me is the ultimate tease, and my hips lift from the bed.

"Rix," I groan impatiently. I might never have done this before, but right now, I need it. I need it so badly. "Please."

In a flash, he's off the bed and shoving his boxers down his legs.

My eyes drop to his dick, and my breath catches.

I may have had my hand around Wilder's, but I never really registered what that size might look like.

But seeing it standing proud of Rix's body... holy hell.

Do I really want to do this?

He crawls back into the bed and gets comfortable between my thighs.

His dick bobs, brushing against my pussy, making my entire body tense at the sensation.

He drops over me once more, his hand landing beside my head as his lips move to mine.

His other hand is on my thigh, gently caressing me.

"Do you have any idea how perfect you are?" he tells me, his eyes bouncing between mine.

My nose tickles, and a huge lump crawls up my throat.

"I love you," I blurt.

It's not news to me. I'm not shocked by my confession, but it seems that he is.

"Y-you..."

"Rix," I breathe, my voice cracked with emotion.

"I love you too, Elle. I always have."

A soft smile plays on my lips as I fight to hold my tears back.

Now is not the time for a sob fest.

Releasing my thigh, he holds his dick, dragging the head through my folds.

His eyes rip from mine in favor of watching.

"Go on," I encourage. I might be a little anxious over what's about to happen. We've all heard the horror stories of women's first times. As much as I'd like to savor this moment, I also kinda want it done so we can move onto the much more relaxed and hopefully less painful second, third, and fourth time.

"I-I—" He swallows thickly. "I don't have any condoms. I wasn't expecting—"

"It's okay. You know I'm on birth control." He literally came with me and held my hand as I had the implant put into my arm a couple of years ago.

"Are you sure?" he asks with a small frown pinching his brows.

"Never been surer of anything in my life," I assure him. "I want to feel you. We've waited all this time; there shouldn't be anything between us."

At this, he moves his dick lower, nudging at my entrance.

My muscles tense.

"Relax, please," he begs.

I suck in a deep breath and will my body to loosen up.

"Okay?" he asks hesitantly.

"Just do it."

He nods once before pushing the head of his dick inside me.

"Oh god," I gasp, making him still instantly.

"Does it hurt?" he asks, looking horrified at the thought.

"N-no," I stutter, trying to decide exactly what I'm feeling right now. "It's just... weird."

"Reassuring," he laughs. "If it helps, you feel fucking incredible."

His words light me up inside—that is, until he pushes a little deeper and a bolt of pain shoots through me.

"Fuck," he grunts, able to read it on my face,

He lowers himself over me, resting on his elbows beside my head.

"I'm sorry," he says before slamming his lips down on mine, trying to distract me as he punches his hips forward, sinking all the way inside me.

I cry out, but Hendrix swallows it with his kiss.

He freezes, waiting for me to get used to the invasion.

His kiss continues, and I happily lose myself in it.

I'm having sex with my best friend.

He's inside me right now.

Hendrix's dick is—

"Oh," I gasp the second he moves. "That's—"

"Okay?"

"Y-yeah, I think so."

"I won't last long," he promises. "You feel... this is..."

"It's okay."

"I want to make you feel good too."

"You are. You do," I promise him.

"You're hurting," he says with a deep frown.

"It's nothing. Keep going. Please."

So he does. He pulls out almost all the way before sinking back inside me.

With him hovering just above me, I get to see exactly

how it affects him. Undiluted pleasure washes over his face.

It's everything.

"So much better than my hand," he muses, making me laugh. "Oh shit," he grunts when I clench around him. "Shit. Shit. Fuuuuuck," he groans, flying over the edge. His dick jerks inside me as his entire body stills. His face morphs just like it did earlier when he got off on me.

So. Fucking. Sexy.

His groan rips through the bedroom loud enough to let Wilder know what's happening, but I don't care. He can listen all he likes.

"I'm sorry, I couldn't—"

"Shush," I whisper, grabbing his cheeks and dragging his lips to mine as his dick softens inside me.

I kiss him as deeply as I can, letting my hands roam over his body. I love the way his muscles bunch and pull as my palm slides down his back.

He kisses across my jaw before sucking on my earlobe.

"You've made me hard again," he whispers, gently thrusting into me.

"Whoops," I say innocently.

"You're trouble," he teases before grunting, "Christ," when I roll my hips.

"I want to watch you come. I need to feel you come. Tell me how."

My heart melts for him.

"Flip us. It's my turn."

I cry out as he does as he's told, and not two seconds later, I'm on top of him with his dick still buried deep inside me.

"Use me," Rix says with a smirk on his face.

His nerves from earlier have lessened, and despite asking for my help to get me off, he seems at ease.

"You have no idea what you're asking for," I confess, circling my hips slowly to get a feel for it.

There's still a little pain, but nowhere near enough to stop me.

The feeling of fullness is one I've never felt before, and knowing that it's Rix... fuck. It's all-consuming.

"Jesus," he groans, his jaw popping. "You have no idea how incredible you feel."

Pride washes through me.

"Show me how to make it just as good for you."

Reaching for his hands, I lift them to my breasts. He already knows what to do here, but I'm happy to give him the guided tour.

He squeezes my heavy breasts and pinches my nipples as I slowly begin to move up and down on him.

Each time I sink back down, taking as much of him as I can, the pain lessens, giving way to something so much better.

"Love having your hands on me," I moan, circling my hips, testing out what I like best. I guess that's the thing about losing your virginity with your best friend; there's a level of trust and understanding that you might not have with someone else—someone else who's already got this shit figured out.

I slide one of his hands down my stomach and over my mound.

"But how about we try here?"

He swallows nervously as his fingers graze my sensitive skin for the first time.

"Oh god," I moan as I show him just how I like it.

"Shit. You just clenched so hard."

Together, we work my clit as I continue to move up and down his length.

As my release approaches, I leave him to it, confident that he knows what he's doing, and lean back.

He studies me with complete fascination and awe. It's a heady feeling, and one I don't think I'll ever get bored of.

"That's it," I gasp. "Yes."

"Fuck, you look so hot right now. I love watching you."

"Yes. Yes," I chant, my movements becoming more and more erratic.

He rubs my clit harder and faster before pinching my nipple with the other hand and I shatter, freefalling into nothing but pure bliss.

I've no idea what comes out of my mouth, if anything. All I can focus on is the pleasure.

It's like nothing I've ever felt before.

I'm just coming back when he grunts and his dick pulsates inside me, filling me again.

"Holy shit," I breathe, collapsing against his chest.

"Yeah, that," he agrees with a delirious chuckle. "We could have been doing that all this time. We're such idiots."

I laugh along with him, high on the endorphins he's released in me.

"I love you, Hendrix Kemp."

"I love you too, Noelle Bell."

Despite not wanting this to be over, with Hendrix's arms banded around me, I find myself drifting off to sleep.

I know that I need to go and clean up, but I can't find it in me to move.

I'm too content. Too sated.

Too... happy.

15

WILDER

It's an asshole thing to do, but I turn the volume down on the TV so I can listen to them.

I figure that it's better than last time because at least I'm not standing at the door, watching.

I can't help myself. It's the most action I'm going to get while we're here. I may as well live vicariously through them now they've figured their shit out.

Although, I can't say I'm all that jealous of them navigating their first times. Awkward as fuck. I could happily go through the rest of my life without having to think about mine.

Sex, now that I know what I'm doing is so much better.

At least I can share some of my knowledge with my brother. He's always waved me off in the past when I've attempted to give him advice. But he needs it now, especially if he wants to keep making Noelle scream.

He's already come once, and fast.

Fucking pussy.

He needs to build up some stamina.

Not that I can really comment. I pretty much blew the second I got it in on my first time.

Fair play though, he didn't roll over and go straight to sleep. He's being a gentleman and making sure she gets hers, too.

I try to imagine what they're doing right now, what position they're in.

The need to see if I can open their door and watch through the crack is strong, but I resist.

I've done enough creeping today.

Slouching back farther on the couch, I spread my thighs and let out a pained sigh.

Watching them, hearing them, is making me horny as fuck.

"Rix," Noelle cries, not making the situation any better. "Please."

"Fucking hell," I mutter to myself as I angrily shove my shorts over my ass, letting my aching dick free.

Closing my eyes, I wrap my hand around my length and try to imagine that it's hers.

She felt so fucking good earlier. Too fucking good for a simple hand job.

Her hesitance and lack of confidence should have been a turn-off. I'm sure that with any other woman, it would have been.

Noelle, though? She's different.

"Oh god, yes. More," she begs, her voice getting louder and more uncontrolled.

She's getting close.

I work my dick harder, faster. I have this weird need to finish with her.

I don't understand it, and I put every effort I can into trying not to figure it out.

"Yes, Rix. Yes. Yes," she screams as her orgasm finally takes her.

Rix's groans rip through the cabin as he finds his release right alongside her.

"Fuck," I grunt. "Fuck, fuck." My hips jump from the couch as my dick jerks and I come over my own hand.

Merry fucking Christmas.

With a pained sigh, I sink lower, both physically and mentally.

This was not the vacation I was expecting.

I take a couple of minutes before I give myself a talking to and go clean up.

It's almost an hour later when the sound of someone moving around fills the cabin.

Someone slips out of the bedroom and footsteps move toward the bathroom. When that door doesn't close, I take it as an invitation and go and investigate.

I find exactly what I was expecting: Rix standing at the toilet, taking a piss.

"Shit," Rix hisses.

"Problem?" I ask, making him jump and almost piss up the wall.

"Fuck off," he grunts.

"No can do," I say resting my shoulder against the jam. "Everything okay?"

He shakes his head. "I made her bleed," he confesses quietly.

"It didn't bother her, from what I heard."

I jump when his hand slaps against the wall in front of him. "Fucking asshole."

Keeping his back to me, he moves to the sink and begins to clean up.

I leave him to it and head for the kitchen for a drink, knowing that he's going to follow.

Pulling out two glasses, I grab the bottle of vodka from the freezer and pour two shots.

I only have to wait a minute before footsteps move my way.

"Goodbye to your virginity," I say holding up the glass. "I've been waiting years to celebrate this."

"I fucking hate you," he mutters, grabbing the glass and doing the shot without clinking it against mine.

"Pussy," I quip before doing the same.

It burns, but in a good way.

"Another?" I ask but pour it long before he has a chance to answer.

He shakes his head but does the shot anyway.

"So, how was it?" I ask, hopping up on the counter, ready to hear all the juicy details.

"I thought you were listening," he says, copying me and sitting on the opposite counter.

As I look up at him, I get hit with a strong sense of déjà vu.

We used to do this as kids in our shitty trailer kitchen. Honestly, I've no idea how the rotting cabinets took our weight, but they did. We used to spend hours sitting there shooting the shit. Most often alone, but sometimes with Noelle too.

"I was," I confirm, not that he needs it. "Was it everything you hoped it would be?"

"More," he whispers with a smirk on his lips.

"Oh yeah?"

"Yeah. It was... everything. She's everything."

"Took you fucking long enough to realize it."

"I've always known," he admits. "I just thought she deserved better."

"Oh, fuck off. How could she do any better than you?"

"You," he blurts, making me throw my head back and laugh.

"Me? Fuck off. I don't come anywhere close to standing up to you, let alone being better."

He shakes his head, refusing to believe me.

"She had to show me what to do. I had no idea."

"So? That's fucking hot. And it's better than you fumbling around in all the wrong places. Trust me, girls don't like that."

"Oh really?" he deadpans.

"I never had a Noelle to guide me. Just porn."

"I bet that was hella helpful."

"No, not really."

We fall silent, Rix losing himself in his memories and me drowning in my regrets.

I'd have loved to have a Noelle. Sure, she's always been in my life, but not the way she's been in Rix's.

I've never told him before just how jealous I've always been of them.

"I'm still pissed at you, you know," he suddenly says.

"Yeah," I agree. "I know. Wouldn't expect any less, to be honest. I took something that wasn't mine. But hey, at least you know I didn't fuck her."

"Well, that makes it all better," he mutters.

"Nothing will make it better. I shouldn't have—"

"Then why did you?"

"Because I'm a selfish asshole."

The words float around the kitchen, but for long seconds, Hendrix doesn't respond. Instead, he just sits there wearing nothing more than his boxers with his fingers gripped so tightly around the edge of the counter, his knuckles are white.

He's angry, I get it. But if I'm being honest, I'd rather he hit me again than force me to open up. He knows I hate talking.

Probably exactly why he's doing it, a little voice pipes up.

The ultimate punishment for my crime.

"When we were dancing," I start, taking myself back to that night, "there was something different about her. And then when she left, I couldn't help but follow her. I needed more. Her body spoke to mine in a way no other woman's ever had.

"I followed her to the bathroom and caught the door just before she closed it.

"I didn't give her a chance to react. I just pinned her back against the wall and lifted her veil."

The shock I felt at that moment rendered me useless for a few seconds. Long enough that she could have run. But she didn't.

"I couldn't believe it. Hell, for at least a minute, I don't think I did. But she stayed there with her back against the wall, looking at me with wide eyes. Wide, hungry eyes that begged me to do something."

"Did you know what the date was?" I ask.

I hang my head. "To start with, no," I confess.

"Would it have made any difference if you had?"

"Honestly, no. She needed an escape. It didn't matter what from. In that moment, I just knew that I needed to give it to her."

He stares at me, and for once, I can't read what he's thinking.

"I can't regret it, Rix. I won't regret it. She was spiraling. If it weren't me, then it could have been—"

"I know. And weirdly, I'm grateful that you were there to take care of her. Not sure this morning was necessary, though."

I hang my head.

"She's ensnared me in her web, Bro. Couldn't help myself."

"She's mine," Hendrix growls possessively.

"I know." I hate how dejected and sad my voice comes out. "You should get back to her," I say, hopping down from the counter. "She might wake up wanting round three."

Rix's eyes light up at the suggestion.

"Welcome to adulthood, Bro," I mutter as I walk out of the kitchen.

The rest of this trip will be hellish if they're going to be fucking every few minutes.

After making use of the bathroom, I strip down to my boxers and attempt to get comfy on the couch. The cushions are lumpy and the blanket is scratchy, but it's all I've got. If I didn't think it would earn me another punch to the face, I might mention joining them in an actual bed, but I could do without the pain.

Hendrix is still crashing about in the kitchen, tidying up the mess I probably should have dealt with while they were fucking.

I'm busy scrolling through the bullshit on my feed when he appears.

"Bet you wish you were in Austin, huh?" he asks.

"You have no idea," I mutter, although honestly, I'd much rather spend the holidays with those I love than getting fucked up with the team. I'm just not going to admit that out loud.

"Christmas Eve tomorrow."

"Fantastic," I deadpan. "More cheesy movies."

"We can watch *Die Hard.*"

"*Die Hard* isn't a Christmas movie," I mutter, knowing that it's going to start an argument.

"*Die Hard* is a—"

I glance at him, and it cuts off the rant he's about to embark on.

"We'll deal with that tomorrow," he says before walking toward the bedroom. "Can you do me a favor?"

"Sure."

"When it's just the two of you up in the morning, don't fucking touch her."

"Wouldn't dream of it, Bro. Not unless you're watching."

All the air rushes from his lungs, but he doesn't respond. At least not until he's at the bedroom door and bids me goodnight.

The cabin falls quiet. Only the sound of the smoldering fire can be heard.

I guess some would describe it as peaceful. To me, it's hell.

It was never peaceful where we grew up, and if things did go quiet, it was a warning for what was about to come.

Silence puts me on edge. It always has, and it probably always will.

Picking my cell back up, I turn the volume down and put some music on—anything to fill the silence. If I don't, it'll allow space for my thoughts, and those really aren't necessary.

The less I think about Hendrix crawling into bed with Noelle and wrapping her up in his arms on the other side of the wall, the better. I don't need to think about what it felt like for him when he pushed inside her for the first time, or the way she tasted on my fingers this morning.

Has he eaten her out yet? He'd fucking love that.

Her too, of course, assuming he figured out what to do.

Maybe I'll have to teach him...

My dick twitches at the thought of spreading her legs

and feasting on her pussy, of getting her taste from the source, not second-hand from my fingers.

Fuck. No.

He needs to be doing it.

I could watch, though. Make sure he does it right.

She looks beautiful when she comes; I bet it would be even better with his face between her thighs.

I fall asleep with a raging hard-on, and the dreams that float through my head in my slumber mean that I wake up the exact same way.

These next few days are going to be hard. Pun fully intended.

16

NOELLE

Just like yesterday morning, the cabin is silent when I wake up with the sunrise.

Hendrix is out for the count. He doesn't show a single sign of being aware of me slipping from the bed and pulling clothes on.

As I leave the bathroom and head toward the kitchen for my morning hit of caffeine, I assume that Wilder is either still sleeping or out for his morning run.

I soon discover that I'm very wrong when I step into the living room and find him wearing only a pair of shorts and doing push-ups in front of the couch.

All the air rushes from my lungs at the sight of his muscles rippling beneath his skin.

Hendrix is fit, his body toned and defined. But Wilder's... it's in an entirely different league.

Unable to stop myself, I stand there with my mouth agape and watch.

He moves so effortlessly. It's addicting. Too addicting.

"I know you're watching," he says roughly, scaring the ever-loving shit out of me.

"What the fuck, Wilder?" I gasp, my heart beating uncontrollably.

He stops and climbs to his feet. He's got the cockiest smirk playing on his lips that I think I've ever seen, and I kick myself for getting sucked in.

"Enjoying the show?" he asks, combing his sweat-damp hair back.

"Why aren't you out running?" I hiss, needing to take the heat off me.

"You saw the weather warning yesterday, right?"

"Yeah," I muse.

"Go look outside."

Ripping my attention from him, I march over to the windows and gaze out.

"Oh shit," I breathe.

"Indeed. I could have opened the door, but it would have caused a snowslide."

"A snowslide?" I ask, still staring at the mass of perfectly white snow on the other side of the window. I know I said I was hoping for a white Christmas up here, but this is something else.

"Yeah, a landslide but with snow." I don't look back, but I know he's rolling his eyes at me.

"Right," I mutter.

"It's going to get worse today," he explains as a gust of wind whips across the top of the snow, causing a huge cloud to engulf the cabin.

"Right," I repeat.

"I hope you ordered enough food, because there's no way of getting more."

"We'll be okay," I say absently.

"I guess all we need to worry about is entertaining ourselves, then. Although, I'm not sure that you and Rix will have an issue with that. How was last night, by the way? Sounded epic from where I was sitting."

My cheeks blaze. I knew at the time that he'd hear everything. But while I was with Hendrix, lost in our own little world, it didn't matter.

Now, in the harsh light of day and standing in front of his twin brother, it's very different.

"No need to be shy," he says, his smirk still firmly in place as he takes a step forward to whisper in my ear, "I rubbed one out listening to you."

My gasp rips through the cabin a beat before he chuckles.

"Go and make your coffee, Rebel," he demands before walking to the coffee table and drinking some water.

His throat ripples as he swallows, and despite knowing better, my eyes drop to his chest, his abs, and then his crotch.

My mouth runs dry when I find a tent in the fabric.

Shit. He wasn't joking, was he?

Before I embarrass myself even more, I make a beeline for the kitchen, leaving him to do his thing.

When I return to the living room, he's moved on to sit-ups.

Keeping focused, I grab my book and curl myself into my favorite reading chair, seeing as the swing seat is out of action today.

If it weren't so cloudy, it would allow me to watch the sunrise as well as the open fire, assuming someone had lit it.

So instead of enjoying the beautiful scenery outside of the cabin, I'm forced to try and ignore what's happening on the inside.

Snuggling under the blanket, I open my book and stare at the words.

It works for a couple of pages, but then Wilder begins doing burpees, and I can't help but lift my eyes.

Just like the sit-ups, it's effortless. If it weren't for the light sheen of sweat on his skin, I would think he wasn't even trying.

"Got to a boring bit of your book, huh?" he guesses, although fuck knows how he's aware I'm looking; he's got his back to me.

"You're an asshole."

"Tell me something I don't know," he quips as he continues jumping up and down.

"You make me feel unfit and fat," I mutter.

He clearly wasn't expecting the comment, because he stops on his feet and turns to look at me.

"You might be unfit, but you certainly aren't fat." He stares at me with such intensity that I instantly regret the comment.

"When was the last time you exercised? Other than last night, of course." He winks, and I roll my eyes.

"Uh..."

"Too long ago. Put your book down and get over here," he demands, placing his hands on his hips.

"Um... I'm okay. Thanks, though."

Ripping my eyes from him, I pretend to start reading again. In truth, it's impossible with his gaze boring into me.

"Noelle," he growls. "You need to be in tip-top shape for all the sexercise you're going to get now. Gotta put some work in."

"I really don't. What the hell?" I shriek when he steals my book and coffee and places them on the side before ripping the blanket from my lap and grabbing my hand. "Oh no," I cry, attempting to run away.

"Nope. We're doing this. Warm up first, then I'll put you through your paces."

"This is really unnecessary. It's Christmas Eve, for fuck's sake."

"Even more reason to be doing it. Burn off some calories before all the feasting."

"I don't like you very much right now."

He quirks a brow. "Only right now? Okay, let's stretch."

Resigning myself to my fate, I follow his orders and do as I'm told.

"I thought we were warming up. This is yoga."

"Same thing. We're stretching your muscles and beginning to get your heart pumping."

"There's been plenty of that recently," I mutter, mimicking him and moving into a downward dog.

"Sex is good for the soul."

"Yours must be suffering right now then," I tease. "When was the last time you went this long?"

"I'm not a complete man-whore, you know," he mutters, attempting to sound offended.

"Just a partial one, then?"

"Pain in the ass," he breathes before moving us through a few more poses.

I hate to admit it, but I quite enjoy it.

Despite the banter, it's quite relaxing.

The weather might be all kinds of awful outside, but inside, it's calm and peaceful.

I focus on my breathing as we transition and feel the weight of the past few days lift.

"Okay, now it's time for some work," Wilder says, jumping to his feet and jogging on the spot.

"There is something wrong with you," I grumble.

His need to keep moving, to keep busy is exhausting.

I know it's a coping mechanism and his way of dealing with life, but it's hard work to watch.

"Jumping jacks. Squats. Sit-ups. Push-ups," he lists.

"Seriously?"

"Seriously," he says, coming to a stop in front of me. "Ready? Twenty jumping jacks." He begins leaving me standing there, the opposite of ready, as he begins counting. "Come on, don't be a pussy."

"Fuck's sake."

I do one and am swiftly reminded that I'm not wearing a bra. My boobs aren't that big, but then I'm pretty sure every pair is too big for unsupported star jumps.

"I'm too much of a woman to be doing this, Wilder."

His brow wrinkles in confusion.

"Boobs and jumps don't mix."

"And you think a dick and balls do? Hold them down if you have to. Or better idea, let me."

Rolling my eyes, I forget about the top half of the star movement, grab my boobs, and jump with him.

By the time he gets to twenty, I've done no more than eight, but I'm already sweating and out of breath.

Why people do this for fun is beyond me. It's torture.

"Squat time," Wilder says happily.

"Slave driver," I mutter, ripping Hendrix's hoodie off and throwing it onto the chair I should be relaxing in.

"Hmm, much better," Wilder says, making a show of checking out my body.

"Rix will hurt you again," I point out.

"It'll be worth it," he muses, rubbing the bruise on his cheek Rix gave him yesterday.

"If you say so."

"Okay, squat for me. Let me see your form."

Rolling my eyes, I do as I'm told.

"Stick your ass out. More. More."

"I hate you."

"That's it. Now, ten reps."

"Five," I barter.

"Ten."

I groan, aware that I'm not going to win.

I get to seven before my thighs are trembling, and not in a good way, and I collapse on the floor.

"You really are out of shape, huh?" Wilder asks, looming over me, his signature smirk on full display.

"And you really are an asshole."

I close my eyes as he drops to his knees, praying this torture can be over.

It's Christmas; we're supposed to be enjoying ourselves.

"On your back, feet on the floor."

I crack one eye open to find him waiting for me impatiently.

"I bet you say that to all the girls," I deadpan.

"No, not one of them requires this much work."

"What you mean is you sleep with easy jersey chasers."

"Works for me," he says as I get into position.

The second my feet are down, he grabs my ankles.

"Cross your arms over your chest and lift."

Before doing as I'm told, I lift my hand to my head. "Yes, Boss," I salute.

When all he does is glare at me, I get to work, figuring that the sooner I pacify him, the sooner it'll be over.

"One," he counts. "Two. Three."

Then it begins to get hard.

Four and five come slower, and then I get to six, and before I manage to get up, a voice booms through the cabin.

"I thought I told you not to touch her."

"Dude, don't get your panties in a knot. I'm holding her ankles."

"And making her exercise. Noelle hates exercise."

"I can tell," he deadpans.

"Hey," I cry. "I'm doing my best here."

Wilder quirks a brow as if to say, 'Really?'.

"Rix, your brother is being mean to me. I was quite happy sitting there and reading my book," I argue. "Look what he's made me do."

Rix's footsteps get closer until I can see him.

But unlike I'm expecting, he doesn't make Wilder stop. Instead, he claims the chair I was pulled from and instructs his brother to continue.

"What?" I shriek in utter disbelief. "You're supposed to be on my side."

Hendrix holds up his hands in surrender before sitting back to get ready for the show.

"Fucking hell."

"Four more," Wilder says, sadly not forgetting that we're not done.

"And then it's jumping jacks, right?" Hendrix says hopefully.

"No, you're too late. Wilder's already watched me do them."

I can't help the wide grin that spreads across my face as Rix's jaw ticks with realization.

"I thought it was weird that I had to do them naked, but I trust him."

Rix is on his feet faster than I thought possible.

"You fucking ass—"

I can't hold it; I burst out laughing.

Thankfully, Wilder releases my feet and I'm able to stand. The second I do, I rush between them, just in case I started something.

"I'm joking," I breathe, pressing my palms against Rix's chest and staring up into his eyes.

"Good. Because if there's going to be any nakedness, I need to be involved."

My heart somersaults and my first thought is whether Wilder told him about my book and what he read yesterday morning.

"O-okay," I stutter, following Hendrix's line of sight toward his smirking brother.

If I ever needed a reminder that these two can communicate with only their eyes, then this is it.

17

HENDRIX

As much as I might hate Wilder for what he did, I also trust him.

Hell, I trust him with my life, which means I trust him with Noelle.

Possibly a little too much.

Ducking down, I let my lips brush against her ear as I whisper, "You're dirty."

She gasps, not expecting my words.

"I think it's time we clean you up."

Taking her hand, I drag her behind me as I march through the cabin.

"I'll finish this on my own then," Wilder sulks behind us.

"I would suggest you attempt to make breakfast, but we'd actually like something edible."

"I'm not that useless."

"We didn't buy Ramen noodles," Noelle teases, more than aware that it's pretty much the only thing Wilder can make for himself.

He's done remarkably well to avoid learning,

considering all three of us have basically brought ourselves up.

"I can do more than noodles," he mutters. "I can make toast, too."

"We'll deal with breakfast after..."

I pull us into the bathroom and push her up against the door the second we're inside.

"After what?" she manages to ask before I claim her lips.

We might have gone a lifetime without kissing, but that's over now, and I want to do it any and every chance we get.

Her hands land on my waist before sliding under my shirt. My skin erupts with goosebumps, and the shudder of desire that follows goes right down to my toes.

Hitching her leg up around my waist, I press the length of my body against hers, gently grinding against her.

Images of last night fill my head as my cock gets impossibly hard.

I want to experience that all over again.

"Hendrix," Noelle moans when I drag my lips away from hers and kiss down her throat.

"Never going to get bored of hearing that," I confess. "How are you feeling?"

"Wilder forced me to work out," she sulks, making me chuckle.

"I'll hurt him for that later, but I meant after last night."

"Oh," she gasps as I suck on the patch of sensitive skin under her ear. "I... I feel great."

"Not sore?"

"Not sore enough to stop me from doing it again."

Heat floods through my veins and I pull back so I can look into her eyes.

"Yeah?"

She laughs, her expression softening, and she reaches up to cup my jaw.

"Yeah," she agrees.

"Okay, but later. Right now, I want to take care of you."

Releasing her, I force myself to take a step back and sink my hand into my sweats to rearrange my boner.

"Are you sure?" she asks, studying me with desire filling her eyes.

"I'll always take care of you first," I confess before spinning around to start running the bath.

In only a minute, steam fills the room and white fluffy bubbles explode before me.

"You're cute," Noelle says, stepping up behind me as the sweet scent of the bubbles fills the air.

Spinning toward her, I take a step closer and stare down into her eyes.

"Get naked," I demand.

"I'll show you mine if you show me yours," she teases before grasping the bottom of her tank and pulling it up her body.

It's not just the sight of her bare chest that takes my breath away; it's her confidence, too.

When I don't move, she rests her hand on her waist and pops her hip, waiting for me to follow suit.

"I ran this bath for you," I tell her.

"And I'm not getting in it without you," she counters.

My mouth opens and closes, but I quickly find that I have no argument. I mean, how could I? Noelle wet, naked, and covered in bubbles. That's my idea of heaven.

Without missing a beat, I reach behind my head and drag my shirt off, abandoning it on the floor with hers.

"Better," she muses before reaching out and tucking her fingers into the waistband of my sweats.

My breath catches, and it only gets worse a second later

when she suddenly drops in front of me, dragging the fabric down with her.

My cock springs free and bobs right in front of her face.

I swallow thickly, trying to imagine how she'll look, how she'll feel if she were to—

"Fuuuuck," I groan when she leans forward and licks the tip.

Sucking her tongue back into her mouth, she pauses, deep in thought.

My heart jumps into my throat.

What if she didn't like that?

Do I taste funny?

But as I'm starting to lose myself in my anxiety, she makes a decision and leans forward again, her lips parting.

"Oh fuck," I groan, my hand moving of its own accord, my fingers threading into her hair, holding her in place.

She stares up at me with her big, emerald green eyes and her lips stretched around my cock.

It's... it's...

"Fuuuuck," I groan when she sinks lower on me.

Her hands lift, one wrapping around my hip, the other holding the base of my cock.

"Christ, Noelle. That's— fuck, that's good."

She continues to suck me, experimenting with speed and technique.

I love it all. Every single second of it.

I want it to last forever, but as is the case when it comes to being intimate with Noelle, the end comes too soon.

"Shit, Elle. Shit. I'm gonna... fuck."

I really try to warn her, I do. But one second my release is approaching and the next it's slammed into me with the force of an eighteen-wheeler.

I'm still deep in her mouth when my cock jerks and ropes of cum spurt from the tip.

Her eyes widen in surprise, I assume as it hits the back of her throat, but she doesn't pull back. She gags, but it doesn't put her off.

I stare at her on her knees with my cock in her mouth, and I'm hit with a whole new level of awe for my best friend.

My girl.

My one and only.

"I love you," I blurt, unable to say anything else in my post-orgasmic state.

Finally, she pulls back, releasing my softening cock before wiping her lips with the back of her hand.

"You're amazing," I say before reaching down to lift her to her feet and slam my lips on hers.

I can taste myself when I sweep my tongue against hers, but I don't care. I can't. I'm pretty sure she could do anything right now and I'd go along with it. I'd give her anything and everything she could possibly want.

As our kiss continues, I slide my hands into her shorts and panties and push them over her hips, letting them pool at her feet.

With my hands firmly planted on her hips, I walk her backward toward the bathtub.

"I hope I got the temperature right," I say into our kiss, confident that I've nailed it, before effortlessly lifting her tiny frame from the floor and placing her into the water.

"It's perfect," she breathes after a beat.

A smile curls at the corners of my lips before I kick off my sweats and boxers from around my ankles and step into the water with her.

Sliding my legs on either side of her, I encourage her to lie back on me.

Water and bubbles slosh over the side of the tub, but neither of us makes a move to do anything about it.

"This is nice," Noelle muses, resting her hands on my forearms that are wrapped around her middle.

She shrieks when I sink us lower, causing even more mess.

"It's better than nice. And what you just did... fuck."

"You liked me sucking your cock, huh?"

"Yeah," I muse, my brain misfiring from hearing her talk like that. "It was amazing."

"Good, because I'm doing it again," she states confidently.

"Only if you have to," I tease.

"I want to do everything with you, Rix."

"Sounds perfect," I whisper as I press kisses to her shoulder. "I owe you now, though."

"You don't owe me anything."

"I blew too fast last night. You deserved better than that. And I'm not the kind of guy who's happy to take and not give."

"That's good to hear. What are you—Rix," she gasps when my hand slides down her stomach and doesn't stop until my fingers graze her clit.

"Are you sore?" I ask again as I gently tease her.

Honestly, I've no idea what feels good or what I should be doing here, but much like her sucking my dick, I'm willing to experiment until I get it right.

Her legs fall wider, giving me the space I need and in turn, a little hope that maybe it doesn't feel awful.

I remember everything she showed me last night and try to mimic it.

"No," she breathes, her hips jumping as I hit the right spot. "There. Keep doing that."

So I do. Her breathing increases, the movement of her chest becoming more and more erratic.

Wanting to give her more to push her over the edge, I grip her breast with my other hand.

"Yes," she gasps.

Her hips roll in time with my movements, and her moans and mewls get louder, letting me know that I'm doing an okay job.

"I want to make you come," I whisper roughly in her ear.

"Keep going," she moans, her grip on my thigh tightening to the point her nails dig into my skin.

"You're amazing, you know that?" I breathe. "So sexy. Watching you fall apart is everything. So much better than I've been imagining all these years. I've wanted to touch you like this for so long."

"Yes, yes," she chants as her body begins to tense. "Rix."

Her body convulses and her back arches as she rides out her pleasure. Watching her is enthralling.

I'm obsessed. Utterly fucking obsessed.

"Oh my god," she breathes as she begins to come down from her high. "My vibrator is going in the trash,"

I still as an image appears in my mind.

"You have a vibrator?"

She laughs. "Of course. I might not have been with anyone before, but a girl still has needs."

"Don't get rid of it," I demand.

She twists her head back to look at me, a wicked smile playing on her lips.

"Oh yeah?"

"Hell yeah."

Happiness dances in her eyes as she curls up on my chest. I'm hard again, I'm pretty sure it's going to be an issue going forward, but neither of us makes a move to do anything about it. We're too content being in each other's arms.

We relax in the tub until the water becomes too cold and our stomachs are rumbling.

Thankfully, it doesn't smell like anything is burning outside of the bathroom, so I can only assume that Wilder decided not to embark on cooking breakfast in our absence.

After wrapping Noelle in a warm, huge fluffy towel, I wrap another around my waist, scoop up my discarded clothes, and pad through to the bedroom, leaving her to finish up.

With clean clothes on, I go in search of my brother.

I find him laid out on the couch with his eyes closed, a pair of AirPods in, and his cell resting on his chest.

Curious, I walk over and pluck one from his ear.

His eyes pop open as I put it into my own. Instantly, a deep growly voice erupts and my brows pinch.

I was expecting music, or maybe a sports podcast. But this...

'My mouth waters and my fists clench as I watch him spread my girl's thighs and lean forward.'

Reaching out, I grab his cell and stare down at the screen.

"This is the book Noelle is reading," I state, recognizing the cover immediately.

If he's embarrassed to be caught, then he doesn't show it.

"Do you know what it's about?" he asks simply.

"Romance," I say confidently.

"Yeah, but what kind of romance?" he probes, suddenly jumping to his feet, pushing the other AirPod into my ear and hitting play again as he stalks off.

'I shouldn't want to watch as another man goes down on my woman,' the narrator continues to growl. 'But right now, I'm harder than I think I've ever been in my life. She's enjoying herself, and that means everything to me.'

18

WILDER

I walk away from my brother with a smirk playing on my lips and desire flooding through my veins.

The walls in this place are far too thin. I know exactly what they were doing in the bathroom. His groans and her cries for more gave them away in a heartbeat.

I was once again left hard as fuck as the sounds of them enjoying each other filled my ears.

Did I really think that finding the audio version of the book that Noelle is reading was going to help? No, not for a second, but I was intrigued.

Now having listened to an hour or so, I'm even more curious.

As I leave Hendrix behind, the bathroom door opens and Noelle steps out wrapped in a towel.

I stop and make a show of checking her out.

Honestly, I can't see anything, but the way her cheeks have reddened by the time I get back to her face makes me wonder if she's aware.

She tightens the fabric around herself before dropping her eyes and moving toward the bedroom.

"Are you done in here?" I ask.

"Yep, all yours."

"Thanks. Not sure I'll have as much fun as you did, though." I'm about to close the door when a thought hits me. "Elle?"

"Yeah?" she says looking back over her shoulder.

"When you're done, can you help me make breakfast? Hendrix is... busy."

We both look in the direction of the living room and find Hendrix standing at the windows, gazing out at the blizzard beyond.

"He looks swamped," Noelle jokes.

"You've no idea where his head is at right now. I'll be ten minutes," I promise before closing the door behind me and instantly shoving my shorts down my thighs.

My semi bobs free, and I stare down at it with a sigh.

"I'm doing my best here; don't taunt me," I muse before laughing at myself and stepping into the shower.

I get blasted with ice-cold water for a few seconds, but it does very little to wash away my lingering desire, or the images the audiobook helped to draw in my head.

I've messed around with group sex before. I've tag-teamed girls with friends, and I've had multiple girls at once —good times. But they've always purely been about fun and pleasure. And alcohol. There was a lot of alcohol.

If something were to happen here, it would be so much more than those previous times.

It would be something that would have the power to build or break relationships that have lasted a lifetime.

My heart rate picks up as the weight of the seed I'm planting really takes hold.

I mean, sure, it might be that I plant and water this seed as much as I want, but it never goes anywhere.

Hendrix has been in love with Noelle his entire life.

Why should he even consider sharing her with me? So what if we've shared everything our entire lives? Maybe this is where we part ways. Take different paths…

But then I think of his statement earlier…

"If there's going to be any nakedness, I need to be involved."

Needing to put a stop to my overthinking, I tip my face to the water and wrap my hand around my shaft.

If I take the edge off, it'll make everything easier, I lie to myself.

Images of Noelle pinned between me and Hendrix fill my mind, and I allow myself the freedom to take it wherever I want until I'm spilling my seed into the shower tray.

After cleaning up, I dry myself off, wrap a towel around my waist, and head out.

Hendrix is standing in the exact same place as he was earlier when I return. He's so lost in the story, he doesn't even hear me approach.

With a silent chuckle, I pull my bag from behind the couch and rummage through for a clean pair of boxers.

Movement behind me lets me know that Noelle is approaching, and I act before she can slip into the kitchen.

Standing to my full height, I drop my towel.

It pools at my feet for a beat before she sucks in a sharp breath.

Pretending to not know she's there, I spin around, barely covering myself with the fabric in my hand.

"Oh shit, sorry," I say with a smirk.

She knows me too well and sees straight through it.

She's busy rolling her eyes as hard as she can and pretending not to check me out when Hendrix finally gets with the program and spins around.

He sees Noelle first—obviously— but the second he sees her looking at me, his eyes turn my way.

"The fuck, Bro?" he barks, but his question is soon forgotten when Noelle glances at him and notices that he's been enjoying his time at the window.

Glad I'm not the only one to rock a semi while listening to a man growling in my ear.

Fuck. I am never saying that out loud. Ever.

"What's going on?" Noelle asks suspiciously.

"Hendrix has been enjoying his first audiobook. Haven't you, man?"

Rix's lips open and close as he debates whether he's willing to confess or not.

"An audiobook?" Noelle asks, looking impressed.

"Uh..."

"What are you listening to?"

With her focus on Rix, I quickly pull my boxers on and watch them interact.

Hesitantly, Hendrix lifts my cell and shows Noelle.

"That's what I'm reading," she says, confusion laced through her tone.

"You inspired me yesterday," I explain, helping Rix out. "And I thought I could inspire Rix too. It really is an interesting read."

Noelle's mouth opens to respond, but after a second or two, she clearly decides that she doesn't have any words to offer.

"If you want to make breakfast, you're going to need to put more clothes on," she finally says, turning her eyes on me.

"We should play it through the Bluetooth speaker. That way we can all enjoy it," I suggest.

Noelle's lips purse with frustration. "I don't think that's necessary," she says before spinning on her heels and marching toward the kitchen.

"Clearly not an audiobook fan," I mutter as I pull a pair of shorts and a T-shirt from my bag.

"You're playing with fire," Hendrix warns darkly.

I still with my arms in my t-shirt and look at him.

"If you're not interested in getting a little hot, then all you've got to do is say. We're stuck here for the foreseeable future; as far as I can see, we either die of boredom watching endless Hallmark movies, or we have some fun.

"Which would you rather do?"

"Don't worry, Wild Child," he mocks, using the nickname our sister gave me years ago. "I'm having plenty of fun."

"But you could be having more," I say as he walks toward the couch, putting my AirPods back in as he goes.

"I thought you were having a cooking lesson," he prompts before dropping onto the couch and getting comfortable.

"Yeah," I muse, taking off toward where Noelle is already crashing around in the kitchen. "What are we making?"

"Waffles," she says with a wide smile.

"Okay, great. Where do you want me?"

She grins at me, and I can't help but wonder what she's really thinking about.

My eyes drop down her body again, taking in every one of her curves in her leggings and loose t-shirt. Our innocent little Noelle knows exactly what she's doing... she's braless beneath that shirt.

"Oh yeah, I like where your dirty mind just went, Rebel. They do say that it's the quiet ones you should be wary of." I close the space between us, making her suck in a sharp breath. "And you're one of those, aren't you? Well, unless you've got my brother between your thighs. Then you're not very quiet at all."

"Y ou didn't do any of this, did you?" Hendrix asks a while later when I lower a massive plate of waffles to the middle of the table. Noelle follows me with a plate of bacon and sausage, and a bowl of fruit salad.

"I helped," I scoff.

"That's true, he did. You can see his first attempt in the trash."

I let out a frustrated huff as I remember why I don't cook.

It's not that I just choose not to, I can't, and it fucking irks me that I'm bad at something. "They weren't that bad," I mutter.

"I've seen less burned charcoal," Noelle points out, making Hendrix laugh.

Asshole.

"That's cool, laugh it up. Just remember that I'm better at a whole host of things that Hendrix hasn't even attempted yet."

"Low blow," Rix mutters as he helps himself to two waffles before piling bacon on top and drizzling the whole lot with syrup.

"True though. Elle, when you want to experience what a real man can do, you come let me know."

She shakes her head, laughing it off as she takes the seat beside Rix and places a kiss on his cheek. She can deny it all she likes; I saw those dirty thoughts in her head in the kitchen.

"So, how's the book? Anything happened that we need to know about?" I ask Rix, loving the way his cheeks heat.

"Yep, they killed the other guy," he says without missing a beat.

Noelle snorts, aware that losing a lover isn't a story arc in the book we're now all reading or listening to.

"With pleasure, you mean. I'm assuming he went all the way with the other guy's woman. I didn't get that far."

"You should continue listening. I'd hate to ruin it for you."

"I'm sure you wouldn't."

Anticipation crackles between us.

We're all thinking the same things, or at least I think we are.

The question is, are we going to do anything about those thoughts, or are we going to spend the next few days skirting around the idea before returning to Trinity and forgetting all about it?

Sure seems a shame to do that and not make the most of this opportunity. We may never get it again. We all live very different lives, and despite sharing a house, I'm hardly ever there. It's not like we'd be starting anything serious.

I'm more than aware that Noelle belongs to Hendrix. She always has and always will. Doesn't mean that I don't appreciate how hot she is.

I'll never try and steal her away. They belong together. And I... I belong to being wild and carefree, just as my name suggests.

My fate was written for me when our parents decided to make me the wild one, and I'm okay with that.

It's not like I'll have time for a serious relationship if I manage to live out my dream and make it to the NFL anyway. There isn't a week that goes by where a player's doomed relationship isn't splashed across the internet for everyone to enjoy.

I'm not interested in that. And I certainly wouldn't want to drag someone as sweet as Noelle into that life.

She needs a man like Hendrix. Someone who will be

able to quietly give her the world, not someone like me who'll inevitably cause her pain and heartache without even lifting a finger.

I look up and watch them interact, and my heart aches in my chest.

I'm happy for them. I am.

I really do hope they manage to get the happily-ever-after they've always craved with each other.

19

NOELLE

"Whoa," I whisper when the lights flicker around us.

We've spent the afternoon chilling out in the cabin; I've been reading, and, embarrassingly, both Hendrix and Wilder have been listening.

They offered to do it as a group, but I point-blank refused. It was bad enough knowing that they were listening to the same group sex scenes that I was reading. Doing it together...

My emotions war over how I feel about it.

I want to say that I would be totally mortified.

But...

I also fear that it would be incredibly hot.

Wilder has made no secret of his ideas about us getting down and dirty together. Sure, his comments may appear to be in jest, but he's being serious. Or at least as serious as Wilder can be.

He's always chasing the thrill, so it's no real surprise as to where his head has gone while we're all stuck here.

"It said it's going to get worse before it gets better," Hendrix says.

All afternoon we've been listening to the wind howl around the small cabin.

There's something so comforting being in here all snug and warm with the fire raging while chaos reigns outside.

I may not have planned for the snow to be this bad, but this is the exact thing I wanted. To be away from reality for a few days with absolutely nothing to do.

The lights flicker again, and we all look at each other.

If Hendrix is right and this is the beginning of things getting worse, then we could be in for a fun Christmas Eve.

"Do we have candles?" I ask, trying to think if I've seen any emergency supplies should the worst happen.

"Uh..." Hendrix starts. "I'm not sure, but we should probably look."

"Stop panicking," Wilder scoffs, taking life about as seriously as he usually does. "Even if we have a blackout, it won't last long."

I glance at him before looking back at Hendrix. He nods, and we both climb to our feet.

"Just in case."

"See, this is why it's taken you guys this long to bump uglies. You always worry about the future."

"At least we plan. If a disaster happened, we'd be somewhat prepared. You'd be—"

"Less boring?" Wilder asks with a smirk.

"Call us boring all you like, at least if the power goes, we'll have located the candles and— Fuck," Hendrix barks as we're suddenly plunged into darkness.

"You were saying?" Wilder teases.

It's dark.

Really fucking dark.

We're in the middle of nowhere. There's no light pollution, and with the thick cloud covering and heavy snowfall, there isn't even any moonlight to help.

"This is your fault," Hendrix snaps, making me roll my eyes. I've lived through years of their sibling bickering; I really should be used to it by now.

"How could this possibly be my fault? I didn't go and blow the board out."

"If you weren't banging on about us being boring, then we might have had a chance to find the fucking candles already."

"Well, you are boring. Listen to you."

"Okay, as fun as this is..." I say, hesitantly putting my book down. When the lights come back on, I'm going to be pissed if I've lost my page. "How about we actually go and look for those candles? Put your flashlights on," I demand.

"Oh, I do love a girl who knows what she wants," Wilder mocks.

"If I could see you, I'd punch you," Hendrix mutters a second before Wilder's cell lights up the room.

"Come on then," he taunts.

"Focus," I say, snatching Wilder's cell and using it to illuminate my way to the kitchen. "Do something useful and help," I shoot over my shoulder.

Hendrix follows me and begins rooting through the cupboards in search of something that will help.

"Anything?" I ask after a few minutes.

"Nope. Wilder, get your ass in here."

"You've taken my cell; I can't see fuck all."

"Stop being a pussy," Hendrix snaps.

"Pussy? I'm right there," he says, footsteps moving our way.

"Give me strength," Hendrix mutters.

I remain quiet, trying to keep focused on my search, but I'm coming up empty.

We can't spend the next... however long with only cell phone flashlights to guide us.

There has to be something.

Wilder's cell buzzes in my hand, and I glance down to see a message from someone called *blonde with no panties*.

Fucking Wilder.

"What was that groan?" Hendrix asks, making me aware that I didn't keep my reaction internal.

"Wilder's in the middle of a booty call," I explain. "Classy one, because he doesn't know her name."

"What's new there?"

"Hey," Wilder complains, stealing his cell back. "Oh fuck," he gasps. I glance back to see his eyes wide. "Name doesn't matter. She's still not wearing any panties."

"Jesus, you're a whore," Rix snaps.

"Look," Wilder says, flashing the image on the screen at Hendrix.

"I don't want to fucking see that."

"Why? Is Noelle's better?"

"Of fucking course it is. That has nothing on hers. Fucking perfect."

I'm grateful I'm shrouded in darkness, although I can't help but wonder if my cheeks burn so bright I turn into my own light source.

"Oh yeah?" Wilder muses.

"Can you both just stop?" I hiss.

"Sorry," Hendrix mutters while Wilder states, "What? You've compared our dicks."

"Yeah, and you probably don't want to know the outcome of that," I deadpan before demanding that Hendrix follow me toward the closet in the hallway.

If the emergency supplies aren't in the kitchen, then that's where they'll be.

They have to be.

I refuse to believe that we're now stuck here in the dark with nothing more than three shitty flashlights—assuming we can locate my cell, that is.

The person I message the most is here in this cabin with me; I've barely touched it since we arrived.

It takes a bit of searching, but eventually, Hendrix and I manage to locate a box that is full of candles, matches, and a couple of flashlights.

Together we set them up around the living room and flop back on the couch.

"Now what?" Wilder asks, dropping into the chair opposite.

"Uh…" Hendrix starts.

The room glows with the flickering candlelight, and the scent of vanilla floods the air.

"Not much really," I mutter.

We might have some light, but I'm not sure it's enough to read.

This was not part of my plans.

"I know," Wilder suddenly says, leaping to his feet and rushing out of the room with his cell leading the way.

"That didn't sound good."

"At least we know he won't be cooking," I quip, vividly remembering our little lesson earlier.

"True."

A bottle clinks, and my stomach knots.

This isn't going to end well.

My eyes lock with Hendrix's and I see the same hesitation dancing in his.

"Vodka," Wilder says, holding up a bottle and three glasses as he emerges.

The candlelight glints on the glass, and my dread grows.

Bad idea.

Really bad idea.

But...

"Bottoms up, kids," Wilder says the second he's poured us all a shot and passed them out.

"What?" he asks when we both just stare at him. "What else are we going to do? This is the best we've got." To prove his point, he lifts the small glass to his lips and swallows it down.

He pulls a face and groans as it burns before turning his gaze on us.

"Come on, I hate partying alone."

"We're not partying," Hendrix mutters.

"Fuck that, Rix. Take off those boring panties and put on your party ones instead. It's Christmas. We're fucking stuck here. And we can't even warm up a pizza. It's time to get drunk, baby."

Wilder pours himself a second shot, and by the time he lifts it to his mouth, I've decided that I'm with him.

He's right. It's Christmas. We've got to embrace the situation we've found ourselves in.

"Let's do this," I say happily before drinking the shot. "Oh my god," I gasp, instantly regretting it.

"Your turn, Rix. You can't have your girl going wild without you."

I've no idea if it's meant to be an innuendo, but I do know that the twins' eyes collide, Rix's narrowing in warning and Wilder's lighting up with excitement.

A swarm of butterflies erupts in my stomach. I have first-hand knowledge that partying with Wilder leads to trouble.

But is it the kind of trouble I'm willing to get involved in tonight?

Like he said… there isn't anything else to do.

"Refill," I demand, thrusting my glass out.

Wilder's face lights up with excitement.

"Good girl," he praises, making something warm flood through my system.

Only Hendrix has said those words to me before. My parents never gave me any kind of praise, no matter how hard I tried or how well I did.

"What are you waiting for then? Put some music on," I demand, getting to my feet. "I thought we were having a party."

I begin dancing long before Wilder finds a suitable playlist. My skin tingles with awareness, but it doesn't stop me.

Looking back over my shoulder, I find Rix watching me with intrigue.

We've done a lot together over the years, but we've never really partied. Unlike Wilder, it hasn't been a part of our lives.

Sure, there have been plenty of times when we've drunk too much, but there was never dancing and joy. It was more about drowning our sorrows.

By the time Wilder started hitting the party scene, I was too focused on Nick, and Hendrix was right here with me.

Partying and enjoying ourselves, no matter how fake it might have been, felt wrong.

But now… for once, it feels right.

I came here to relax, to let go, and now more than ever, I've got the opportunity. I'm going to grab it with both hands and see where it leads me. Even if it is directly into trouble.

Finally, music floats through the air, a deep bass thumping through my body and making me move in time.

The soft candlelight makes it so much more sensual and I let go, forgetting about everything that usually keeps my muscles pulled tight and embracing the moment.

"Oh hell, yeah," Wilder announces happily before I sense him join me on my makeshift dancefloor.

There isn't much space inside the cabin, and it only feels smaller now we're in total darkness. But it's also comforting.

I'm safe here. Possibly safer than I've ever been with two guys I trust with my life.

Wilder might be a loose cannon, but he'd do anything to protect me.

Hendrix too.

Just like I'd do for both of them.

The warmth of his hard, strong body spreads down my back a beat before his hands land on my hips.

I'm hit with a strong wave of déjà vu.

Now I know the identity of the man I was dancing with that night, it's obvious. I kick myself for not figuring it out sooner.

If I were in a better state of mind, maybe I would have realized the touch was too familiar, that I knew his scent.

Hell, let's be honest, if I were in a better place I wouldn't have found myself off my face and at a college party in the first place.

I let out a sigh as I lean back against him, my body moving with his effortlessly.

A deep growl from the other side of the room brings me back to Earth. I attempt to jump away from Wilder, but his grip on me is too much.

He spins me around, forcing me to face Hendrix.

His eyes are dark, but it's not anger. It's something much more dangerous than that.

It's desire.

My stomach knots and everything south of my waist pulls tight.

I want to blame the vodka, but that would be unfair.

This has been building since the moment Wilder invited himself on this little trip.

Some may even say it's been inevitable.

And who would I be to stop the inevitable?

20

HENDRIX

My skin feels too tight and my heart is racing as I stare at the two of them together.

They've stopped dancing. But it doesn't matter. He's still touching her.

Anger bubbles up within me. But it's not enough to make me do anything, to force me to make him stop holding her. Because there is something else there, too. And he knows it.

Over Noelle's shoulder, his eyes hold mine.

Daring me. Taunting me. Challenging me.

He knows that my natural instinct is to protect her.

Hell, to protect myself, too.

The road we're going down here is risky and dangerous.

But I'm not sure I'm strong enough to try and stop it.

And even if I was, do I want to?

The song changes, and the second the beat drops on the new one, Wilder begins moving.

He rolls his hips, grinding himself against Noelle's ass, and my fists curl in my lap.

His smirk grows, the twinkle in his eyes getting brighter.

He lives for this shit. Always has, and always will.

I, however, have always run in the opposite direction from anything even remotely risky.

I'm the safe and dependable twin, and some days, I'm okay with that. Being the boring one. But more often than not, I crave a little of what Wilder has. I wish I could let go of everything that holds me back and just... have fun.

"Dance with me, Elle," he growls in her ear when she's slow to join him.

Her eyes hold mine, concern dancing in them.

She's waiting for me to freak out. She'll be able to read on my expression that I'm close to the edge.

But I'm not.

I'm not going to do what either of them expects of me.

Just for one night, I don't want to be the boring one.

Just one night.

So instead of jumping up and ripping her from his hold, I sit back and force my body to relax.

I uncurl my fists and spread my legs as I suck in a deep, calming breath.

"Do as you're told, Elle," I demand making her lips pop open.

Pride for myself warms my stomach.

I can do this.

I can embrace my inner Wilder and live recklessly for once.

It takes her a second, but hesitantly, she starts to move.

I watch them, my eyes jumping from Wilder's hands on her hips to her face.

She hasn't taken her gaze off me once.

He might be the one touching her right now, but I'm very much the one in control.

I feel more powerful than I have in my entire life.

With my eyes still on them, I blindly reach for the bottle of vodka. Ignoring the glass before me, I twist the top off and take a shot.

If you can't beat them, join them, right?

It burns down my throat before warming my stomach and sending a little extra confidence through my veins.

"Are you just going to watch us?" Wilder taunts. "Or are you going to man up and join us?"

The need to take the easy route burns through it. It's what I'd always do.

But that was then; this is now.

Sitting forward, I rest my elbows on my knees.

"Is that what you want, Noelle?" I ask, focusing on her desire-filled, glassy eyes.

She bites down on her bottom lip. It's the simplest of reactions, but it hits me right in the dick.

The image of her on her knees in the bathroom for me earlier hits me out of nowhere, and my temperature spikes.

"Yes," she breathes. Her voice is barely loud enough to be heard over the music blaring from Wilder's cell, but I don't need to hear it; I see the answer.

Pushing to my feet, I saunter over. The second we're in reaching distance, she holds her hands out for me.

Without overthinking it, I twist my fingers with hers and lift her arms over my shoulders as I step into her body.

Taking her face in my hands, I lower my lips to hers and kiss her as if we were alone.

Wilder's attention burns, but I push it aside.

Fuck him.

He's the one who takes exactly what he wants. For the briefest moment, I wonder how it must feel with the shoe on the other foot, but then I remember that I'm not caring about anyone but what Noelle and I want for once, and I push it aside.

Together the three of us move to the music, and eventually, I release her lips, resting my brow against hers instead as we try to catch our breath.

The vodka makes my head swim a little, and I can only imagine that she's feeling it too.

"You okay?" I mouth.

A lazy smile appears on her swollen lips.

"More than okay," she confesses, continuing to dance between us. "How could I not be while pinned between two hot twins?"

"Hot, huh?" Wilder asks.

"Oh, pipe down," Noelle laughs. "Your ego already knows how hot you are."

"Maybe so. It's still nice to hear it from the woman who's rubbing her ass against my cock, though."

I still, his words hitting me harder than I expected.

Noelle's eyes bounce between mine, probably waiting for me to freak out.

I'm not going to, though. Instead, I take the other road, shocking the shit out of both of them.

"Is he as hard as I am?"

Noelle gasps while Wilder's face beams with pride.

Weird thing for him to be proud of me for, but I'll take it.

Pressing myself harder against her stomach, I wait for her response—not that I need it. Call it twin intuition or whatever.

"Yes," she finally breathes.

Fuck.

This is crazy. Crazier than anything I've ever done before.

Noelle pushes up on her toes and whispers in my ear.

"Stop overthinking. Just enjoy."

Her hands slip to my ass and she squeezes.

"Y-yeah, I am," I promise, letting myself be taken away by the beat of the music.

I've never really danced before. Sure, Noelle and I have messed about over the years. But we've never danced. Not like this.

My lips find hers again, and we make out like no one is watching, despite the fact someone is very closely observing our every move.

Suddenly, Noelle's lips are ripped from mine as a loud moan spills from her lips.

I glance down and instantly discover why. Wilder's hands are cupping her breasts.

My heart jumps into my throat as my fight or flight kicks in.

Rip them off; rip them fucking off, one voice screams. All the while, I have another voice demanding I let it go. To roll with the punches and see where it leads us.

It's a hard battle, but one I insist on fighting because I know it'll be worth it.

All the air rushes out of my lungs as I stare down at his big, calloused hands against her tiny, soft body.

It's wrong, but at the same time... it's so right.

"Pinch her nipples," I rasp, unable to believe I'm saying the words. "She likes that," I add as his hands move.

"Oh god," she moans, her head falling back against Wilder's shoulder, her eyes closing as she focuses on the sensation.

She's still wearing my hoodie, but I know for a fact that she's only got a thin tank beneath it.

"Kiss her neck," I demand, allowing myself to throw caution to the wind now we've started.

Wilder's eyes hold mine firmly before doing anything.

We've touched on this enough over the last couple of days for him to know that I'm intrigued. But I'm not sure he thought I would be brave enough to act on it.

Noelle is mine. She's always been mine. But...

Watching the way her face morphs as he touches her. Knowing that she's enjoying it...

Fuck.

It's a head fuck that I think I'm okay getting on board with.

With his eyes still locked on mine, he leans forward.

If it's possible, my heart rate picks up even more and I swear to god, it stops entirely the beat before his lips brush her skin.

She whimpers as he kisses her, and a potent shot of desire goes through me.

Holy shit.

Ignoring Wilder, I focus on Noelle.

Her eyes are wide open now. Wide and full of undiluted desire, but there's also fear there.

"It's okay," I assure her quietly. "Enjoy it."

She continues to stare at me with hesitation in her dark green eyes.

Needing to prove that I mean what I'm saying, one of my hands wraps around her waist, a few inches from where Wilder is still pinning her in place against him, and I cup her jaw, the opposite side to where Wilder is kissing her.

Leaning forward, I rest my brow against hers.

"You want to stop, we stop," I promise her.

She nods. The movement is so slight that I probably wouldn't notice if I weren't touching her.

"I love you," she breathes.

My heart swells just like it has every time she's said it since we embarked on this thing.

Fuck. It's only been a day.

How is that even possible?

Sure, we might have only been intimate since yesterday, but we've been together for our entire lives, we just hadn't realized it.

"Oh," she gasps, her breath rushing out of her, and when I look over, I find Wilder sucking a hickey into her neck.

A wave of possessiveness rushes through me. Closing the couple of inches between us, I crash our lips together.

She kisses me with even more desperation than she did earlier.

Her tongue tangles with me, her body silently begging for more.

It terrifies me.

Wilder is more than likely in his element right now. He does this kind of thing every weekend. He knows exactly what to do, where to touch, and how to make her feel good.

I'm still learning.

Dragging my lips from hers, I kiss down the other side of her throat, my hand sliding up to her breast, squeezing and pinching the way I know she likes.

The fabric of her hoodie bumps against my hand, and when I look down, I find Wilder's fingers wrapped around it.

Releasing my hold on her, I allow him to drag it off, leaving her standing in only her thin tank and tiny shorts.

Her nipples are peaked and obvious behind the fabric. The sight of them makes my mouth water.

"That's better," Wilder muses. "What do you think, Rix?"

"Hot," I muse, letting my eyes trace down the lines of her body. "Really fucking hot."

"Now, that's what I'm talking about." Wilder's fingers

thread into Noelle's hair and he gently tugs her head back, twisting her exactly as he wants her.

He stares at her, his eyes darting between her eyes and her lips.

He wants to kiss her.

I stand there with my chest heaving, waiting...

He leans in, going in for the kiss, but right before their lips touch, she tenses and blurts, "I'm hungry."

A laugh erupts from my throat as I watch Wilder's face fall and Noelle step back.

"Uh... yeah," Wilder muses, rubbing at his scruff-covered jaw. "Good idea. That's totally what I was thinking too."

"Sure you were," I laugh, reaching for Noelle's hand and tugging her into my side. "What are you thinking?" I ask, my eyes bouncing between her glassy ones.

She's buzzed, that's more than obvious. It's probably for the best we eat before this gets out of hand.

Together we navigate our way through the almost darkness into the kitchen.

She pulls the refrigerator open, but unlike normal, the light doesn't come on.

Stepping up behind her, I shine my flashlight into the dark space to illuminate our options. They're pretty limited considering we only have a fire to cook on right now.

"Cheese. We need cheese."

21

NOELLE

y body burns red hot, and my heart pounds a million beats a second as I stare aimlessly into the refrigerator.

I was hoping the cool air might help with my current situation, but all it does is remind me that I shouldn't have opened it.

We've no idea how long this blackout is going to last; we don't need all the food in here getting warm before necessary.

Apparently, there is no limit to my recklessness. If you can compare opening the fridge in a power outage to dirty dancing with twins.

My chest compresses and a huge sigh passes my lips.

"Noelle?" Rix's voice is deep and raspy in a way I'd never really heard before this trip. Hearing it also isn't the bucket of ice water I really need pouring over me.

"I'm okay," I whisper, finally reaching for what I came in here for.

I wasn't lying. I am hungry. And more than that, I need something to soak up the alcohol.

I don't usually drink, and when I do, it's not shots of vodka. And something tells me this is only the beginning. The three of us... we have a lot of night ahead of us.

My stomach knots with a mixture of excitement, anxiety, and anticipation.

Both of them had their hands and their lips on me.

Desire coils between my thighs and a little regret seeps in that I stopped it.

Should I have kept going?

I shake my head, trying to reconcile the old me and this bold new version.

Who knew that getting just a taste of what real sex is like would turn me into this... this...

An erratic laugh erupts from my throat as I wrap my fingers around a block of cheddar and spin around to face my best friend... my... boyfriend?

I'm hit with such a huge wave of reality, I'm not entirely sure how I remain on my feet.

Everything has changed.

Sure, that happened the night of the Halloween party.

I did this when I allowed Wilder to continue touching me.

I regretted it. Even on the drive here, on our first day, it was my biggest regret. Knowing how much it would hurt Hendrix to learn the truth. But now, suddenly, I regret nothing.

Okay, that's a lie. There may be a tiny part of me that is regretting bailing on that situation out there in favor of... cheese.

Fucking cheese.

What was I thinking?

"Are you sure you're okay?" Hendrix asks.

It's pretty dark in here, with only a couple of candles and his cell illuminating the small room, but that doesn't stop me from seeing the deep frown pinched between his brows.

"Yeah," I say, forcing as much conviction into my tone as possible. I fail; the only thing I sound is drunk. "Help me get this together?" I ask, returning to the refrigerator for more cheese.

"Of course."

A comfortable silence falls between us as we work side by side like we have a million times before. But while it might be relaxed, it's impossible to ignore the elephant in the room.

My breath catches and my stomach knots when footsteps float our way. It was inevitable. Wilder isn't the kind of guy who sits around and waits for things to come to him. He's a go-getter in a way that I know Rix wishes he was too.

The second he steps into the room, I freeze. The images from what happened out in the living room only moments ago slam into me.

My hand trembles as I try to get some crackers out.

I've no idea if Hendrix and Wilder can see it in the dark, or just sense it, but both of them move closer.

Wilder's hot breath washes down my neck as he steps up behind me, and a violent shiver races down my spine.

The length of his hot and hard body presses against my back.

Without thinking, I lean into him.

It feels good, familiar, comforting.

His hand lands on my hip, grounding me, reminding me just how good it felt being pinned between them.

Hendrix's hand finds mine, and he entwines our fingers.

Instantly, the final few tense muscles in my body relax.

Right now, I feel like I belong more than I ever had in my life before.

Wilder's hot breath rushes down my neck again before he leans even closer.

"What happens in a blackout stays in a blackout," he whispers, his lips brushing the edge of my ear.

My breath catches.

Is it really that easy?

Could we carry on what we started out there earlier and then wake up in the morning like it never happened?

No. There is no way.

I already know it's impossible to forget the things that Wilder Kemp is capable of.

I've tried. I've tried really fucking hard.

Almost as soon as his words have floated away, he turns the tables on me once again.

"This was a good idea," he says leaning around me and quickly cutting off a corner of the blue cheese before me.

He throws it in his mouth and then turns to get us drinks.

"It's red wine or port with cheese, right?"

"That's very sophisticated of you," Hendrix mocks.

"What? I can do sophisticated when it's called for."

Hendrix snorts, unwilling to believe his brother's bullshit.

"When the fuck is it ever called for? I've seen the girls you spend time with; I can confidently say, it's not for them."

"Hey," I argue, unable to keep my mouth shut.

"You don't count, Elle," Hendrix assures me, leaning in to brush a kiss on my cheek. "You buck every single one of Wilder's trends when it comes to women."

"She's hot."

"Every other trend."

Wilder wants to argue, I can sense it, but he knows that Hendrix is right.

I'm not a jersey chaser. I'm the total opposite. I only ever watch football to support Wilder and be there for Hendrix as he does the same.

I don't really care for the game. And I have even less interest in screwing my way around any team for bragging rights.

I can understand why most people would look at what happened between Wilder and me and pull a face.

I'm not the kind of girl he'd ever go after.

He's not the kind of guy I'd ever be interested in.

But when we came together that night, something happened.

Something I've been unable to forget.

"I'll take that as a compliment," I mutter, finishing off our platter of cheese and crackers.

"I would; he hooks up with some right dogs."

Shaking my head, I pick up the plate and head toward the door so we can eat in the dim candlelight of the living room.

"We don't have either of those options," Hendrix says, going back to Wilder's first point.

"And I'm not having any more vodka," I add.

"Beer it is then," Wilder states as I lower the plate to the table.

"N-no, I'm not sure—"

"It's Christmas. What's the worst that can happen?" Hendrix asks, using my own words against me.

"Do you really want to go there?" I ask, dropping into the middle of the couch without thinking.

Hendrix takes one spot beside me, and only a few seconds later, Wilder takes the other after placing three beers on the coffee table.

"Well, this is cozy," he muses, reaching for a cracker and loading it with a soft cheese.

"There is another chair," Rix grumbles, copying his twin and throwing a loaded cracker into his mouth.

"You're funny," Wilder mocks.

They both fall quiet as they devour the food before us, but I quickly find that any appetite I did have has vanished, and it only gets worse every time one of them brushes against me.

"What's that?" I ask when Wilder returns from the kitchen a while later with a bag of something in his hand.

He holds it up with a grin playing on his face.

"Who wants s'mores?"

"Nah, I'm good," Hendrix says, falling back onto the couch.

"You're gonna miss out, man," Wilder teases.

I narrow my eyes at him, trying to figure out what he's planning.

"Elle?" he asks, knowing just as well as Hendrix that I can't refuse a s'more.

I scoot to the edge of the couch, ready to stand as Wilder holds his hand out for me.

I stare at it frozen. It would be so easy to slip my hand into his and allow him to pull me toward him, but...

I glance back at Rix.

"Go," he encourages with a soft smile playing on his lips.

With a single nod, I lift my hand and allow Wilder my pull me from the couch.

The heat of the fire licks up my body as we approach.

This is it. This is the kind of cozy Christmas I dreamed of.

S'mores in front of the fire is my kind of heaven.

Wilder passes me a couple of sticks while he rips into the bag and pulls out a giant marshmallow. Holding out a stick, he places it on the end, and I move it toward the flames.

I watch enthralled as the marshmallow begins to melt and toast.

"Did you bring the—" My question is cut off when he pulls a packet of Graham crackers from... somewhere.

He opens them for me before spearing his marshmallow and holding it out next to mine in the fire.

Once I'm happy, I sandwich my marshmallow between the crackers and lift it to my mouth.

"Ow," I complain as it burns my tongue, but it's not enough to stop me. "So good," I mumble.

Wilder's eyes turn on me as I battle with my s'more. The gooey marshmallow drips down my chin.

My body burns hotter with his attention, and it only increases when Rix's voice floats through the air.

"Do it," he instructs.

Wilder continues to stare at me, his eyes darting between mine and my lips.

"Rix, I haven't—"

"Do. It," Rix repeats.

The fire sizzles beside us, forcing us to look over.

"Ah, damn," Wilder complains as we watch his fallen marshmallow melt and burn on a smoldering log. "Well, it looks like I'm going to have to share yours now."

Before I have a chance to react, Wilder leans forward, wraps his hand around the back of my neck, and drags his tongue up my chin.

My gasp fills the air, and as he pulls my bottom lip into his mouth and sucks, I stop breathing entirely.

He's not kissing me, not really, but damn.

Fire burns through my veins as he pulls back and looks at me with smoldering, heavy-lidded eyes.

"Delicious," he muses.

Finally, I suck in a deep breath before absently lifting my s'more to my lips again.

I eat it, but I don't really register it. I'm too lost in Wilder and the promise of his kiss. Not to mention the searing gaze of Hendrix from the couch.

Trying again, Wilder pushes another marshmallow onto his stick and holds it into the flame.

The air around the three of us crackles louder than the fire, anticipation making it hard to breathe.

As I continue eating, I look back at Rix.

His eyes are firmly focused on me, and his sweats clearly show the evidence of how he feels about what he just demanded Wilder do.

I'm stuck with the sudden urge to crawl over and take care of him.

I lick my lips, remembering just how he tasted earlier in the bathroom.

"Later, dirty girl," Wilder muses, able to accurately read my mind. "Every gentleman knows that the girl is meant to get their pleasure first."

I swear I get whiplash I turn to look at him so quickly.

His smirk is pure filth, and it makes everything inside me coil tightly with desire.

"Here," he says, holding out his perfectly toasted s'more for me. "I'm all yours."

22

___

WILDER

I watch her lips part as I move the melted marshmallow closer.

My dick twitches the second I brush it across her lips. It's stupid. It's innocent and nothing like what I usually get myself into, but fuck, I'm pretty sure I'm more turned on right now than I've ever been in my life.

I've barely even touched her.

I want to, though.

Fuck do I want to.

Hendrix wants me to as well.

He's so fucking curious about all of this. If the situation weren't so hot, it would almost be cute.

The marshmallow leaves a sweet, sticky trail on her bottom lip, one I'm desperate to lick away, but I refrain for now.

The creak of the couch behind me doesn't come as a surprise. It was only a matter of time before we cracked Hendrix's resolve to come a little closer.

"Are you going to take it?" I ask, my voice deep and raspy before I push the pillow of sweetness into her mouth.

Her eyelids lower as the sugar explodes on her tongue, and she groans in appreciation, but she doesn't get to fully enjoy it because Hendrix appears beside her.

His fingers grip her chin and he turns her head to face him. My own lips part in time with his before he leans forward and does exactly what I was craving.

He licks across her lips, sucking the sweetness from her equally as sweet skin before diving in for a kiss.

I sit there on the floor in front of the fire, unable to do anything but watch them make out.

Their tongues twist and the sound of their lips smacking rivals the crackling of the fire.

It's hot. So fucking hot.

I'm not sure if Hendrix has found his confidence, or if it's the mix of vodka shots and beer, but he doesn't so much as hesitate as he reaches out and cups Noelle's breast, pinching her nipple through the fabric.

She gasps and he deepens the kiss further.

It ends almost as fast as it started, leaving both of them, and me, breathless.

"She needs more," Hendrix demands before plucking another marshmallow from the bag and pushing it onto the stick that I'm still holding between us.

"Don't you think she's sweet enough?" I tease as I move it toward the fire.

"Not quite," Rix muses, not taking his eyes off Noelle for a single second.

Noelle doesn't say a word; something tells me that she's too lost in her lust fog to really decipher what's happening.

Instead, she reaches for her abandoned stick and grabs another marshmallow.

Music from my cell continues filling the air around us as we watch our marshmallows toast.

Once mine is done, I hold it up between Noelle and Hendrix.

Rix shakes his head. He's never really been one for sweet treats. Noelle and I, though...

She leans forward, her lips parting, and I do the same. With our eyes locked, we both take a bite of the same marshmallow, our lips only millimeters apart.

My heart slams against my ribs, my entire body screaming at me to kiss her.

The taste I had a few minutes ago was nowhere near enough.

Hendrix watches us, his eyes burning almost as hot as the fire.

Suddenly, he reaches out and snatches the stick and the remainder of the marshmallow from me.

"Kiss her," he demands roughly, giving me little choice but to dive right into what I need.

We might have got a little dirty at Halloween, but I didn't kiss her.

I want to say that it was a conscious decision, but it wasn't.

I wanted to. Fuck did I want to.

Her lips were pink and glistening. I was fucking desperate to. But I knew that as much as me touching her would hurt Rix, kissing her would be worse.

He may have had zero experience with women, but kissing Noelle would be crossing a line I wouldn't be able to come back from.

Now, though...

He's telling me to.

No. He's demanding I kiss her.

What red-blooded man could ever say no to that?

My lips part at the same time as hers and our tongues

collide. If it's possible, the sweetness already coating my mouth only gets sweeter.

Cracking one of my eyes open, I check on Rix, but it's instantly obvious from the way that he's watching us that it's okay.

Confident that he's not about to impale me on a stick and shove me into the fire, I give Noelle everything I've got.

Wrapping my hand around the back of her neck, I encourage her to rise up on her knees.

Shuffling forward, I press our bodies together as I slide my hand down her back until I grab her ass.

"Oh god," she breathes as I drag my lips from hers in favor of her throat.

Her neck ripples as she turns to look at Rix, and then she swallows thickly.

I can only imagine what she finds in his expression.

"S'more?" Noelle rasps, lifting her marshmallow up to Rix.

"I've got a better idea," I announce before he has a chance to respond. "Take this," I demand, plucking the stick from Noelle's hand and passing it to Rix.

The second he has it, I lift Noelle from the floor and carry her over to the couch.

"I think Rix has his sight set on a whole different kind of dessert," I explain as I lower us, setting Noelle on my lap with her back to my chest.

"What are you—oh god," Noelle cries when I tuck my fingers under the straps of her tank and drag them down her arms, exposing her to both of us.

Her arms fly up to cover her bare tits, but I catch them.

"No," I warn. "Rix." I command him over with nothing more than a jerk of my chin.

The second the still-warm marshmallow is in reaching

distance, I snatch it from his grasp and brush it over Noelle's nipple.

"Shit," she gasps, arching from my chest.

Leaving a sticky trail behind, I move to the other side.

"She's all yours when you're ready, Bro."

Hendrix watches us with intrigue. His eyes are blazing and every muscle in his body is pulled tight, although none more than the most important one in his pants.

I know how he fucking feels.

He moves closer, his eyes locked on Noelle's tits before he ducks down and swipes his tongue across her sticky skin.

"Oh god," she cries, arching once again. Her hands find mine and she grips them hard.

"She likes that," I assure him, encouraging him to continue. Not that he looks like he needs it as he switches to the other side.

While he goes to town cleaning her up, I lift the cooling marshmallow to her lips, feeding her.

She's a little more distracted compared to when I fed her earlier, and in the end, I take a bite and let her steal it from my lips.

Hot. As. Fuck.

No sooner has she swallowed it do I thread my fingers into the back of her hair and drag her lips to mine, kissing her as Rix sucks on her nipples.

Now this is how you fucking celebrate Christmas.

She moans into our kiss, and if it's possible, it makes me even harder.

"Oh god. More," she begs the second we part.

"Yeah?" I ask breathlessly as I stare into her blown eyes.

She swallows almost nervously before both of us look down at Rix.

He pauses, his lips hovering just above her left tit.

"Give her more, Rix," I instruct.

His mouth opens and closes as he thinks.

Moving the marshmallow back to her body, I draw a line from between her tits all the way down her stomach. Hooking my feet around hers, I give her little choice but to spread her legs and keep going, showing Rix exactly where he needs to be.

"You eaten your girl out yet, Bro?"

Rix's eyes dart to mine. There's now a little fear there with the unfiltered desire.

I'll take that as a no, then.

"Strip her," I demand, allowing her legs to close again to make it easier for him.

His eyes hold mine for another second before he looks at her, waiting for her permission.

It takes her a moment, but she nods her head and whispers, "Please."

Without missing a beat, Rix drops to his knees and eagerly tucks his fingers beneath the waistband of Noelle's shorts.

He drags both them and her panties down her legs, and the moment he's unhooked them from her ankles, he reaches for her tank that's bunched up around her waist and pulls that from her body as well.

"You're beautiful," I breathe when she squirms self-consciously on top of me. "So fucking hot. Can you feel how hard I am?" On the off chance she can't, I roll my hips, ensuring I poke her in the back.

"Yeah," she whispers.

"Rix is too. He wants you so fucking bad. You want him too, don't you?" I ask as I drag her legs apart again.

"Yes."

"How wet is she, Rix?" I ask, giving him little choice but to stare right at her pussy.

His throat ripples as he swallows.

She might only be illuminated by candlelight, but he can see more than enough to tell how much she needs this.

"Really wet," he rasps.

"You want to taste her?" I spread her legs wider, leaving her completely exposed and ready for the taking.

He rubs his jaw, his tongue sweeping across his bottom lip as he tries to imagine what it might be like.

"Yeah," he confesses.

"So, what are you waiting for?"

I know exactly what's holding him back. It's what holds him back in most things in life. His confidence.

"I-I don't—"

"Rix, please," Noelle begs, probably as aware as I am about the issue. "I need you."

Their eyes lock for a moment, just long enough for a short, silent conversation to pass between them, Rix places his hands on Noelle's knees and slides them higher.

She trembles from his innocent touch alone.

"Yes," she breathes as he gets closer to where she needs him. "RIX," she cries when he drags the pad of this thumb across her sensitive flesh.

"She's going to taste so fucking sweet, man," I tell him.

He glances up, needing reassurance from both of us before he ducks down and leans forward.

"Oh shit. Yes, yes."

"He hasn't even touched you yet," I point out.

"But he's going to," Noelle points out before her entire body locks up and she cries out.

Fuck.

I look down her naked body, watching as my brother licks up the length of her pussy, getting his very first taste of the woman he's been fantasizing about for years.

Should I feel bad about intruding on such an intimate

moment between them? Probably. But I don't. I really fucking don't.

"That's it, Bro," I praise as Noelle's hips roll against his mouth. "Tell him how good it feels."

"So good," Noelle breathes. "Keep going."

His eyes flash with pride before he gets back to it.

I let him work solo for a few minutes, allowing him to find his flow. Noelle moans and mewls as he explores her body, finding all the bits that get her going. But I soon get impatient to join in.

"Oh shit," she cries when I cup both her breasts.

Rix looks up and his movements falter as he watches me tease her right alongside him.

"If you want me to stop then—"

He shakes his head. "Let's make her scream."

I chuckle. "You don't have to tell me twice. Suck on her clit," I demand before pinching her nipples at the same time.

"Oh my god," she cries.

Rix and I have always been pretty in sync, but like this, we work together perfectly to bring Noelle to complete ruin.

It is fucking beautiful.

23

NOELLE

Holy shit.

Oh my god.

Fucking hell.

With my eyes locked on Hendrix between my thighs, my release surges forward, slamming into me with the force of a freight train.

Hendrix's mouth and whatever he's doing with his tongue never falters, and Wilder's fingers only tighten on my nipples. It hurts, but it's so fucking good.

I'm aware that there is noise falling from my lips, but I've no idea what words I'm saying.

I'm lost, so freaking lost in a level of pleasure I never thought really existed. I've read about mind-numbing releases that tilt your world on its axis, sure. But I thought they were a myth made up by romance authors, just like our dream book boyfriends.

But no.

Apparently, these things are very, very real.

"Fucking hell," Wilder rasps in my ear. "You're enjoying having Rix eating your pussy, huh?"

His dirty words send another, smaller, wave of pleasure shooting through me.

My entire body trembles with aftershocks, and it only gets worse when Rix finally sits up.

His mouth is glistening with my juices and he's got the most incredible smile on his face.

Wiping the back of his hand across his mouth, he pushes to stand. At the same time, Wilder sits forward, pushing me with him. I'm so limp and sated, I don't have a choice. I'm not sure I could hold my own weight even if I wanted to right now.

But then I drag my eyes down his body from his incredible mouth to his heaving chest and then his—

My mouth runs dry as I take in the massive tent in his sweats.

"Look what you did, Noelle," Wilder says, his warm breath rushing over my neck and down my chest, making my nipples pebble again.

I'm achingly aware that I'm sitting here between them completely naked while they're fully dressed. But as I continue to stare at Hendrix's reaction to him eating me, it becomes less and less of an issue.

All I can think about is him. About making him feel as good as he just did me.

Fuck. It was incredible.

"Go on, Elle. No need to be shy," Wilder encourages. "We're both big boys; we can handle it."

He shifts a little beneath me as he says the words 'big boy' to tell me what he really means.

Fire burns through me as crazy thoughts about comparing the two of them flicker through my mind.

They're twins. They're so similar in every way...

"Noelle?" Rix rasps, his voice so thick with desire, I barely recognize it.

I glance up and swallow thickly when I see a little fear in his eyes.

Fuck that shit. Hendrix has nothing to be scared or anxious of right now.

I want him.

Reaching out, I tuck my fingers under the waistband of his pants and drag them down, taking his boxers too.

His dick springs free. It's painfully hard, the end purple and glistening with precum.

"It's not going to suck itself," Wilder quips when I take too long to jump into action.

"Wild," Hendrix grunts.

"What? I'm just saying."

Something tells me that the two of them are glaring at each other over my head, but I don't bother to look, and I'm pretty sure that Rix forgets all about it when I finally lean forward and lick.

"Oh shit," he grunts, his hips thrusting forward in search of more.

"That's what I'm talking about," Wilder praises, his hands wrapping around my hips to hold me in place.

"You're weird," Rix mutters as I continue to tease him.

"It's fucking hot, man. You can't argue with that."

"N-no, I—" I sink down on Rix's cock and all his words evaporate.

His fingers slide into my hair and he gently holds the back of my head as I set my rhythm.

The sounds he makes as I suck him ensure that my desire continues to simmer just beneath the surface, despite the mind-blowing orgasm they both gave me. The situation doesn't get any better when Wilder's hands begin roaming, either.

"She's squirming on my lap, Bro. She fucking loves sucking you off."

"G-Good," Rix stutters.

Rolling my eyes up his body, I find him staring down at me with nothing but awe in his expression.

Hollowing my cheeks, I take him even deeper.

"Y-you... you want Wilder to get you off again?" he asks, making liquid lust pool between my thighs.

Is that even a question?

I nod. Wilder might not be able to see it, but Hendrix sure feels it.

"What are you doing?" I ask in a panic when Hendrix steps back, pulling his dick from my mouth.

I watch in confusion as he drags the coffee table closer to the single chair and then falls down into it. Wrapping his fist around his cock, he demands, "Get on the coffee table, ass in the air, and continue what you started."

I look from him to the coffee table, my head spinning.

"What are you waiting for?" Wilder growls behind me, and before I know what's happening, he's taken over and I'm deposited in place.

Leaning forward, I rest my palms on either side of Hendrix's thighs and stare at him as I arch my back and shamelessly thrust my ass in the air.

"Like this?" I ask innocently, my teeth sinking into my bottom lip.

Hendrix rubs his jaw as he takes me in. "Fuck, yeah. You're perfect, Elle. Fucking perfect."

"She really fucking is. Look at this pretty little pussy," Wilder muses from behind me.

He moves and a rush of air flows over my heated skin. I wiggle my hips, desperate for more.

"And just look how needy it is, too."

"She's not the only one," Hendrix grunts as his fingers find purchase in my hair again, gently pushing me down onto his dick. "Make her scream, Wild."

I suck in a sharp breath through my nose as a pair of hot hands land on my hips.

Oh god.

A whimper rumbles in my throat as a warm stream of air blows across my pussy. My back arches further as I offer myself up to him.

This is wrong. So fucking wrong.

But also... so right.

I work Hendrix, trying to focus on his pleasure over my own. But it's hard. Really freaking hard.

"If you stop sucking, I'll stop licking," Wilder warns. "You got that?"

"Yes," I breathe, pulling off Hendrix for a second.

"Good. Let's see who can hold out the longest."

"Wilder," I squeal when he licks up the length of my pussy.

I'm so sensitive from Rix already. I don't think there's going to be much competition over who's going to fall first.

"Get to work, Elle. You only get yours if Rix is getting his."

"How very selfless of you."

Wilder chuckles darkly. "For now," he mutters before latching onto my clit and making me scream. Although the sound is soon cut off when Rix thrusts his dick between my lips.

I try to focus, I really, really do. But Wilder's tongue...

Rix was good. Really good. But Wilder's experience shines through and in only minutes, I'm trembling from head to toe, desperately trying to hold off the inevitable.

Every few seconds, I remember that I'm supposed to be doing something and I suck on Rix's dick, but it's a pathetic attempt at best.

I guess it's a good thing that Wilder can't see how badly I'm doing or he'd stop.

"Come for us, Noelle," Rix demands.

My eyes fly open and I look up at him.

His jaw is clenched tight, his nostrils flaring, and his eyes are almost entirely black.

He looks downright dangerous.

The sight of him being so turned on by this is the final straw and I shatter, coming all over Wilder's face as Rix watches.

"Good girl," he whispers as I ride out every inch of pleasure.

Wilder pulls back, leaving my pussy clenching around nothing as the tail of my release fades away, and I shriek when he suddenly spanks my ass.

"Always the quiet ones," he mutters to himself before pushing to his feet and walking around the coffee table, where I'm still hovering over Hendrix's hard dick.

Wilder has lost his shirt, and I feast on inches upon inches of tanned and toned skin.

I swallow nervously as he pushes his hand into his shorts, squeezing his dick.

"But I think you've got more in you."

"There's nothing in me," I quip, my eyes widening as I hear my own words.

Wilder throws his head back and laughs.

"Knew there was more to you than meets the eye," he confesses before shoving his shorts down, letting his dick spring free without a care in the world.

"Wilder," I gasp as he kicks the coffee table I'm awkwardly perched on.

"Sit on the edge," he demands, wrapping his fist around himself and stroking slowly.

Absently, I do as I'm told, I'm too enthralled watching him—watching them—to consider what I'm doing.

This is insane.

I've got both Kemp twins before me with their dicks in their hands. And they're hard because of me.

What is this life?

My blood is like lava as I sit on the edge of the table, waiting for more instructions.

Whore, a little voice says in my head.

But I don't care.

Right now, there's a very good chance I'd do anything they asked of me.

"Get on your knees and suck Rix again. You're neglecting him."

Before Wilder has even finished talking, my knees have hit the floor and I've got my lips wrapped around his dick.

"You look so good on your knees for him, Elle."

My eyes dart between the two of them as I bob back and forth on Rix's dick.

Wilder continues stroking himself as he watches me.

"Fuuuck" Rix groans, his fingers threading through my hair and gripping tightly enough to cause a bite of pain.

I don't complain, though. I can't. Not while I have the pleasure of watching him fall apart.

"That's it. Be a good girl and let my brother come down your throat."

I moan in response, loving the sound of that.

"You're fulfilling all of his filthy dreams right now, do you know that?"

I nod. I do know. Because Rix—both of them—are fulfilling mine too.

"Good, Bro?"

"So good," Rix groans.

Sensing that he's getting close, I'm up my speed, sucking a little harder.

My lungs burn for air and my eyes begin to water, but I

don't give in. I want Rix to experience the most incredible high after what he's given me.

"You suck his dick so good. Are you going to suck mine too and let Rix watch?"

At his words, Hendrix's cock thickens. He groans loudly before his length jerks in my mouth and he spills down my throat just like Wilder said he was going to.

I take it all, eagerly swallowing him down.

"Fuck. Noelle. Fuck. Fuck," Rix chants as the sound of Wilder jerking himself harder mixes with their combined heaving breaths.

I pull back from Rix just in time to watch Wilder reach his climax.

"Fuck," he barks before stepping closer and coming over my tits.

All three of us watch in silence as it drips over my skin.

"Oh my god," I whisper after a few seconds as the lust haze fades and reality seeps in. "Did we really just..." My words trail off because yes, I really am sitting here as naked as the day I was born, and Rix and Wilder's dicks are both hanging free in front of me.

I stare up at both of them, terrified that I'm going to see regret, or anger, or disappointment. But I didn't find any of it. I just find two very happy, sated faces smiling down at me.

Holy hell, I just hooked up with both of the Kemp twins. At the same time.

I really am a whore.

"Shower?" Rix asks, holding his hand out to help me up.

"U-uh," I stutter as I climb to my feet. "Yeah, probably a good idea."

24

NOELLE

Hendrix is silent as he leads me toward the bathroom. My anxiety spikes with every step we take.

After closing the door, cutting us off from Wilder, he releases my hand and leans into the shower, turning the water on.

I'm so lost in my own head that I don't think about our current situation or that the room is only illuminated with candles like the rest of the cabin, but the second he pushes me under the powerful stream of water, it all comes crashing down quickly.

"It's freezing," I shriek, attempting to jump straight back out of it. But Hendrix doesn't allow it. Instead, he reaches for the shower gel and squirts a generous amount into his palm.

He starts with my breasts, and I try not to think about why.

His touch feels so good, but the heat of his palms is nowhere near enough to make me forget about the ice water that's sluicing over both of us.

He washes himself down just as quickly, and only a minute or so later, he's killed the water and is wrapping me in a huge fluffy towel.

"Hendrix?" I whisper, achingly aware that he hasn't said a word since we walked away from Wilder.

His eyes bounce between mine, and no sooner has he wrapped a towel around his waist than he reaches up and cups my face in his large hands.

My breath catches. There's so much emotion in his eyes it's impossible to decipher everything he's feeling right now.

Closing the space between us, he rests his forehead against mine as he releases my face and wraps his arms around my body, tugging me against him.

My heart thunders and my head spins with a mixture of alcohol and anxiety.

Did we just fuck everything up by doing that?

Does he think I'm a whore?

Does he think I want Wilder more than him?

"Stop," he whispers. "Everything you're thinking, stop it right now."

My brows pinch in confusion and my lips part to respond, but he doesn't give me a chance.

"Come on," he says, suddenly releasing me. He takes my hand again and tugs me into the bedroom.

The living room is in silence, and concern for Wilder floods through me.

Is he regretting what just happened? Is he worried about the fallout?

I almost laugh at myself when I realize what I'm doing. Wilder doesn't worry about things that have happened. Hell, he barely spares a thought for things that are yet to happen.

The bedroom is in darkness, and Hendrix leaves me at the end of the bed while he lights some candles.

It's romantic, or at least it should be.

When he turns back around after lighting the final candle, his brows furrow when he finds me chewing on my nail.

"Hey," he says softly, reaching out to pull my hand free. "Are you okay?"

"Rix," I breathe.

"Shit," he curses, ripping his eyes from mine in favor of staring down at his feet. "You're regretting it, aren't you?"

"What?" I gasp, shocked by his words. "N-No, I'm not regretting anything. I'm... I'm worrying about you and what happened and—"

He cuts me off with his lips.

"Stop," he murmurs into our kiss.

Unhooking the towel from under my arms, he lets it drop to the floor before leading me to the bed.

We're still wet, but I'm also cold, so I don't argue when he holds the sheets back and encourages me to slip in.

He follows me not a second later after losing his own towel.

Sliding his body right against mine, he wraps his arm around my back and holds me as close as possible.

"You're incredible," he whispers, kissing the tip of my nose.

I shake my head. "I haven't done anything."

He laughs. "Oh, you've done plenty, Miss Bell."

My cheeks blaze red hot.

"Oh my god," I breathe before tucking my face into Hendrix's chest. "I can't believe we did that. I blame the vodka."

He chuckles, sliding his hand up and down my back supportively.

"There doesn't need to be any blame, Elle. We did it because we wanted to. Because it was hot."

"It was really hot," I confess against his chest.

"Exactly. We're all consenting adults. There's nothing to be ashamed of."

"I know. I do know that. It's just..." I let out a sigh and pull my head out of its hiding place.

"It's just what, baby?" Rix asks softly.

"We've only just started. Don't you think that going from nothing to threeways with your brother in the blink of an eye is a bit much?"

He smirks.

"Maybe. But did it feel right?"

I think for a moment. "I wouldn't have done it if it hadn't. You wouldn't have either."

"No," he muses.

"Were you really okay with it? Watching him... touching me?"

He bites down on his lip. For a moment I almost believe he's thinking, but I quickly learn that he's trying to stop his grin from breaking through.

"Rix," I cry, playfully slapping him on the shoulder.

"What? Trust me, if it were anyone but Wilder, I'd have real fucking issues with it. But it's Wild. I trust him. He won't hurt you. And let's face it, we both know he's had enough practice to ensure he'll make you feel good."

Hell, didn't he ever.

"I know but... you don't and—"

"You're worried that I'll compare myself to him?" he finishes for me.

"Yeah. I know that we already fucked up. I don't want to give you any reason to think that I want him more than you. I don't. He's fun, sure. But it's you, Rix. You're the one who owns my heart." I press my hand to my chest, right over the organ in the hope it helps prove my words.

"I know," he whispers. "It's me and you, Elle. It was always meant to be. Having some fun with Wilder while we're stuck here doesn't change that."

"This is crazy. You have to know that."

He laughs again. "Oh, I know."

We don't say anything else. Instead, his lips find mine and we make out for what feels like hours before I finally fall asleep in his arms.

I wake with a start.

It's late. Later than I've woken in a really long time.

The sun isn't shining, but it's light out.

I don't move; instead, I keep my head on the pillow and watch Rix sleep.

He looks so peaceful, so content.

Unable to stop myself, I think back to last night.

He told me that he was okay with what happened, but concern still knots up my insides. Wilder and Hendrix have a close relationship, I know that better than anyone. But I'm also aware of how frustrated Rix can get with his brother.

Rix sees Wilder as the 'better' twin. I hate it. Just because Wilder got better grades at school and can catch a football, it doesn't make him a better person. But Hendrix has always felt like he's in Wilder's shadows, fighting and failing to stand up.

I find it hard to believe a little bit of that didn't slip in last night.

Our friendship—our relationship—might be solid, but insecurities aren't that simple.

It tells me a lot about the trust he has in me, in our connection.

He's right, and as far as I'm concerned, there isn't anyone else in the world I want—would ever want—more than Rix, and it warms my heart to know he feels the same way.

I'm so lost in my own thoughts that when something—someone—moves behind me, I almost scream bloody murder, or at least I would if a large hand doesn't cover my mouth.

"You think really loudly," Wilder whispers. "Woke me up."

He shuffles forward, and I suck in a sharp breath as his hot skin lines up against mine, the hardness of his morning wood against my ass.

He's naked.

We're both naked.

"What are you doing?" I whisper once he deems it safe to remove his hand.

"Well, I was sleeping."

"B-but you sleep on the couch," I counter.

"The fire went out. It got cold, fast. Rix said I could join."

"He did, did he?" I accuse.

"I swear, he did. You were already asleep when I came in."

"Hmmm," I mumble, unsure as to whether I believe him or not.

"Didn't realize just how much I lucked out until I got in and found his hot little naked body to cuddle up to."

"Wilder," I gasp when he drops his hand to my bare breast.

"What? Rix won't have an issue. Remember, what happens in the dark—"

"It's not dark," I point out.

"Fine. What happens at the cabin, stays at the cabin."

"You're insufferable."

"Maybe, but you also know that I'm right. You remember just as vividly as I do the way he watched us last night. He fucking loved it. You did too."

"I don't remember you complaining either."

"Fuck no. I'd never complain about that kind of action."

He continues teasing me, pinching my nipple and palming my breast.

"You were something else last night," he muses.

"Not sure what got into me."

"Well, it wasn't either of our dicks, unfortunately."

His words shouldn't cause a reaction in me, but damn it, they do. Just the thought of having one of them inside me does weird things to my insides.

"O-oh, I like where your mind is going right now, little rebel."

"I've no idea what you're talking about," I argue.

"Like I said, you think loudly. Plus, I know you better than you think I do. I'm not as oblivious as my brother. I know that you've been looking at him with sex eyes for years."

"I have not," I argue, although weakly, because he's right. As soon as I was aware of Rix in that kind of way, I wanted him.

"You have. You've been imagining what his dick might feel like inside you for years."

I squeeze my eyes closed as my cheeks heat. I can't count how many times I laid in bed over the years, many times with him right beside me, imagining what it would be like if he reached over and pulled me to him.

"Want me to prove it to you?"

"Wilder, what are you—Oh Jesus," I gasp as his hand sinks between my thighs.

Every muscle in my body screams for me to stop him, to keep him out, but one brush of his fingers against my clit and my body betrays me. My legs part and I allow him to drag his fingers up my aching core.

"See?" he whispers, his breath rushing over my neck and down my back, making me shiver. "You're soaking just thinking about Rix's dick."

"Y-you need to stop," I argue weakly.

"No, I don't," he states, continuing to circle my clit.

"Reach for his dick," Wilder whispers. "Make his Christmas by waking him up with your hand wrapped around him and your needy moans in his ear."

I hesitate, but only for a few seconds. My hand slides across the small space between us and find him hard and ready for me.

I study him, looking for any sign that he might be awake and aware of what we're doing. But there's nothing.

"He hard?" Wilder asks.

"Y-yeah."

"Bet he's dreaming about you."

Heat surges through me at the thought of me featuring in as many of Hendrix's dreams as he has in mine.

"Or maybe he's dreaming about watching you with me. Kinky fucker seems to really like it."

"Wilder," I moan when he pushes two thick fingers inside me.

As if he can hear, Rix's dick jerks in my hold.

"That's it. Ride my hand while you jerk him off."

"Oh god."

As he works me, Wilder grinds his cock against my ass, searching for some pleasure of his own.

"What do you think he'd do if he woke up right now?

Suck on these addictive tits, or slide his dick straight into this tight, wet pussy?"

"Either. Both," I pant, imagining every possibility.

"And what about me? Would I get your hand? Your mouth? Or your ass?"

"Shit. Oh god, Wilder," I cry, his filthy words and the image they conjure up enough to push me over the edge.

But I'm not alone, because as I come down from my high, I register the movement of Rix's cock in my hand, and more so the sticky residue that's sliding down my skin, and when I open my eyes, I'm met with his heated blue ones.

"Oh my god. I'm sorry, I—"

Lifting his hand, he presses two fingers to my lips, cutting me off.

No one says anything for long seconds as my heart rate returns to normal, and just when I think he's going to up the ante again, Wilder presses his lips to my shoulder, giving me a chaste kiss.

"Merry Christmas, little rebel," he says before rolling away and climbing from the bed.

I want to stop him, but then Hendrix reaches for me and pulls me into his body, his lips stealing mine and completely consuming my thoughts.

25

HENDRIX

I was awake the moment she moaned.

I heard everything. But as much as I wanted to open my eyes and join in, I wanted to listen more.

There's a part of me that wants to rip his hands clean from his body every time he touches her. But there's a bigger part that's desperate to watch. To see what he does. To watch her fall apart for him. As much as I love doing it myself, there's something magic about watching the two of them.

I can't really describe it; all I do know is that I fucking love it, and right now, I'm happy to go along with that.

It's just for a few days. For once in my life, I can throw caution to the wind and focus on fun and pleasure. I can be like Wilder when I really want to be.

Any hesitation or flickers of jealousy were eradicated when her hand wrapped around my dick.

I'm a part of this. I haven't been forgotten while they get their kicks. Knowing that makes my heart swell and my cock get even harder.

"Obsessed with you," I mutter into our kiss long after Wilder has left us to it.

Watching him leave was weird, but it also confirmed to me that he's fully aware of what's happening here.

He might have been allowed to play, but Noelle is mine. For now, he's just an added bonus.

A thought lingers about how that must make him feel. He's not used to being the one on the sidelines watching all the action. But for once, I push concerns about everyone else side and focus on me.

On me and Noelle.

Fuck. I never thought I'd get to say that.

A moan rumbles deep in her throat as she hitches her legs up higher around my waist, letting my hard-again dick graze her pussy.

Will she ever stop affecting me so much? Fuck. I really hope not.

Our hands roam as our kiss continues. Neither of us of cares about the morning breath situation; being connected to each other is way more important.

Reaching between us, my cock jerks as she wraps her hand around it, lining the head up with her entrance.

"I need you," she confesses into our kiss.

I squeeze my eyes closed tightly, wishing I could savor those words forever.

Reaching for her ass, I position her exactly where I want her before gently thrusting forward.

Her pussy is wet and slick from the release that Wilder gave her, making my entrance easy.

"Oh god," she whimpers as a heavy breath punches from my lungs at the feel of her squeezing me so impossibly tight.

"I'm never going to get used to this," I confess, resting my brow against hers, our eyes locked.

"Me neither."

Gripping her ass tighter, I thrust harder, needing to be deeper, needing to imprint myself on her soul so she never forgets this.

"I love you," she whispers as I gently rock us.

It's not the kind of hot and heavy fucking that a part of me wants to embark on right now; it's soft, sweet, and fully loaded with emotions to the point my eyes begin to sting.

Fuck. I can't cry while having sex with Noelle. She'd dump me for Wilder in a heartbeat.

Sensing the shift in me, she slides her hand up my back, wraps it around my neck and drags my lips back to hers.

Our kiss is as gentle as our lovemaking, and it doesn't really make the situation any better.

We're finally doing it. Noelle and I have finally pushed through the barrier that has been holding us back all these years, and fuck me is it good.

"I want you to be mine, Elle. Forever," I blurt.

Her eyes open, the green glittering with desire and love.

"I am. I always have been."

My hold on her tightens as my hips pick up pace.

"I love you so much," I whisper as I roll her onto her back.

Wrapping her legs around my waist, I sit up and watch where my dick disappears inside of her.

Best. Sight. Ever.

Needing to feel her coming, I lick my thumb and press it gently to her clit.

"Rix," she gasps, her hips jumping.

Pride and accomplishment rush through me. I might not have made her come yet, but it's a good start.

Maybe I'm not so bad at this, after all.

"Oh my god,' she gasps, her fingers twisting in the sheets beneath her.

"You look so good full of my dick, Elle. So fucking hot. Can you feel how deep I am inside you?"

Her pussy clamps down on me as her eyes shoot open.

"What?" I ask, fearing I just did something wrong.

"That... that dirty talk. So fucking hot."

A wide smile spreads across my mouth.

"I didn't know you had it in you," she confesses.

"There's only one of us with something deep in them right now, Noelle."

Dropping over her, I rest on one arm as I drive into her harder, continuing to tease her clit.

"Look at you, taking my dick like a good girl."

"Shit. Rix," she gasps.

"Fuck, you feel so good. I want you to come all over me, then I'm going to fill you up."

"Yes, yes, yes," she chants before exploding.

"Good girl," I praise, rutting into her for the final few times before I deliver on my promise.

I collapse on top of her before flipping us once again and resting her on top of me.

Pulling the covers back over our heated bodies, I wrap my arms around her and hold her tight as our breathing returns to normal.

Despite there being a million and one things that need to be said between us, both of us remain silent, just soaking up the moment.

"Merry Christmas," Noelle giggles.

Her laughter is infectious as I can't help but join in.

"Best one yet, I'd say."

"Most pleasurable, for sure," he teases.

"No pressure for next year, huh?"

She giggles again, and it lights something up inside me

before she lifts her head from my chest and looks into my eyes.

"Is this... this is real, right? Me and you," she asks, making my chest ache.

"Yes," I assure her, cupping the side of her face gently. "Why would you even think it wasn't?" My eyes bounce between hers, desperately trying to figure out what has her on edge all of a sudden. "I love you, Noelle. You're the only girl I've ever seen, the only girl I've ever wanted. It's always been you."

She sniffles, and my grip on her tightens as if it'll help hold her together.

"I love you too. It's just—" She rips her eyes away from me and looks at the wall that leads to the living room.

My heart slams against my chest. I'd say I've been dealing with my insecurities pretty well over all this.

Noelle has told me honestly that I'm the one for her, and I trust her more than anyone else on this planet. But if she were to change her mind...

"He complicates things."

"You want him too?"

Her eyes snap back to mine. "No. I mean, yeah. Kinda. I want him the way we had him last night. I don't want him like this," she says, reaching out and dragging her thumb over the pillow of my bottom lip. "You're my ride or die, Rix. Always have been, always will be."

Relief floods me.

"But I enjoyed last night. I know it's not conventional, or normal in any sense of the word, but it was—"

"Hot?" I finish when she hesitates to find a word.

"Yeah."

"What we do with Wilder doesn't affect us. When we leave this place in a couple of days, I want it to be with my hand in mind. I want to return to Trinity as a couple. I want to move into your room and have this every single morning."

"And Wilder?" she asks.

"Wilder will... no doubt go back to his normal life with the team."

I study her, trying to get a read on how she really feels.

"I don't want him to think that we dropped him just because the vacation is over."

A breath I didn't realize I was holding spills out of me.

"I'm pretty sure he'll be fine."

He does this kind of thing most weekends. It's nothing new, and I've no reason to believe that he's suddenly going to become interested in having anything serious with anyone.

He's a free agent, and something tells me that he always will be. Life would get too boring and mundane for him otherwise.

"Yeah, you're right," Noelle finally says. "As fun as this is, I'm also really excited to be this new us at home."

"Me too, baby,' I say, flipping her again and making her squeal.

I t's at least another hour before we leave the bedroom. The sheets are a twisted-up mess on the floor, and the chill in the air has been long forgotten.

Naked, we dart across the hallway and into the freezing-cold bathroom.

"Oh my god," Noelle shrieks, hopping from foot to foot on the tiles.

Safe to say the power hasn't returned.

I stand there watching her hop, taking in her peaked nipples and bouncing tits.

Could there be any better sight on a Christmas morning?

My eyes drop, and I discover there is. Noelle's cum-slick thighs.

I did that.

I fucking did that.

Reaching for her hand, I tug her closer and pin her against my body.

"Warm," she muses, curling into me.

"Take a piss, and be fast," I say before releasing her again and striding toward the basin to brush my teeth.

She gasps as her ass hits the seat, and I shamelessly watch her in the mirror.

I will never, ever get used to seeing her like this.

Naked, and all mine.

"Are you really going in there?" Noelle asks in horror when I reach to turn the shower on.

"Quickly, yeah. I want to be nice and clean for you."

"Oh yeah?" she teases, wiggling her brows.

I smirk. "Watching you suck my dick is the best thing I've ever seen," I tell her honestly. "I'm not giving you a reason not to do that again."

She smiles at me as she picks up her toothbrush and loads it with toothpaste.

Resting her hip against the counter, she watches as I step under the ice-cold water and clean up. There's so much naughtiness in her eyes that even the cold doesn't affect my semi.

I hope I never stop wanting her.

"What are you thinking about?" she asks around her toothbrush.

"Bending you over right there and fucking you in front of the mirror so I can watch your reaction."

Her chin drops, and she only just catches her toothbrush before it tumbles to the floor.

"I've had years of fantasies about you," I confess as I cut the water and move closer. "And I have every intention of living out every single one."

With a peck on her nose, I grab a towel and then march toward the bedroom.

WILDER

The second I crawled out of bed, I fucking regretted it. With the power still out, it was fucking freezing.

Nearly two hours later, despite having started a fire and embarking on a grueling training session, I had failed hopelessly at distracting myself from both the cold and the situation I'd walked away from the bedroom.

I knew what happened after I left. The sounds of Noelle's moans were a harsh reminder of what I could have been getting involved in.

But I'd already pushed my luck. Getting her off like I did this morning was a risk.

Hell, getting involved last night was a fucking risk. But at least we were all drunk. In the hard light of day, Hendrix's opinion of me touching his girl might have been vastly different.

Call me a pussy, but I didn't really want to hang around long enough for him to kick me out of bed so he could have his girl to himself.

No one kicks me out of bed. I'm either the one calling

time on our rendezvous and leaving, or I'm the one kicking her out of bed.

They're usually too busy begging me for another round...

I let out a pained sigh as I continue with my workout. After all, there's fuck all else to do. It's not like I'm about to go and cook Christmas Day breakfast.

I'm pretty sure I've already ruined their vacation enough at this point.

Or have I?

Giggles erupt from the bedroom again, causing yet another sigh to pass my lips.

I'm happy for them. I am. It's taken long enough. But also... watching them makes me feel more lonely than I ever have in my life.

I've always surrounded myself with people for a reason. But I'm nothing but the third wheel at this party, and I hate it.

I push harder, forcing myself to work through the pain. I need it. It's the perfect distraction from everything I refuse to dwell on.

If I were in Austin with the guys right now, I wouldn't be having any of these issues.

I'd be blissfully ignorant and probably in bed nursing a hangover from the epic night before.

What exactly I did to deserve the airline fucking me up the ass quite this badly, I've no idea.

They fucked me over good, that's all I fucking know.

The giggles and happiness get louder, and I've no choice but to look up when the happy couple emerge.

"You have to be shitting me," I mutter.

"What?" Elle mocks. "I think they're cute."

"Matching Christmas sweaters are never cute," I

deadpan. "And plus, you weren't even a couple when you bought those," I point out.

"Aw, you're just jealous that she didn't buy you one too," Rix mocks, unaware of just how close to the mark that comment hits.

"Fuck off," I scoff. "You won't catch me dead in a matching sweater to a girl, no matter how hot she is."

They both laugh at me, looking entirely too happy about this whole situation.

It's as infuriating as it is amazing.

I had my head between Noelle's thighs last night. She came over my fingers this morning, and Hendrix isn't beating the shit out of me.

Fucking Twilight Zone here in Canada or some shit.

"One day, you'll eat your words," Hendrix tells me smugly.

Shaking my head, I continue with what I'm doing. I might have been lonely with them locked in the bedroom, but now that they're here, I'm not sure if seeing them all loved up in person is worse.

"Breakfast?" Noelle asks, gazing up at Hendrix like he's just hung the moon.

"Yeah, I'm starving."

"I wonder why," I mutter.

"Jealousy really isn't a good look on you, Bro."

"Not jealous. I've got plenty of pussy just waiting for my attention. All I gotta do is video call one and boom," I say making a little explosion gesture with my hand.

Noelle's eyes darken with something before she mutters, "Lovely," under her breath and disappears into the kitchen.

Hendrix and I stand there in silence for a few seconds as she crashes around.

"You good?" he finally asks me.

"Yeah, of course," I lie. "You?"

"Fuck, yeah. It's Christmas, and it started with being inside Noelle."

"Hendrix," she moans, clearly listening to us.

"What? I'm excited about it."

Noelle chuckles and leaves it there.

"You both deserve it."

Rix's mouth opens and closes as if he wants to say more, but no words pass his lips.

"Just spit it out," I demand.

He moves a little closer and lowers his voice. "We both enjoyed last night. Is that weird?"

"Only if you want it to be. Sex is sex. Pleasure is pleasure," I say with a shrug. "There's no shame in enjoying it in whatever form it comes in. Embrace it while it lasts, I say."

"And you're okay with it?"

"Bro," I laugh, although there isn't much genuine happiness in it and more self-loathing than I'm used to. "Of course I'm fucking okay with it. It was hella hot. As long as you're good, I'm good. And anyway, something needs to liven this vacation up."

"You didn't need to come," he says for the millionth time.

"And where would you be right now if I hadn't?" I raise a brow to emphasize my point. When he purses his lips, I follow up with, "Exactly, you'd still have blue balls and would be pining after Mrs. Claus in there.

"Being the nice one only gets you so far in life, Rix. Every now and then, you just have to be a little bit naughty." I wink before continuing with my sit-ups, letting him go and help his girl out.

I've no idea what she's cooking in there; we still have no

electricity. I guess it's going to be cereal all around... assuming they bought some.

"That's the last log," I say as I drop it into the fire, watching the embers fly out and land on the hearth.

"Shit," Rix hisses.

"There's more though, right?" Noelle asks, sounding a little terrified that on top of surviving with no electricity, we're now going to freeze to death.

Okay, probably a little bit dramatic, but it's really fucking cold even with the fire. I can't imagine what this little wooden shack would be like without it.

At least we can snuggle... snuggling is fun...

"Yeah, they're out in the woodshed."

"Outside?"

"Yeah. That's generally where people keep their wood pile."

"All right, smart ass," Noelle hisses.

But despite knowing what we have to do, all three of us just sit there.

"I made breakfast, so I think this job is for you two."

"I've been keeping the fire going. Rix, what have you done today?"

"Made Elle come."

"So did I," I counter. "Try harder."

Rix glares at me from his seat next to Elle on the couch.

"Fine," he huffs before pushing to his feet. "It can't be that bad."

"Put a coat on," Noelle calls after him.

"What happened to my little rebel?" I ask teasingly.

She sucks in a breath, but her only response is to narrow her eyes.

Following Rix to the door, they exchange a few words I can't hear before he slips his feet into his sneakers and pulls his coat on like the good little boy that he is.

I shake my head. "So fucking whipped already."

"There are worse positions to be in," he shoots over his shoulder before reaching for the front door.

It's still snowing out, but it's nowhere near as heavy as it was yesterday, and the wind has eased off, too. But that doesn't mean even an inch of the snow surrounding us has melted.

Curiosity has me climbing to my feet and following them.

I can only imagine what he's about to—

"Oh fuck," Hendrix shouts as an avalanche of snow spills into the entryway.

"See, snowslide," I announce smugly.

"W-what?" Rix barks as he stares at the mess before him.

"Now what do we do?" Noelle asks in a panic as the wind proves my previous point wrong and whips around all three of us, making us shiver and wrap our arms around ourselves.

"We need to move it," Rix says helpfully.

"Where to? That's taller than me out there."

She's not lying. Where the wind has blown the snow against the side of our cabin, it's almost unscalable.

Exactly why I didn't want to be the one to open the door.

Honestly, we'd probably have been better climbing out of a window. If I were less of an asshole, I might have pointed it out, but this is too funny.

"The bathtub?" Rix suggests.

"You want us to shovel all this with... something and dump it in the bathtub?" Noelle echoes in disbelief.

"Well, does anyone have a better idea that doesn't involve flooding the cabin?"

When we both stay silent, he continues. "Right, should we go and find something to shift this with?" He marches into the kitchen, leaving Noelle and me in the entryway.

"He really shouldn't have opened this door," I point out.

"You didn't do much to stop him."

"Neither did you," I shoot back.

"Hey, at least it gives us something to do."

Noelle lets out a pained sigh. "I could think of other things we could be doing..."

I step closer and wrap a loose lock of hair around my finger.

"Oh yeah? Care to share?"

Her cheeks flush, letting me know that we're most definitely on the same page here.

"Elle, Wilder, get your asses in here," Rix demands.

"Boring," I mutter, spinning around to find him standing in the middle of the kitchen with bowls in hand. "You're serious about this, aren't you?"

"Deadly. Now start shoveling. The faster we can fix this, the faster we have logs and warmth."

"Fucking hell, this was not the kind of Christmas Day I signed up for."

"You're telling me," Noelle agrees as she takes her bowl and moves back toward the snowslide.

"This is going to take forever," Rix mutters as he shovels his first bowlful.

"Should have thought of that before opening the—"

"Unless you have something helpful to say, will you please shut the hell up?"

Noelle catches my eye, and we both erupt in laughter like naughty school kids.

It takes all of about five trips to the bathroom to deposit snow before I make a decision. "We need alcohol for this." With that announcement made, I take off for the kitchen and retrieve the bottle of vodka from last night.

There's less in there than I remember, but it'll get us started. And hopefully, help keep us warm in the process.

"Are you serious? That's not going to help," Rix complains.

"Will you stop being such a stick in the mud? Elle is up for it. Aren't you, little rebel?"

I hold the bottle out for her after I've taken a shot and wait.

Her eyes dart between mine and the bottle.

The old Noelle, the one I've known all my life, would most likely say no and continue on sober. But this new wild version of her... yeah, she's more likely to let go.

"Let's be honest, it's not going to make this situation worse, is it?"

"Good girl," I praise when she swipes the bottle from my hand and swallows down two shots.

"Rix?" she offers.

He lets out a heavy sigh but thankfully shakes off the seriousness and takes the bottle.

"To Christmases we'll never forget," he says as a way of a toast before chugging down a couple of mouthfuls and getting back to work.

He isn't wrong. This is most definitely a Christmas we're all going to remember.

27

NOELLE

"Oh fuck, it's fucking freezing," Wilder bellows as he and Hendrix finally scale the snow mountain outside the cabin.

Laughter peels out of me as I watch them horse around.

"You fucking asshole," Rix barks as Wilder hits him square in the face with snowballs.

"Oh my god," I breathe, unable to do anything but watch them with a wide smile on my face.

I'm supposed to be cleaning up, but they're too addictive.

Ice-cold air whips around me, but I'm burning up from the number of trips I've done to the bathroom to remove this epic snowslide. The vodka also helps.

Wilder grunts as he gets hit square in the junk.

"Prick," he gasps, clutching at himself.

Both of them have bright red, rosy cheeks, and there are white clouds of breath surrounding them.

We grew up in California; there was no snow. But if there were, I could see this exact scene playing out with a younger set of Kemp twins. Happier Kemp twins, ones that weren't subject to the kind of shitty childhood we all were.

We had our moments, sure, but there was never that much opportunity for playing and just being carefree kids. There was always something to worry about, always someone to look after, even if it was ourselves.

"It's okay, Noelle can kiss it better later," Wilder teases, shooting me a wolfish grin that hits me like a lightning bolt and goes right down to the tips of my toes.

A filthy image appears of me on my knees for them both in my mind, and another wave of heat rushes through me.

"You're supposed to be getting logs," I point out, hoping that my voice doesn't betray me.

They both look at me. Hendrix studies me closely, while Wilder just smirks.

"Oh sure, you're thinking about logs right now," Wilder teases.

"She's thinking about something hard," Rix agrees. "But I don't think it's logs."

"Will you both stop and just do your job? It's cold."

"Us do our jobs? I don't see much action happening with you either, Miss Bell," Rix mocks.

"I should lock the door and make you both sleep out there," I warn.

"She wouldn't; she loves us too much," Wilder says confidently.

"She loves one of us. The other just tagged along for the ride," Rix quips.

Wilder lets the comment flow over him like it's nothing. I can't help but wonder if it's as easy as he makes it look.

Nothing fazes him. He has the thickest skin of everyone I know.

But is that who he really is? Or is it a coping mechanism

for everything he's been through? Is it survival more than anything else?

Shaking the morose thoughts from my head, I force out, "Just get the damn logs," before turning my back on them in favor of finding the mop to fix the mass of puddles surrounding my feet.

"Slave driver,'" Wilder mocks, making me smile.

It takes a while, I dread to think just how much snow they need to trudge through and then move to stand a chance of getting at the logs, but eventually, Rix appears with an armful.

"Are they dry?" I ask the second he emerges from the mass of white.

It's the one thing that could ruin this whole little log-retrieving mission. If they're wet, then really, we'd be no better off than letting the fire go out.

Well, actually, we'd be worse off, because we've had the door open for fuck knows how long now, letting any warmth we did have out.

We'd be royally fucked and freezing fucking cold unless a miracle happened and the power came back on.

It could happen at any moment. Heating, hot water, the oven... they could come back at any time.

There's a part of me that can't wait. But weirdly, there's another part of me that's enjoying a step out of reality.

And after all, who knows, when the lights come back on, what the three of us experienced last night and this morning could be over.

"Amazingly, yes. They're pretty cold though," Hendrix says, ripping me from my thoughts.

"I'll get them in front of the fire and hope for the best," I say, taking them off him.

What was a roaring fire when we embarked on this little mission is now nothing more than glowing embers.

"Shit," I hiss.

I have zero knowledge of fire making, but I do the best I can and pile up some logs on the embers, hoping they'll catch. Then I return to the door to take another armful of logs from Wilder.

We continue until we have a wall full of stacked logs.

"You two should come in," I say, my fingers brushing Hendrix's frozen ones as he passes me more logs. "I think we have enough for a while."

The snow is beginning to get heavier now, and the light is vanishing quickly. It's time to call it a day.

"Yeah," Rix replies, his response curt as his body begins to tremble.

"Shit, you're freezing."

"You'd better warm me up then," he says, stepping into me after I've added his logs to our stack.

"Oh my god," I squeal as he wraps me in ice-cold, his wet shirt soaking into mine, arms pinning me in place.

"Hmmm," he moans. "Warm." He tucks his frozen face into the crook of my neck, and I shiver.

"Oooh, I'm missing snuggles," Wilder announces happily before the front door slams shut and his heavy footsteps thump over.

He abandons his logs before the length of his body presses against my back. I want to say his warm body, but it's anything but.

"Ew, and you're wet," I complain as he wraps his arms around both of us, the two of them pinning me between them.

"And now I'm getting you wet," Wilder mocks.

"You're insufferable," I mutter.

"You love it," he counters.

"Take it off," I demand.

"Your wish is my command," Wilder says, moving back an inch so he can do as he's told.

"Now you're wet, you should do the same," Rix points out, staring down at me with blazing eyes. "Then you can really warm us up."

His hands wrap around the bottom of my sweater and he drags it up.

"No, the fire. It's—"

"Blazing, just like your body," Wilder says as the cool air surrounds me.

Trust Hendrix to take my tank too.

My nipples pebble as I stand there between them, the soul focus of their attention.

My hands lift to cover myself, but Wilder's fingers wrap around my wrist, stopping me from hiding.

"Let him see what he owns now, little rebel," Wilder rasps in my ear, sending heat straight between my thighs.

With his eyes locked on my chest, Rix reaches behind him and drags his wet sweater and t-shirt from his body.

My mouth runs dry at the sight of the skin he reveals as the sound of the fire coming to life crackles around us.

"Something tells me things are about to get nice and hot in here," Wilder mocks.

"So hot," Rix mutters absently as he shoves his pants from his hips, leaving him in his boxers.

"Aren't they wet too?" I ask, my eyes on the tent in the fabric.

"They are. But it's Christmas. You need to have something to unwrap."

"Dude, that's fucking cringe," Wilder quips.

"If you don't want her to do the same to you, all you've got to do is say."

Wilder's grip on my wrists tightens, and his warm breath tickles down my neck and over my chest.

"Is that what you want, Rebel? Do you want to unwrap our cocks like Christmas presents?"

Oh my god.

Is this even real right now?

A whimper rumbles in my chest. It's all the answer Wilder needs.

"I think that was a yes."

His lips land on the patch of skin that connects my neck to my shoulder. A shudder of desire rips through me, my skin erupting in goosebumps.

"I think she's the one who needs unwrapping now we've started," Hendrix growls, his eyes jumping between my bare tits, my mouth, and my eyes.

"Now there's an idea. And what will we do with her once we've unwrapped her?"

My thighs brush together in the hope of squashing the ache between my legs the more the two of them taunt me.

"Noelle," Hendrix rasps as he watches me.

Dropping to his knees, he reaches out and tucks his fingers into the waistband of my shorts, pulling both them and my panties down my legs.

Cool air rushes over my heated skin, making me even more desperate for what's to come.

"How does she look?" Wilder asks when Rix sits back on his haunches and looks up at me.

"Perfect," he breathes. "So fucking perfect."

"Please," I whimper impatiently.

I'm not sure at what point I turned into a needly little whore for these two, but I have. And I can't control it.

Wilder pushes his foot between mine and kicks my legs wider, letting Rix see what I'm hiding between my thighs.

"What about now? Is she wet for us?"

Hendrix swallows roughly before licking his lips in preparation.

"Y-yes. So wet."

"She tastes so good, huh? I swear, her sweetness is still on my tongue from last night."

My chest compresses, and all the air in my lungs rushes out.

Why are they both so good at this?

Okay, sure, Wilder has had plenty of practice. But Hendrix... he's surprised me in the best possible way.

The air crackles loudly as Hendrix's eyes lock on mine.

There is so much love and adoration within his gaze, it makes a lump crawl up my throat.

"You want my mouth on you, baby?" he asks, his voice deep and rough.

"You know I do."

"And what about Wilder? What do you want him to do?"

I shrug one shoulder, or at least I attempt to. Wilder's grip is unforgiving, leaving me mostly immobile.

"Whatever he wants to do. He can watch or he can join."

Wilder's deep chuckle fills the room, making all my hair stand on end. "Now there's an offer I can't refuse.

"Naughty girl." Along with the awe and adoration, I swear I see some pride in there too.

"Rix, suck on her tits. We're not going anywhere near her pussy until she's begging for it."

Holy shit. These two are going to kill me.

But damn, what a fucking way to go.

Pushing up on his knees, Rix brings his lips within touching distance of my nipples.

His hot breath rushes over my skin and I shamelessly arch my back, thrusting my tits forward.

The second I brush his lips, a potent shot of desire rushes through me.

"Oh god."

"Good start. But we're going to need a lot more than that for you to get what you want, little rebel."

With my eyes locked on Rix's, he pokes his tongue out and flicks my peak.

My entire body jerks.

How can one simple touch cause such a powerful reaction? How can they have so much control over my body?

It's equally as terrifying as it is thrilling.

"More?" Wilder asks.

"Yes, more. So much more."

Rix's eyes flash with determination before he leans forward and sucks one of my nipples into his mouth.

"Rix," I cry, my arms jerking against their binding with my need to reach for him.

"Nope, not going to happen. You need to be a good girl and let us have our way with you."

"Oh god." My entire body sags with need as Rix switches to the other side.

He kisses, nips, and sucks, driving me to the brink of insanity.

I cry out, plea, and beg for more. I'm not aware of the words that spill from my lips as he builds me higher and higher.

I'm so close just from this alone. I have a feeling that the second someone touches my clit, I'm going to explode.

"Please, please. I need you," I cry. "Please."

28

HENDRIX

I've got a problem. A really big fucking problem.

I'm addicted.

Totally fucking addicted.

It shouldn't be normal to need her as potently as I do.

If it continues, I'm never going to get anything else done.

Hell, as it is, I can barely think about anything but her. But now I've had a taste... Now I know what she looks like when she comes, the noises she makes...

Fuck. I'm gone.

Totally fucking gone.

I've always known that I've been in love with her. That's no secret. But I never, ever thought it could be this good.

Sure, Wilder adds to the situation, but he's not necessary. He's an added bonus, if you will. I already know for a fact that when we return to normal life and he's off doing his thing, we're not going to miss him.

Will the three of us do this again after this vacation? Maybe. Obviously, it'll be fun if we do. But I don't for a second think it's required. The chemistry that crackles between Noelle and me is enough.

The intensity of her gaze burns, the heat radiating from her bare body causing mine to increase.

There was a moment when Wilder and I were out in that snow that I never thought I'd be warm again.

But here we are.

All we needed was Noelle.

Wilder said he wanted her begging, and I'm fully on board with the idea as I let my lips brush down her stomach toward where she really wants them.

Her legs are spread, giving me the perfect tease of what I want.

My mouth waters to taste her again.

Being between her thighs last night feels like a million years ago now.

"Oh god," she whimpers as I kiss over her mound before shifting to the side and focusing on her thigh.

"You're going to need to be more specific about what you want here, little rebel."

She sucks in a deep breath, shifting on her feet in the hope of getting relief. It's pointless with the way Wilder has spread her legs, but she's desperate enough to try nonetheless.

"I want you to make me come like you did last night."

"You want one of us to put their mouth on you?" I ask, my lips brushing against her soft skin.

"Y-yes. Please, Hendrix. I need you."

I continue to stare up at her, wondering how long I'm meant to keep this up when she's so temptingly close. "Shit, Wilder," she gasps as he wraps a hand around her inner thigh, lifts her foot from the floor, and opens her wide for me.

"Fuck," I breathe, my eyes feasting on her desperate pussy in the way my mouth wishes it was.

"Beg him," Wilder demands, leaving very little space for argument.

"Please, Hendrix. I need your tongue on me."

"On you where?" Wilder urges.

"On my pussy," she cries, and without thinking, I lean forward and give it to her.

Her taste floods my mouth and I lose myself in the moment.

With one hand on her thigh beside Wilder's, I help hold her open while gripping her hip with the other and pretend that I'm Wilder and have a wealth of knowledge about what I'm doing.

Hearing Noelle's cries of pleasure sure helps me to believe that I'm doing a half-decent job.

"Shit, she's trembling. Can you feel that, Bro?" Wilder rasps.

"Good," I grunt against her pussy.

"She's going to come so hard when you let her fall. Anyone would think she hasn't already gotten hers today."

"Do... do we have to talk about it?" Noelle pants, making Wilder chuckle.

"Making up for lost time," I muse after sucking on her clit hard enough to stop her from saying anything else.

"Fuck, you've got a hell of a lot of orgasms to give her if you're going to do that. You two should have been fucking for at least five years now."

"F-five?" Noelle gasps.

"Fuck, yeah. What did you think I was doing during eighth grade?"

"Whore," Noelle whispers.

"Takes one to know one," Wilder quips.

I'm not sure there is any real comparison between the

two. Wilder has been man-whoring it up for years. Noelle is only just discovering all of this.

We both are.

My chest tightens at the thought of us experiencing it all together.

Just as we should be.

Noelle cries out again as I get back to work, and after a few seconds, Wilder's hand disappears.

My brows pinch as I try to figure out what he's doing.

Pushing Noelle's leg back, she trembles on the one and I pray that Wilder has a good hold of her because I'm not sure I'll be able to catch her should she go down.

"Oh my god," Noelle gasps, her entire body bucking against my mouth, and not a second later, I discover why. My tongue collides with Wilder's fingers as he pushes inside her.

Shit. That's... hot.

With both of us working her, it only takes a few more seconds before she's flying over the edge.

As her cries ring out around the cabin, her fingers sink into my hair as I continue through her release, and when I look up, Wilder has his arm banded around her waist, holding her up.

"Oh my god," she gasps. I sit down and wipe my mouth with the back of my hand.

Her chest heaves, her cheeks are flushed, and her eyes are blown with desire.

I let her leg go, and she settles back on two feet and continues to stare down at me as Wilder's arm moves, his hand cupping one of her breasts.

"Do you like the sight of him on his knees for you?"

Noelle's lips twitch into a smile before she nods.

"I think he loves it too. Are you going to reward him for getting all those logs in and making you come so hard?"

"You both did that," Noelle says, making my breath catch.

"That is true," Wilder muses as I get to my feet. "So, how are you going to reward us?"

My head spins with possibilities, but those filthy thoughts are soon cut off when Noelle wraps one hand around the back of my neck, pulling me down to kiss her. The other hand slides down my body until she's palming my achingly hard dick through my sweats.

"Noelle," I groan.

My clothes are still damp and cold, but I can barely feel them while I'm focused on her. She erases everything.

"Now that's what I'm talking about," Wilder mutters, keeping his body pinned against her back, squeezing her breasts and pinching her nipples.

Noelle's hand slips from my neck a beat before Wilder grunts before whispering, "You naughty little rebel. You want our dicks, don't you?"

She groans into our kiss. It's the only kind of confirmation I get before her hand sinks inside my sweats, fisting my dick and stroking gently.

Wilder hisses, and I can only imagine that she does the same to him.

In a rush, I shove my sweats over my ass, letting my dick spring free and giving her easier access for whatever she intends to do next.

"I love you," she muses before suddenly sinking to her knees.

"I love you... fuck," I grunt when she takes the head of my dick into her mouth. "Too... fuck."

Twisting my fingers in her hair, I hold her in place, encouraging her to sink lower.

How the fuck have I gone almost nineteen years of my life and only just discovered how fucking good this is?

Maybe Wilder isn't such an idiot after all.

Speaking of… he moves around Noelle, kicking off his shorts as he goes, leaving him completely bare, and comes to stand next to me.

He wraps his hand around himself and strokes.

Noelle's lips don't leave me, but her eyes focus on him. They start at his face, then drop, watching him work himself.

When she looks back at me, I see the question as clear as day in mind.

'Can I?'

Fuck.

My heart races, my body temperature rises, and my hands begin to tremble as adrenaline and desire collide.

There's a part of me that wants to say no.

Wilder has got everything he ever wanted in life. Why should he get this too?

But also… the thought of watching her sucking him off…

I can't get it out of my fucking head.

We've gone this far already and… what happens in the cabin stays in the cabin?

I nod once and she releases me, a huge puff of air rushing over me before she looks at Wilder's dick.

She shuffles a little closer on her knees, watching as he pleasures himself. But before she does anything, she looks back at me again.

'It's okay,' I mouth. "I love you. Always have, always will."

Wrapping her hand around me, she leans forward and licks his dick.

Watching it is like a punch to the gut but in a weirdly good masochistic way.

"Christ," Wilder grunts. "Keep going. Show your boy here how good you look doing this."

She glances at me again, but this time she doesn't wait for my approval. Instead, she sinks lower on his cock.

All the air escapes Wilder's lungs as he hits the back of her throat.

"Good?" I ask, aware that Wilder has done this a million times over. He must have pretty high expectations and Noelle has now given all of two blowjobs, and I've got zero experience to compare it to.

"So good," Wilder groans, holding the back of her head as he slowly begins moving his hips.

She works him for a few seconds before pulling back and returning to me.

Wilder and I have shared pretty much everything in our lives, but I'm not sure anything compares to this moment.

She alternates back and forth between us, and all too soon, my balls draw up and I get the tingles that this is about to be over.

"Fuck, Rebel. You're gonna make me blow," Wilder rasps, letting me know that I'm not alone.

The head of Noelle's mouth finds me again, and no sooner has she taken me to the back of her throat than I come.

A loud groan spills from my throat as I let go, pure, unfiltered pleasure surging through me.

Noelle swallows me down before licking her lips and turning to Wilder.

It takes him a few more seconds, but he soon follows me, his bark of pleasure echoing around the cabin.

The two of us collapse on the couch, both breathless, sated messes, while Noelle lingers on the floor.

"Come here, Elle," I demand, holding my hand out for her after pulling my sweats back up.

She instantly snuggles into my side and I hold her tightly.

"You're amazing," I tell her honestly.

"You too," she says, smiling up at me with wide eyes.

She's not drunk, not even close, but I can see the evidence of the vodka we finished off earlier. It's certainly lowering all our inhibitions, that's for sure.

"That was some way to celebrate getting the logs in and not flooding the place, huh?" Wilder teases as he gets up and throws another two logs onto the fire.

Since we managed to close the door, it's gotten significantly hotter in here. Although to be fair, there was a point where I wasn't sure if it was possible to get colder.

"What are we doing for dinner?" he asks as he pulls a clean set of clothes from his bag.

"Whatever we can find that doesn't need cooking," Noelle says.

A thought hits me, and it's out of my mouth before I can catch it.

"We're leaving tomorrow."

"Are we?" Wilder asks. "I'm not sure we stand a chance of moving your car yet."

"Shit," Noelle hisses.

"I'm down for extending this vacation if you two are," I offer.

"We probably don't have a choice unless a miracle happens overnight," Wilder points out.

We all fall silent, and I can't help wondering if they're hoping for a little more time together before we have to return to reality, like I am.

29

WILDER

I barely get any sleep, and I'm awake long before Noelle and Hendrix the next morning.

After our special celebration for getting the logs in, we cleaned up, raided the kitchen for any kind of food that didn't need cooking, and started an epic board game battle.

It was like we were kids again after finding something worthwhile at the thrift store to keep us entertained for an afternoon.

Noelle and Hendrix sat at one side of the table, being all cute and couple-y, and I sat on the other, watching them and feeling all kinds of anxious.

I wasn't able to put my finger on why, and I'm still struggling this morning.

Once again, the cabin is freezing. My entire body erupted in goosebumps the second I threw the covers back, because yes, I slipped into bed with them again last night. I told them it was because of the cold, and yeah, it was, but also... there was more to it than that.

I didn't want to be out on the couch on my own. I didn't

want to be lonely, wondering what they were doing without me. I wanted to be close to my people.

I start the fire, which thankfully is a little easier now the logs are warmer, and then move to the windows. It's pointless; it's still dark, and I can't see if we're still snowed in or if that miracle I mentioned last night happened or not.

I hope it hasn't.

I'm not ready to go back to Trinity yet.

I should be. I should be pumped for the New Year's party the team is hosting in a few days. I should be excited to get training, to finish the season off as we started, strong and fucking proud to be Titans. But I'm struggling to find any kind of enthusiasm for any of it.

My head is firmly here, and it doesn't want to leave.

Staring out, I watch as the orange glow behind the snow-covered hills in the distance gets brighter.

A new dawn. A new day. But nothing really ever changes.

I—we'll—always just be the kids from the shitty trailer park in California.

I'll always be the uncaring crazy one, and Hendrix will always be the thoughtful, sensible one.

I might have secured my scholarship at Trinity, but he's the one who really worked for it. He's the one who deserved it. They both do.

I just... I can throw and catch a football.

A heavy sigh spills from my lips, fogging up the cool glass before me.

I have no idea how long I stand there, drowning in the dark thoughts that I don't usually allow in. The orange gets brighter, allowing me to see the mass of snow. It should brighten my mood, knowing that we're not going to be able to leave today, but it barely touches it.

A throat clearing behind me makes my heart skip a beat,

and when I spin around, I find Noelle standing in the middle of the living room. Hendrix's hoodie drowns her, hanging almost to her knees. Her hair is piled on top of her head, and she's still got a crease in her cheek from the pillow.

She looks cute as hell.

I squeeze my eyes closed, attempting to banish that thought about my brother's girlfriend. After what we've done, it should be the least of my concerns. She was literally on her knees sucking my dick less than twelve hours ago. Thinking she looks cute is nothing.

"Are you okay?" Noelle asks quietly as if she's speaking to a terrified animal.

I hate it. I hate that look in her eyes that tells me she doesn't think I'm holding my shit together right now.

I have to hold my shit together.

I always hold my shit together.

It's who I am. It's what everyone expects of me.

Pulling my mask on, I force a smile onto my face.

"Of course. Rix still sleeping?" It's a stupid question and one I regret the second it falls from my lips.

Hendrix has never been a morning person. It was always our time. Mine and Noelle's. Although, I now realize that I never appreciated it as much as I should have.

I never appreciated her as much as I should have.

"Y-yeah," she stutters, narrowing her eyes in suspicion as she moves closer. "Are you—"

"The snow hasn't disappeared, and the electricity isn't back," I blurt like an idiot.

"Have you checked the weather?" she asks, humoring me.

"My cell died."

"Late-night video call with Miss No Panties?" Noelle deadpans.

There's no kind of hesitation in her reaction, and it just confirms what I already knew.

She's seeing this situation for what it is. I'm just here for the pleasure.

It's cool. I get it. That's who I am.

Usually, I don't care.

Girls can use me all I want as long as I get mine.

But there's something different this time.

"Nah, she doesn't really do it for me."

"Ah, just a one-time wonder, huh?"

"I barely even remember her. She was... meh."

"Meh? Wow, remind me never to ask you for a reference on all this."

"That's not... Shit, Noelle, I—"

"I'm joking," she says, ripping her eyes from mine and focusing on the outside. "At least the sun is shining today." Positivity radiates from her.

I want to say it's contagious, but...

"Maybe it'll melt fast and we can head home later. What time is check-out?"

"Uh... eleven, I think."

"The road trip home should be interesting," I muse.

It's bullshit small talk, and I hate it. It puts my teeth on edge, but I don't know what else to do.

"I'm going to call the rental people, see what we can do when they're open," she explains.

"You think they're going to answer this time?" I say, thinking of the number of times she tried and failed when we first got here.

She shrugs.

"Did you... did you want to work out?"

Her question makes me give her a double take, and I stare down at her like she just asked me to go to the moon.

"You want to work out?" I echo.

She shrugs again. "I feel like you need to. That or—"

"You probably don't want to go there," I warn, predicting what she's going to say next.

"We'd have to wake Rix up, and you know what he's like if he hasn't had enough sleep," Noelle teases, making me laugh.

"He woke up quite happily yesterday morning. I think we could convince him."

"You're trouble."

"You've only just realized that?" I taunt, moving into her personal space.

Her breath catches as she gazes up at me, her lips parted as if she's ready to accept my kiss.

Dropping my head, I brush my lips against her ear and whisper, "Did you want to go and find a sports bra today, or do I get to watch them bounce again?"

She laughs before playfully slapping me on the shoulder.

"You'll probably be pleased to know I didn't pack one," she confesses as she lights a couple of candles.

"That is very pleasing news. Let's get our blood pumping then."

"Can't wait," she deadpans as she pulls Hendrix's hoodie off and gets into position for our first drill.

"We should do this every morning," I announce before starting us off with some gentle yoga positions.

"Okay, that's great. Thank you, bye," Noelle says before hanging up the phone and turning to look at the two of us sitting on the couch with a packet of chips each. Breakfast of champions.

We're almost out of food that doesn't require cooking. Something is going to have to happen soon.

"We've got an extra day. Apparently, there are snowplows expected today that will help clear our way out."

Another day...

I really shouldn't be as happy about that as I am.

"Any news about the power?" Hendrix asks.

"They're working on it. Could come back any minute."

"I fucking hope so," I mutter, dramatically throwing my half-eaten packet of chips onto the coffee table. "I need decent food and a hot fucking shower."

"We know," Hendrix deadpans.

"Fuck off. Noelle and I showered after our workout this morning. Not our fault you were too busy snoring."

Hendrix narrows his eyes at me. "No, you didn't."

I quirk a brow.

"Don't listen to him," Noelle says. "Do you want to borrow this?" she asks, holding up the battery pack she found to charge her cell so she could make the call.

"No, it's okay."

"But what about all your devoted female fans?" Hendrix asks.

"They can wait," I state. "I kinda like being cut off. It's... peaceful."

They look at me for a few seconds like I've sprouted an extra head.

"What? You don't agree?"

"Oh no, we agree. We booked this place for a reason, remember?"

Pushing to the edge of the couch, I walk over to the fire and load it up again.

"What do you want to do today?" I ask.

"We haven't played Monopoly yet.."

"We're not playing Monopoly," Hendrix barks.

"Oh come on, it's been years since that... incident."

"I've still got the scar," Rix says pointing to his chin.

"I was young and stupid," I reason.

"What's changed?"

"He's no longer as young?" Noelle offers up.

"Look, if I promise not to throw anything, can we play?"

"No," they both cry at the same time.

"We can do Clue" Hendrix offers.

I roll my eyes. "It's not the same."

"No, it's Clue and the only people who are getting hurt are make-believe."

"You two are boring."

"I think we've proved in the last couple of days that we're anything but boring," Hendrix mutters.

"Okay, I'll give you that. So if it's no to Monopoly, how about we fuck all day?"

Shaking their heads, they share a look before moving toward the table. Noelle grabs Clue and together they get it set up.

I once again get a flashback from our childhood.

Hendrix would always do the setup while Noelle would read any of the necessary instructions out loud so that he wouldn't have to.

Even as young children, they were basically a couple.

They've always been endgame, and despite this vacation being a little... unconventional, I'm glad I was able to have a hand in pushing them even closer together.

We're an hour into the game, all three of us keeping our cards—or our lead pipes—very close to our chest when the lights flicker.

"Oh my god," Noelle gasps excitedly, but when nothing else happens after a few seconds, we return to the game, our hope diminished.

But the flickers keep coming over the next thirty

minutes, and then finally, the cabin is illuminated and the clunks and grinds of everything kicking back to life fill the air.

All three of us let out a laugh of disbelief. But for as much as we've been desperate for the power back, none of us rush to do anything with it.

Instead, we just keep playing.

The TV stays off, the speaker remains quiet, and the only sound filling the small cabin is our laughter as we accuse each other of murdering Mrs. White.

Honestly, it's one of the best days I've had in a while.

For the first time in a long time, I'm relaxed. I've dropped my mask; I've let a few of my insecurities in, and the world hasn't ended. In fact, it's actually gotten a little bit easier.

I look up at the couple opposite me.

It's them.

They gave me this. I'll be forever grateful.

30

NOELLE

"It's so good to see your faces. I missed you yesterday. Christmas wasn't right without you," Lorelei gushes through the screen.

Hendrix had reached out to explain the power outage, and we tried to video call her and Kian last night, but our signal wasn't strong enough and they kept freezing, so we had to keep the communication to messages.

Lorelei is right though, it felt weird not having her a part of our Christmas. Although, considering how we spent most of the afternoon, it was probably for the best she wasn't here.

My cheeks blaze as I vividly remember what the guys sitting on either side of me did to my body. Or more so, what I did to them.

Fucking hell, I'm such a whore. And no longer just a book whore...

"Aw, you getting all soppy on us, Sis?" Wilder teases with his usual gives-no-shit attitude.

"I missed my babies."

Kian rolls his eyes next to her. "Bring you away to a tropical island and all you do is moan," he deadpans.

Her head snaps to look at him.

"I have not been moaning," she argues.

Kian smirks, his eyes darting between the three of us. "Oh, she has."

"Dude," Wilder complains. "That shit is not necessary.'

Kian throws his head back laughing as Lorelei shakes hers. She's trying to look embarrassed, but really, she doesn't care. She's too happy.

As she should be.

"So, what did you guys do yesterday?"

"Uh..." Hendrix starts while I shift between the two of them awkwardly.

"We had a snowslide," Wilder happily announces.

Lorelei frowns. "A snowslide?"

"Yeah, some moron opened the door, and boom," he waves his hand out as he speaks. "Snowslide."

"Right," Lorelei mutters before the three of us go on to explain the whole debacle.

"Sounds very festive," she finally concludes.

"Oh, don't worry. We celebrated... in our own way," Wilder deadpans, once again making my cheeks blaze.

Lorelei is going to notice. My stomach knots at the thought of having to explain this to her.

"So, what else is new? Any good gifts I need to know about?"

Hendrix and I sit quietly for a beat, and then predicably Wilder pipes up.

"Rix got a fucking epic gift this Christmas."

"Oh yeah? From you or... no, you don't do gifts," she mocks. "Noelle, what did you get?"

"Go on, Noelle, show Lorelei what you got Rix for Christmas," Wilder encourages.

"Why is it a gift for him? It could be a gift for me," I argue, making Lorelei's brows pinch.

"What did you get?"

"Go on, show them." Before I know what's happening, Wilder has placed his palm on my back and he's pushing me toward Rix.

Hendrix looks over just in time, and after the briefest of eye contact with his brother, he wraps his hand around the back of my neck and brushes his lips against mine in the sweetest kiss ever.

"Oh my god," Lorelei squeals. "Oh my god. Oh my god. You're together. Finally."

We part with a laugh before looking back at the screen.

"Do you know how long I've been waiting for this? Oh my god, I'm so freaking happy right now."

Lorelei goes on and on about how long she truly has been waiting, telling us about all the times she'd thought we'd finally figured our feelings out and she got all excited. It's only when Kian gets bored and asks about when we're going to get to leave that she stops.

"Tomorrow," Rix explains. "Wilder and I are going to see if we can dig the car out."

A sad sigh passes my lips at the thought of leaving this place. It's been everything and more than I could have asked for. So much more.

I look at the guys sitting on either side of me. They look so similar and yet are so different in every other way.

I love Hendrix with all my heart. Always have.

And Wilder. He means a lot to me too. Especially after this week away. And not because of the sex, or the pleasure, but because at times, he's allowed me to see a slightly more vulnerable side of him that no one else gets to.

He's always kept his guard up so high, even with me and Rix, that it's incredible to see it lowered slightly. To have it confirmed that he isn't an unfeeling, football throwing machine, and that there is a man with a heart in there if you spend enough time trying to peel it back.

Thinking about going home and him returning to that version of himself makes my heart ache.

"Is it still bad?" Lorelei asks, making me look out the window. The sun is shining, and although there is still a lot of snow out there, now the plow has been through, there's a lot less. We've even seen cars.

It's a reality check that life is still continuing outside of our little bubble.

Hendrix, Wilder, Lori, and Kian continue talking for another twenty minutes, but I barely react to what's being discussed. I'm too lost in my own head to get involved.

"We're going to go out and find the car," Wilder says once the call is disconnected, pushing to the edge of the couch and heading out.

"Sure," I mutter, speaking for the first time in ages.

Wilder's footsteps get farther away, but Hendrix doesn't follow. Instead, he remains sitting next to me.

"Are you okay?" he asks quietly, shifting so he can look into my eyes.

"Yeah, why?" I ask, attempting to cover up for the fact that I'm not. I mean, I am; there isn't anything wrong. I'm just... unsettled, I guess.

"You're quiet. I don't like it when you're quiet. It usually means you're freaking out about something and don't want to worry me."

My heart skips a beat. This is why I love this man.

Reaching out, I cup his jaw and smile.

"I'm not freaking out. Just preparing to return home. I spent so long waiting for this trip and... it's over already. I'm mourning it, I guess."

"Was it everything you wanted?" he asks despite knowing the answer.

"It was so much more. I'm excited about what's to come for us."

"Me too, Elle. Me too. Are you going to be okay if I go out and—"

"Of course. I'm going to start dinner."

He leans forward and steals a kiss. I get the impression it's meant to be a quick one, but he doesn't pull back.

"I'm not doing this myself. Put Noelle down and get to work," Wilder calls a few minutes later.

I laugh while Hendrix mutters, "Cock block," against my lips.

"Just think, when we get home, he'll go back to the team house and we'll be all alone."

I ignore the pang of disappointment as I say those words and focus on what I'm going to gain instead of what I'm going to lose.

"I can't wait," I breathe.

"Me neither. I get you all to myself."

His words send a wave of heat through me.

I am so ready to embrace this new part of our relationship.

"I'd better go before he drags me out."

"I love you," I say as he climbs to his feet.

"I love you too," he says back as he pushes his feet into his sneakers.

He disappears through the front door, leaving me alone for the first time in... quite a while.

I take a moment to take stock before I get up, put another log on the fire, and then walk to the kitchen. The refrigerator is still stacked with food, but seeing as it hasn't had power for the best part of two days, I question what is actually safe to use.

I'm busy throwing the chicken in the trash when my cell buzzes on the counter.

Assuming it's from Hendrix because quite honestly, no one else ever messages me, I walk over to it.

> Lorelei: Is everything okay? You looked a little lost earlier.

"Shit," I hiss. I should have predicted this.

Lorelei might be Hendrix and Wilder's big sister, but she's just as perceptive and protective over me as well.

> Noelle: Yeah, everything's great.

My thumb hovers over the send button, and the fact I hesitate tells me that I'm sending the wrong thing.

Deleting my previous message, I go with a little more honesty.

> Noelle: Yeah, I'm okay. Things have just been a little weird here.

I feel better about my amendment for about two seconds before I start typing again.

> Noelle: Not bad weird. Just… intense, I guess.

Dots start bouncing immediately, and my anxiety spikes about what she's going to say.

> Lorelei: Can you talk?

I glance out the window and find Hendrix and Wilder in a fully-fledged snowball fight instead of digging out the car.

Noelle: Yeah.

Not a second later, her name lights up my screen with an incoming call.

"Hey," I say, lifting it to my ear.

Abandoning the kitchen, I walk through the living room so I can stand at the full-length windows and watch the antics happening outside.

"What's going on?" Lorelei asks, jumping straight into it. "Aren't you happy with the changes between you and Rix?" The worry in her voice makes me regret the wording of my message more than I already did.

"Of course I am. I love him. I love him so much."

"Okay, so what was I seeing on your face while we were on video call then? That wasn't a crazy happy Noelle."

I let out a huge sigh that she no doubt hears.

"I'm not sure you should be the one I'm talking to about this," I confess quietly.

"Noelle," Lori warns. "It doesn't matter what is it. I'll never judge, you know that."

I do. I do know that. Lorelei has been the best parental figure the three of us have ever had. I'm just not sure she ever needs to hear the words that are on the tip of my tongue.

I take a deep breath and close my eyes, shutting both of them from my vision as I summon the courage to confess. "Rix and me... we may never have happened if..." My words trail off, my stomach knotting.

"If..." Lorelei encourages.

Squeezing my eyes even tighter, I blurt, "If I didn't hook up with Wilder first."

Her gasp of shock rocks through me, and the stunned silence that follows doesn't make me feel any better.

"Okay," she muses as she thinks. "So… you want Rix, right? Not—"

"I love Rix," I say again as if it'll magically fix everything.

"And Wilder?"

I shrug despite the fact she can't see.

"He's Wilder. He's fun and easygoing and—"

"The bad boy you shouldn't want?"

"Something like that," I mutter. She's hit the nail on the head.

Wilder is not my type. Not that it seems to matter.

"How does he feel about all this?"

"I don't know. He's been… different."

"How so?"

"I mean, there is literally nothing to do to keep him entertained here." Apart from one thing that makes my face heat. "He hasn't had his usual distractions. He's been much more pensive, and quieter. He's been thinking more."

"Dangerous," Lorelei says, letting me know she understands.

"Yeah," I muse, holding back what I need to confess.

"Noelle, I can't help if you don't tell me everything."

I both love and hate that she knows me so well.

"The three of us have hooked up. Together," I blurt.

All the air rushes from her lungs.

"Wow. Okay. That sure explains the look on Wild's face when Rix was kissing you."

31

HENDRIX

By the time Wilder and I have finished messing around and crash back into the cabin soaked from head to toe and shivering violently, Noelle has dinner ready.

The scent of spices and tomato fills the air, making my mouth water and my stomach growl.

I didn't realize just how much I'd missed hot food or how hungry I was, but I'm ravenous. And apparently, I'm not the only one.

"Fuck, I need that," Wilder announces behind me before shoving me aside to run into the kitchen.

"I've made tac—" Noelle's words falter at the sight of us. "You're not eating like that."

"W-what?" He gawps, alternating between looking at himself and the food. "I'm starving."

"And you'll still be starving once you've showered and put something warm on. You're dripping all over the floor."

I can't help but snort a laugh at the expression on his face.

With a grunt of frustration, he begins tugging at his sopping clothes.

"What are you doing?"

"Whatever it takes to get food," he announces while wrestling with his t-shirt.

"Go to the bathroom," Noelle complains.

"Rix might eat it all."

An astounded laugh spills from my lips.

"Just go and get dried off; I still need to dish up."

But Wilder isn't having any of it, and in another few seconds, his wet clothes are in a pile on the kitchen floor.

"Can I eat now, please?" he asks, shamelessly walking toward Noelle with everything hanging out.

"You're naked," she points out, her eyes dropping.

A twinge of jealousy pulls at my insides, but it doesn't take hold. I know for a fact that if I were to do the same, she'd be looking at me in the same way.

"And no longer dipping all over the floor. Just one taco, then I'll go and shower. Please. I'm wasting away here. A machine this good needs fuel, Rebel."

"Jesus," I mutter. "I'm going to shower," I say, leaving them to argue this out.

I figure if I hit the bathroom first, I'll get food faster.

"No, I'm not feeding you while you're—argh," Noelle squeals.

I almost turn around and rush back to see what's happening, but I don't. I force myself to keep moving.

Noelle's laughter continues to fill the cabin as I step into the bathroom and close the door.

My own insecurities niggle. I don't want to let them in, but with our return home pending, I'm finding it harder and harder to keep them locked up in the box I shoved them in when we embarked on this... on this... experience together.

Am I enough?

It's a question I've asked myself a million times over the years, but I've never felt it as potently as I do now.

What if we get back and she realizes that I'm not?

Then what?

With my heart racing, I strip off and step into the shower in the hope of washing my fears down the drain.

It's wishful thinking.

I stand there with the hot water running over my body. I'm so lost in my own head that I don't even get to appreciate the temperature or the way it warms me up.

I have no idea how long I stand there motionless, but eventually, the door opens and then a booming voice brings me back to reality.

"Are you trying to starve me or something?" Wilder barks from the other side of the curtain.

"What the fuck, man?"

"You're taking forever. I want to eat."

"Get out," I shout.

"No, you get out."

"I'm not done,' I argue.

"Then you'd better hurry up, because dinner is ready and I'm ravenous. Wash your teeny weeny and get out."

I huff in irritation.

"What? It's not like I haven't seen it a lot recently," he adds. "I already know how much smaller it is than mine."

My lips purse and my teeth grind.

It's not true. I know it's not. And yet, it still knocks me.

What if she prefers his?

"Unless you've got Noelle in there sucking you off—which I know you don't, by the way—finish the fuck up and get out."

"Fine," I hiss, grabbing the shower gel and flipping the lid open as if it's offended me.

I give myself a once-over before killing the water and stepping out.

"Fuck's sake," I mutter under my breath when I find my brother standing in the middle of the room buck naked.

He's everything every guy wants to be, and every inch of what women want. There isn't a single inch of his body that isn't toned and defined. He looks just like the models on the front of some of Noelle's books.

And while I might also be in good shape, I've got nothing on him. Not really.

"What?" he asks as if he doesn't have a care in the world.

"Nothing," I hiss, reaching for a towel and wrapping it around my waist.

"Bro?" Wilder asks, not moving from his spot. "What's wrong?"

"Nothing." Jesus, I'm turning into a woman.

Wilder barks out a laugh, clearly not believing a word I'm saying.

"She loves you, man. You," he states, poking me in the chest, proving that he's not as selfish as many would believe him to be. "She doesn't want me, not really. She wants you."

"Wilder," I complain, not wanting to get into this with him.

"What? It's true. I'm just here for the fun. Tomorrow, she won't even remember me. All she needs is you." The tone of his voice changes as he says those final words, and I swear I see something flicker in his eyes. But before I get a chance to decipher it, it's gone and he's stepping past me.

"Get out there and let her show you herself. Just don't eat all the tacos. I might die of starvation otherwise."

I roll my eyes as the sound of the running shower fills the room again.

He's right, and no sooner has he disappeared behind the curtain than I take off.

The best way to calm my fears is to be with her. Without knowing it, she fixes everything.

I pull on a clean pair of boxers, sweats, and a t-shirt and then go in search of my girl.

I find her laying plates on the dining table. She's wearing one of my hoodies again, and when she bends over, it rises, showing off her legs and letting me know that she's only wearing a small pair of panties beneath.

My cock swells and my mouth waters.

I've always been addicted to her, but these few days away have made everything so much more intense.

It doesn't matter how many times I have her; it'll never be enough. Never.

"I'm not sure what Wilder is moaning about. I'd much rather eat you than the food any day." She stills at my words for a beat before spinning around, resting her ass on the table. Her eyes find mine instantly, alight with excitement and happiness.

"I'm more than happy to be your dinner instead," she says, a wicked smile playing on her lips.

I always knew there was another side to my best friend. But I never could have predicted that she'd be this... filthy. This... perfect.

What am I saying? Of course I knew she'd be this perfect. She's Noelle.

I stalk forward, letting my eyes roam over her body as if she's standing before me naked.

I don't look back up into her eyes until I'm standing right before her, and when I do, the intensity staring back at me punches all the air straight from my lungs.

Wilder is right.

Without letting my thoughts run away with me, I twist

my fingers in the hair at the nape of her neck and tug until I position her exactly where I want her. Then I slam my lips down on hers.

A desperate moan rumbles in her throat as I kiss her, her hands sliding down my arms until she finds my waist and slips her hands beneath the fabric of my shirt. My muscles bunch instantly, my body burning for more of her touch.

Lifting her, I wrap her legs around my hips allowing her heels to dig into my ass, giving me little choice but to take a step forward, closing the final few inches between us.

My own moan fills the air as we slot together as if we were designed to do so.

Tucking my free hand under her hoodie, I let it roam, loving the way she shudders as I do so.

"Christ," I grunt into our kiss when I discover she's braless.

"Oh god," she gasps, her head falling back, breaking our kiss as I pinch her nipple.

Unable to stop kissing her, my lips go to her neck and I lick a line almost up to her ear, letting her sweet taste explode on my tongue.

"Never going to get enough of you," I whisper in her ear.

'Same," she gasps, attempting to grind against me to get what she needs.

The sound of scraping wood startles me as Wilder joins us and takes his seat at the table.

Looking over, I find that he's thankfully dressed again.

"What?" he asks when he glances back at me. "Don't stop on my account. I'm more than down for a little live porn while I eat."

"There's something wrong with you," I mutter as Noelle wiggles to get free.

"Yeah, I'm fucking starving."

Ignoring him, I turn my attention back to my girl. Her eyes are dark and full of hunger. The sight hits me straight in the balls.

'I love you,' she mouths.

My chest tightens as my heart thuds against my ribs.

'I love you too,' I reply. Just please… let it be enough.

Noelle and I take our seats opposite Wilder and grab some food while we can.

"Oh my god, this is so good," I moan around my first mouthful.

I missed hot food.

"It really is," Wilder agrees, having finished his fourth taco already. "It's like the final supper. I'll be back to ramen tomorrow."

The reminder that this is our last night causes a weird reaction.

There's a huge part of me that wants to get back and have Noelle to myself. But I can't deny the other part that isn't entirely ready to leave behind what we found here.

"You really should eat better, considering the high expectations you have of your body," Noelle points out.

"Then maybe you should come and cook for me."

Noelle raises a brow.

"If you lived in the house Lorelei secured for you, then you might get decent food," I point out. "It's not our fault you prefer living with a bunch of sweaty dudes."

"It's good for team bonding," he argues.

"I'm sure it is. Just remember that when you run out of energy on the field."

"Never happened, man. I always have enough stamina. Isn't that right, Noelle?"

"I wouldn't know. Although rumor has it, you can go all night long."

"Aw, little rebel, have you been reading up about my skills?"

Her cheeks burn, but she doesn't back down. I guess that's what a lifetime's worth of friendship does.

"Not so much research as walking through campus and overhearing your hoard of admirers waxing lyrical."

"Well, they do like to make sure they get equal treatment."

"You're gross," I mutter.

"Bro, just because you happily gave Noelle your balls before you knew they even existed, it doesn't mean we all want to be owned by one woman."

"You do you," I say. "Just please try to keep the STIs to a minimum. Kian's medical insurance will only cover so many."

"Fuck off," Wilder barks. "I've never had a fucking STI. I always wrap it, Bro. Always. And anyway, that wealthy motherfucker doesn't have limits on anything."

I want to argue, but I can't. He's right. Kian Callahan is beyond wealthy to the point it makes my head spin when I think about it too much. All that really matters is that he's taking care of Lorelei in the way she deserves.

"And for the record, even if my balls weren't in Noelle's warm hands, I still wouldn't be putting out all over college. You're a whore, brother."

"Loud and proud, baby. Loud and proud."

32

WILDER

I walk into the living room to find Noelle and Hendrix cuddled up on the couch, watching reruns of an old sitcom they've always loved.

The thought of spending a quiet night watching the TV doesn't sit well with me. I was meant to be having the vacation of a lifetime with my boys right now, not being third wheel to my brother and his girl.

I hesitate for a few seconds before inspiration strikes.

Bingo.

I march across the room without any doubts over what I'm about to do.

"What the hell?" Noelle barks the second I plunge us into darkness. Only the brightness from the screen illuminates the room.

"Turn it off," I demand as I connect my cell to the speaker and hit play on one of my favorite playlists.

"No, we're watching it. You can't just—"

"Turn it off," I say again. There's no room for question in my voice, and after a second, Hendrix reaches for the remote, sensing that I'm not messing about.

"I'm not spending another night sitting in the dark," Noelle complains. "Not when we could be—" Her words falter as I light the candles littered around the room, giving us a warm, soft glow.

My skin tingles with awareness as I move around the cabin, but I don't explain myself. Not yet.

Finally, I come to stand in front of them.

"I'll be honest, I didn't want to come on this vacation," I start.

"Oh, you should have mentioned," Noelle deadpans.

"But, I didn't want to spend the holidays alone. The holidays suck. You both know that as well as I do."

"That's not fair," Hendrix interrupts. "Lori has made them good."

I raise a brow.

"As good as she was able to."

Shaking my head, I continue with my point.

"Without her making it bearable, I didn't want to be a part of it. And then my plans went to shit, and the thought of enduring it alone was unthinkable.

"But... I'm really glad I gatecrashed. I know you're probably not. I know you'd have preferred to do this without me, but I'm grateful you let me tag along."

"Wilder—"

"Let me finish," I say when Hendrix tries to interrupt again. "I know things have been... different, and there's every chance you'll look back and regret what we've done here, but I really hope you don't. I hope that after we've returned to normal life, you're able to see this for what it was. A bit of fun and the beginning of you two building your life together. You deserve it. Both of you. More than anyone else I know. All I want is for you to be happy, and for that to happen, you need to be together. I was just getting to the point where I wasn't sure either of you was going to figure it out."

Silence follows my confession, and I instantly regret opening up. Sure, it's easier in the dark, but it's still a weird thing for me to do.

"We don't regret it," Hendrix finally says. "Or at least, I don't."

"I don't either. It's been... memorable."

Both Rix and I laugh at her choice of word.

Memorable.

"As touching as this has been, why are we sitting in the dark for it?" Rix asks.

I let out a heavy breath and comb my hair back from my brow, suddenly uneasy about the proposition I came over here with.

"It's our last night. I don't want to sit around like losers."

Noelle scoffs, and I smirk at her before reaching for her hand and tugging her to her feet.

"How do you feel about one last rodeo, for old time's sake?"

"Old time's sake?" Hendrix asks, sounding amused. "Not sure that saying is appropriate here."

"What? What we've done is now in the past, and I want to remember just how good it was. Don't you?" I ask, tugging Noelle closer.

She gasps as we collide, and I stare down into her big green eyes.

She rolls her lips between her teeth before swallowing thickly.

Her answer is clear in her darkening gaze, but she's not quite confident enough to confess it.

Briefly, she glances over at Hendrix, and the second their eyes collide, she relaxes in my hold.

He's on board with this, and knowing that makes her happy.

Ducking my head, I let my lips brush against her ear. "What do you want, Noelle? This is your last chance to live out this filthy little fantasy of yours."

It's like someone takes a bat to my chest as I hear my own words.

Last chance...

Sucking in a deep breath, I force my own feelings aside and focus on her. That's what all of this has been about, after all.

Her.

Her and them.

None of this has been about me.

I was okay with that when we first started. All I wanted was the high, the pleasure.

Now, though...

Now... I have no fucking idea what I want.

Part of me wants to go home and get back to normal life so I can put all of this behind me and crack on. The other part... that fickle, stupid part wants to stay here and keep this little haven we've created together.

Noelle's eyes drop from mine, and a rush of coldness goes through me.

Sensing her unease, Hendrix stands and reaches out, tucking his fingers under her chin, giving her little choice but to look at him.

"What do you want, Elle? It's okay. Whatever it is."

She thinks for another moment before she looks at me, and then back at Rix.

"I want... both of you."

Hendrix doesn't react, and I can't help but wonder just how good an actor he really is, because there's no doubt that my reaction is clear as day on my face.

He was freaking out in the bathroom earlier, that much was obvious to see. And yet, here he is, encouraging Noelle to live out her fantasy as if it's no big deal.

It's just more proof that he really is the better one out of the two of us.

I know he doesn't feel it. And I get it, I really fucking do. I can throw a football. In many eyes, that makes me something special. But really, it's all bullshit. Who cares about how hard and fast I can throw when I'm nowhere near the kind, compassionate, loyal, loving person he is?

Those things are important. The things I'm good at are nothing in the grand scheme of things. And it's fucking bullshit that people like Hendrix and Noelle don't get the limelight they deserve.

Hendrix has already taken her virginity. He knows what it felt like being inside her for the first time. I'd be lying if I said I didn't want to take one of her firsts for myself too.

"Then your wish is our command."

Without Hendrix's permission, I grip Noelle's chin, turn her to face me, and press my lips against hers.

I need something. I need a distraction.

Anything that will get me out of my own fucking head.

Alcohol and sex. Those are my go-to.

But while I might have the offer of sex on the table right now, the temptation of alcohol is far away.

I want to remember this.

I want her to remember this.

After all, it might be the only time she gets to experience it, and I want it to be everything she ever thought it would be.

"Where?" I ask, barely breaking our kiss.

"Anywhere but out here would be wrong now," she

breathes. "In front of the fire, just like everything else we've done."

"Okay," Hendrix agrees before he steps up behind her and peels his hoodie from her body. She's bare, other than a tiny pair of panties. The sight of her exposed for us makes my mouth water and my dick hard as fuck.

She visibly shivers as the warm air rushes over her exposed skin.

My heart pounds so hard, I can feel it in my ears, and for some reason, when I skim my hands down her sides, they tremble.

I have no idea why I'm so on edge, or why this feels so much bigger than any other time we've been together in the past few days.

But something is different.

Get it together, Wilder.

"You're a naughty girl, Rebel. And to think, I always thought you were so nice."

"Then maybe you didn't really know me all that well," she taunts, suddenly spinning around to give Hendrix her full attention.

I watch as she wraps her arms around his shoulders, presses the length of her body against his, and crashes her lips to his.

With his hands clamped on her ass, he holds her tight and kisses her as if he needs her more than his next breath.

Seconds pass as my head spins with crazy thoughts about how it would feel to have someone kiss me like that because they needed to, not because they wanted to fuck the football player.

Taking a step back, my eyes catch on the fire.

It's beginning to burn out, so I head over and put another two logs on while Noelle and Hendrix are distracted.

Hendrix grunts as I stand back to my full height, and when I spin around, I find him sitting on the couch with Noelle on his lap, grinding down on him.

His hands are everywhere as he loses himself in her, and that weird feeling from earlier that I'm refusing to identify only strengthens.

Without saying a word, I silently walk around the couch, figuring that Noelle didn't really mean what she said a few moments ago and that she'd rather spend the night with Rix. I'll just hang out in the bedroom and hope I can drown them out.

I'm almost out of the room when there's movement behind me. My steps falter, but not as much as the moment my brother's deep voice booms through the air.

"I didn't think you were the kind of guy who runs away from a challenge," he taunts.

"I-I'm not," I stutter, hating that my words don't come out stronger. "I just... you seemed to be enjoying yourselves, so..."

"Noelle told us what she wanted," Rix states, making me feel like a douche for attempting to slip away. "Are you turning her down?"

"No," I say, spinning around to look at them.

Rix is still staring at Noelle, no doubt with little hearts in his eyes. But Noelle's eyes are set firmly on me.

My mouth runs dry at the depth of the desire darkening them.

"I just didn't feel... needed."

Fuck. That confession hurts more than I was expecting it to.

Noelle's expression softens and a small smile pulls at her lips.

"In one way or another, you're always needed with us, Wild."

She sees me.

All the air is punched out of my chest at that realization.

Lifting her arm, she holds her hand out for me.

Unable to do anything but follow her silent command, I walk over and entwine my fingers with hers.

"Last night of vacation," she says. "Let's make it one to remember."

Fuck. She's right about something.

I am never going to forget this holiday, that's for sure.

Once I'm close enough, she stretches up for me.

Predicting what she wants, I meet her halfway, kissing her with as much enthusiasm as Rix just was. Only, it's impossible to miss that there's a part of my kiss that is fueled purely by desperation.

Desperation and sadness.

For them, going home means the start of something new and exciting.

Whereas I can't help feeling like I'm leaving something behind.

33

NOELLE

"Oh my god," I gasp as heat surrounds my nipple.

I pull away from Wilder, but he isn't having any of it. Wrapping his hand around the back of my neck, he keeps my mouth locked to his.

There is something even more intense about his kiss tonight. I figure it's because it's our last time. It can't be anything else, because this is nothing but a game to Wilder.

Although his little speech earlier was much more heartfelt than anything I've heard from him before. Maybe he is feeling a little out of sorts with our time together coming to an end.

But as much as I might want to try and figure out his state of mind, I can't, because his hands tuck under my arms, and I'm suddenly removed from Hendrix's lap.

I cry out into our kiss as Wilder effortlessly lifts me over the armrest and into his body.

Without instruction, my legs wrap around his waist. The second his hardness presses against my core, heat floods through me.

He wants me just as much as Hendrix does. It's a heady feeling.

"Get on your back on the floor," Wilder demands, his lips leaving mine for barely a second.

"W-what?" Rix stutters.

"Now," Wilder barks impatiently.

I can't see what Hendrix is doing, but I hear his movement loud and clear.

"Feet down, Rebel. Hendrix is going to take those panties off for you."

No sooner do I release his waist than the warmth of Hendrix's arms burns up my legs as he guides them down.

My feet hit the floor and his fingers tuck under my panties, dragging them down my legs.

I don't know what he does with them after tugging them from my feet; all I know is that they're gone.

"Now sit on his face, Rebel."

My breath catches at Wilder's filthy demand.

Before I have a chance to argue, he's lowering me to my knees.

I glance down and find Hendrix staring up at me with dark, hungry eyes.

His hands wrap around my thighs and he roughly drags me down the rest of the way, licking me from ass to clit in one swift move.

"Holy shit," I cry, my hands flying out in an attempt to steady myself.

"That's it, Bro. But don't let her come. Not yet," Wilder commands. "We need her desperate and begging before she gets more."

Fucking hell.

These twins are going to kill me.

Hendrix moans in agreement while he sucks, sending delicious vibrations through me.

I startle when fingers thread through my hair and my head is dragged back, so I have no choice but to look up at Wilder.

"Good?" he asks with his signature smirk in place.

Any sign of his earlier hesitation has gone. He is fully invested in this situation now.

I nod as a groan of pleasure rocks through me.

"Good. Now be a good girl and take my dick out."

I nod, or as much as I can with his firm grip on my hair before reaching out and dragging his sweats down his legs.

He's commando underneath, something I made note of the second he emerged from his shower, and his hard dick springs free, bouncing temptingly before me.

"Suck, Rebel. Show me how good Rix is making you feel."

Wrapping his hand around his shaft, he shuffles forward and drags the head across my lips, coating me with precum.

Eagerly, I lick it up before he drags me forward, pushing his dick between my lips.

"Jesus, that's good," he grunts as he takes over my movement.

I've no idea if he's just feeling impatient or if he's aware that I'm pretty useless with what Hendrix is doing between my thighs, but I'm more than happy for him to take control.

I try to imagine how we look right now with only the glow from the fire illuminating our bodies.

Heat floods through me, the thought alone pushing my release forward.

My legs tremble around Hendrix's head as drool spills from the corners of my mouth where Wilder takes what he needs from me.

"Don't let her come," he growls, obviously sensing that I'm getting close.

One hand slides up my stomach before cupping my breast and pinching my nipple.

My whimpers and moans get louder as my release gets closer and closer.

"Hendrix," Wilder warns before pushing his dick deeper.

Sucking in a deep breath through my nose, I will my throat to relax.

They've both given me everything, they deserve the same in return.

"Good girl," Wilder praises. His words, his filthy actions added to what Hendrix is doing push me right the edge.

They both know it, too, because just as I'm about to fall, they pull away.

"The fuck?" I bark, making them chuckle.

Hendrix wipes the back of his hand across his mouth before sitting up.

"Hands and knees, Elle. We're not finished with you," he says before hopping to his feet as I reposition myself.

They share a look. That's all it takes for them to know what the other is thinking.

Hendrix comes around to my head, stripping his clothes from his body as he does, and after shedding his t-shirt, Wilder drops to his knees behind me.

My core clenches at the thought of feeling him pushing inside me.

Will he feel the same as Hendrix? Will I be able to differentiate between them?

A smirk tugs at my lips as I allow that thought to grow.

Sounds like a fun game.

"What's so funny?" Hendrix asks.

"It's certainly not the fact you two have left me hanging," I deadpan.

"Greedy girl," Wilder muses as he gets into position.

"Suck him off, Rebel. Just like you did me. Your boy is feeling left out."

"What are you—" My question is cut off when his warm breath and then his tongue collides with my clit.

I want to say that I'm disappointed it's not his dick stretching me open, but I find it hard to care when he reignites my lost release in only a few strokes.

"Elle?" Hendrix asks, ripping his eyes from his brother and focusing on me.

"Use me," I demand. "Just like Wilder did."

His chest rises as he sucks in a sharp breath.

"I don't want to hur—"

"You won't," I assure him. "Take what you need."

He nods once before wrapping my hair around his fist and lining us both up.

I groan the second his taste explodes on my tongue.

In only minutes, they build me back up until I'm right on the edge again.

"More," I gasp when Rix pulls out for a second to let me catch my breath. But fuck breathing; what I need is more of them. I need the release they're keeping from me.

The two of them share a look, and when Rix frowns, I look back over my shoulder.

Wilder is shaking his head. The reaction makes my chest tighten.

"What's wrong?" I ask, panicking that he's about to back out.

"Nothing. You want Hendrix's dick, Rebel?"

My cheeks burn. I don't know why after what I've already confessed to them, but they do.

"Yes."

"Good."

Hendrix lies back down on the rug then taps his lap, as if I need any encouragement.

He waits until I get into position, then he holds his dick up for me to sink down on.

"Oh my god," I groan as he stretches me open.

Wilder's stare burns into me, making this moment even more intense.

Shit, I think I might just be a little bit of an exhibitionist.

Pushing that realization aside with all the other things I've learned about myself during this trip, I focus on the moment.

Hendrix's hands wrap around my hips and he helps me move as Wilder stands to the side of me, slowly stroking his dick.

It's hot. So fucking hot. But it's still not enough.

"Need you too," I breathe, reaching out for him.

"Fuck," he mutters under his breath before he glances at Rix.

I don't need to look over to know that Rix is nodding in agreement.

Wilder shuffles forward and offers his dick up again.

It's not exactly what I had in mind, but I'll take it.

With one hand on Hendrix's chest and the other wrapped around Wilder's hip, I fully let myself go and be the rebel that Wilder calls me.

"Clit, Rix," Wilder instructs as he watches us fuck right in front of him.

"She allowed to come now, huh?" Hendrix grunts as he thrusts his hips up, forcing me to take as much of him as possible.

"Yeah, I think she deserves it. Don't you?"

Hendrix smirks as the two of them reach for me. Wilder's hand cups my breasts, squeezing with the perfect amount of pressure a beat before Hendrix's fingertips collide with my clit.

"Oh fuck," I gasp as everything becomes so much more.

My body sings as they work me. Every single one of my nerve endings tingles with pleasure, but it's just a tease of what I know they can really deliver.

I want it.

No.

I need it.

So. Fucking. Badly.

I groan as I suck harder on Wilder's dick, my release rushing closer and closer to the surface.

Please. Please, I silently beg.

"Come for us, Rebel," Wilder demands through gritted teeth.

More. I need mo—

He pushes his dick farther down my throat at the same time Hendrix pinches my clit, and I'm fucking gone.

Pleasure races through my body, filling every inch of me.

It's more than anything I've felt before and it feels like it goes on forever. That is, until it's over and then I realize that it was nowhere near long enough.

"Oh my god," I gasp, unable to keep sucking Wilder. Instead, I flop forward onto Hendrix's chest, boneless and sated.

He's still hard and inside me, but his movements have slowed. Each time he thrusts into me, little aftershocks shoot around my body, reminding me of just how epic that was.

I told them I wanted them both, and while that wasn't quite the position I had in mind, it was still freaking incredible.

I had them both.

Both inside me at the same time.

Fuck.

I'm not sure if there's something wrong with me, or if

I've tainted myself with all the smut over the years, but I love being their whore.

I fucking love it.

"Again," I demand despite the fact I can't even sit up.

Hendrix chuckles beneath me before Wilder moves.

I gasp when I feel his fingers slide down to my ass. Excitement floods me, and I suddenly find a whole new lease of life.

"The fuck, man?" Hendrix barks, his eyes wide with shock.

"Oh, pipe down," Wilder mutters before he drags wet fingers up to my ass.

Oh. My. God.

This is what I was talking about when I said I wanted both of them.

Right or wrong, I don't give a fuck. I want to feel them both buried deep inside me. Even if it's just once. I want to know how it feels.

I glance back over my shoulder, ready to tell Wilder to keep going, but when I find his eyes, I discover they're not focused on me, but Hendrix.

There's something passing between them. Something I don't like.

Something that's making Wilder hold back.

"Fuck her, Rix," he commands. "I want to hear her screaming again."

He does as he's told, his hips rutting up sharply, ensuring he hits me so deeply that the tingles of another orgasm begin.

You did ask for more...

With his fingers tangled in my hair, he drags my lips to his, his tongue fucking me as thoroughly as his dick.

"Wilder," I gasp when Hendrix releases me. "Please. I need—"

"Do it," Rix demands.

I howl in delight when Wilder does as he's told and pushes a finger inside me.

It's tight. Weird. Uncomfortable.

But then, Hendrix thrusts again and everything becomes so much more intense.

My second release comes surging forward, and if it's possible, this orgasm is even more powerful than the first.

I completely lose myself to it.

I've no idea how many seconds or minutes pass, but sometime later, I come to, still lying on Hendrix's chest.

His cock is softening inside me, and there's something cold that feels like it's dripping down my ass. Not such a nice sensation.

"Welcome back," Hendrix laughs when he finds me looking up at him. "Good?"

"I think I blacked out."

"Of course you did. We took you to heaven, Rebel."

I shake my head, unable to find the energy to comment on his awful line.

"Bath?" Hendrix asks, and I nod.

A bath sounds perfect.

34

NOELLE

I wake suddenly with my heart pounding. My eyes pop open as I listen to what it might have been.

I may wake up with the sun every day, but that doesn't mean I'm a light sleeper by any stretch. Once I'm out, nothing usually wakes me.

Hendrix is sound asleep before me, his soft snores filling the room, but as I listen, I realize he's the only one.

Gently turning over, I search for Wilder.

Rix and I came to bed after our bath. I was exhausted, and he carried me in before snuggling up with me. I fell asleep safely in his arms with the memories of what we did vividly on repeat in my mind.

Concern nags at me until I have no choice but to roll out of bed and go in search.

He slept back on the couch last night, but he specifically said he'd join us. So... where is he?

Rix's t-shirt is the first thing I find, and I drag it over my head as I make my silent escape from the room.

The cabin is in darkness, so I'm fully expecting to find Wilder fast asleep.

But the second I step into the living room, I find that I'm wrong.

My breath catches at the sight of him hunched over with his elbows resting on his knees and his head hanging low.

It's so dark out here that he's barely more than a shadow, but that doesn't stop me from reading the anguish that's oozing from him.

"Wilder?" I whisper, but despite the cabin being in total silence, he doesn't seem to hear me.

Hesitantly, I move closer. I don't want to scare him, but also... he needs someone right now.

"Wilder?"

This time, his entire body tenses up at the sound of my voice, although he doesn't turn to look at me or react.

I lower myself down beside him, wrapping my arm around his waist in silent support.

It lasts for five seconds before everything changes.

"Don't," he barks as he shoves me away and jumps to his feet.

"W-what?" I stutter as he marches toward the windows.

"Just... don't." His voice is cold, cruel, and... detached.

Nothing like what I've heard from him in the whole time we've been away.

"What's going on?" I ask, ignoring his previous reaction and following him across the room.

"Go back to bed. Hendrix needs you there with him."

"He's sleeping. He doesn't—"

"Just go, Noelle."

I know that I should listen, but there's something in his voice that stops me.

Instead, I move closer.

The wall of floor-to-ceiling windows showcases nothing

but the clear night sky. The stars twinkle and the almost full moon casts everything in a silvery glow. It's beautiful.

My hand lifts to his shoulder, but no sooner has my palm connected with his bare skin than it's thrown off.

"Ow," I complain as my bicep pulls.

As I cradle my arm against my chest, he finally turns to look at me.

His eyes are dark, but not in the way I've become used to in the past few days. There's no desire there. Just anger.

A lot of anger.

"Wilder?" I try again.

"We're done, Noelle. The only person you need to be worrying about is Hendrix. It's time to go back to real life."

All the air comes rushing out of my lungs.

I mean, his words aren't really a shock. Today is the day we all return home and go back to our old lives.

Wilder will go back to partying with the team and hooking up with any and every girl who looks his way. And Hendrix and I will figure out what life is like as a couple.

My heart squeezes at the thought of us embarking on everything together. Officially together, not just best friends who need to figure their shit out.

My brows pinch as I stare at him. But unlike the last few days, I don't feel like I know him. Like we've become closer.

He's looking at me as if I'm a stranger...

A stranger he doesn't like.

"Yeah, we are. But—"

"There's no but. What happened here ended when I came on your ass last night. It was fun, sure. But it's over now."

"But—"

"Forget it ever happened. I have."

His words are like a knife through my chest, and I take a step back as if he physically hit me.

"What are you talking about?" I whisper, unable to gather enough strength to speak any louder.

"You're being just like them," he spits, looking me up and down with his top lip peeled back.

Fury races through my veins.

"Them?" I naively ask.

"Yeah," he muses, pausing before landing his find blow. "The jersey chasers."

My chin drops as hurt seeps through my veins.

How dare he.

How fucking dare he compare me to them.

"I'm nothing like them," I hiss in disbelief.

One side of his mouth kicks up in a smirk. But it's not a sexy one. It's full of arrogance and condescension.

"They always want something more from me. They're never happy with the little breadcrumbs I give them."

My teeth grind as my hands ball at my sides.

"Fuck you, Wilder. Before all of this, I was your friend. I've never been one of them."

I spin on my heels and march away from him, my body trembling with anger and tears burning my eyes. And it only gets worse when I step back into the bedroom and find Hendrix fast asleep where I left him.

I got out of bed because of my concern for Wilder. How fucking stupid am I?

Wilder's never given a shit about me. Not really. I'm just the girl who made friends with his brother and inserted herself into his life.

He never asked for me to be the third wheel, but I never really stopped and considered how my close relationship with Hendrix might make him feel.

A loud sob threatens, and I clamp my hand over my mouth to stop it.

Looking back over my shoulder, I realize that I should have run to the bathroom.

I could have let it all out in there without worrying about Hendrix seeing me.

But it's too late now. I refuse to give Wilder the satisfaction of knowing he's hurt me. Instead, I want him to think that I've pushed everything he just said to me aside and crawled back into bed with his brother.

Fuck Wilder and his bullshit opinions. Who cares if he thinks I'm like one of them? I'm not.

I'm nothing like them.

The only person I care about is snoring softly in the bed before me.

His are the only opinions that matter.

Lifting my hands to wipe the couple of tears that have spilled, I stalk toward the bed.

Peeling Hendrix's t-shirt off, I abandon it on the floor once again and crawl in..

My movement rouses him and he instantly snuggles closer, wrapping an arm around my waist and pinning me as tightly to him as he possibly can.

It's amazing. He makes me feel so safe, so secure, so loved.

So it makes no sense that I immediately burst into silent tears, my body shaking with the restraint it takes not to sob loudly and wake him.

His words and disregard shouldn't hurt so much. Not when I'm wrapped in Hendrix's arms.

But they do.

❄

I barely sleep, and by the time the sun begins to light up the room, my eyes are sore and puffy from crying.

I don't want to get up and face Wilder. But at the same time, I can't lie here and wait for Hendrix to see the state of me.

I don't want to give Hendrix any reason to think he's not enough for me, because he is.

He's everything.

This vacation has just... it's been unexpected, and I need some time to process everything.

I feel like I've got whiplash.

In a heartbeat, we did this epic thing. And just as fast as it started, it ended, and not in a good way, it seems.

I don't want to return home fighting with Wilder. I want us all to go back to our college lives happy and fulfilled.

That might be wishful thinking.

Before Hendrix stirs, I slip from the bed, pull his t-shirt back on, and lock myself in the bathroom.

My race across the hallway is too short to know if Wilder is out there. If he's sleeping or if he's working out. I think the latter is probably more realistic.

Something tells me that he got about as little sleep as I did.

I avoid the mirror. I'm not ready to deal with the reality of how last night has made me look, and instead, I turn the shower on. It's hotter than I'd usually go for, but I ignore the bite of pain as I step inside.

Tipping my face up to the stream of water, I try to purge myself of the emotion he dragged to the surface with his cruel words. I need to be able to walk out of here with my head held high and move on.

All I've got to do is endure a thirteen-hour road trip

home with him, and then we can go about our lives as if nothing happened—if that's even possible.

Even if he has tainted everything with his attitude last night, I'll still treasure our time together here.

I stay in the shower until the water runs cold. It's selfish of me, but I can't bring myself to care. I just need Hendrix to be awake by the time I step out of this room. If I have him by my side, then I can face anything—even his twin brother.

"Hey," Hendrix says when I step into the bedroom and find him pushed up on his elbow so he can see me.

His eyes are hooded and sleepy, and he has a pillow crease in his cheek. He looks cute as hell with his mussed-up hair.

Swallowing down my unease, I plaster a smile on my face.

"Hey," I say, moving toward my suitcase to find some clothes.

"Come here," he demands, holding his hand out.

Unable to deny him, I move closer and cringe as he studies me closely.

I hate to imagine what he can see.

I shriek when he reaches for the towel wrapped around me instead of my hand. "Hendrix," I laugh as the damp fabric pools around my feet.

"Hmm, that's better," he muses, letting his eyes roam over my naked body before he finally reaches for my hand and tugs me on top of him.

"What are you doing?" I squeal as he rolls me over and pins me to the bed. "I'm wet."

His smile grows. "Is that right?"

Playfully, I swat his shoulder. "Behave."

"With you? Never again, Elle."

He lowers his head as if he's going to kiss me, but at the last minute, he changes his mind and goes for my neck.

"Hey," I complain.

"Morning breath," he murmurs against my skin.

"I don't care about that. I want you, whatever way I can get you."

Twisting my fingers in his hair, I drag his head back and crash my mouth to his, immediately pushing my tongue between his lips to deepen the kiss.

With Hendrix's hands on me, everything else falls away, and I focus on the single most important person in my life.

Everything else around us can crumble to pieces, but as long as we have each other, everything will be okay.

It's always been us against the world.

Well, us and... him.

My stomach knots at the thought of him being out there listening to us.

But fuck him.

Why should I care?

He's made his position going forward very clear.

Not our problem if he can't handle us enjoying ourselves without him.

35

HENDRIX

Our journey home has been a very different experience from the one going to Canada.

Noelle and I are still full of excitement; that hasn't changed. However, the reason for the butterflies is very different.

Before we were impatient for our long-awaited trip. Now, I can't wait to get home and fully embark on life as her boyfriend.

My lips twitch with my need to smile just thinking about her being my girlfriend.

I'm a boyfriend.

Her boyfriend.

I'm not sure I'll ever get used to that.

One day I could be her fiancé...

My heart begins to beat a little faster as I think about her with my ring on her finger. That image is quickly followed up by another of her in a white dress walking toward me, and then another of her with a swollen belly.

My dick hardens at the thought of her carrying my baby. Something incredible that we created together.

It's all I've ever wanted.

Noelle and a life together.

I'm so close to having it right now.

There's a part of me that worries it's all too good to be true and that something is going to come along and derail it. But I refuse to let that thought settle, because I know that it'll result in me being the one to cause issues.

I want to enjoy this and everything that comes with it. Even the anxiety, if that's possible.

With my fingers entwined with Noelle's, we drive past the 'welcome to South Carolina' sign.

We're nearly home...

I glance in the rearview mirror at the grumpy jerk in the back and find him fast asleep, just like I have most of the journey.

The only time he's been awake was to video call some jersey chaser and arrange a hook-up for tonight.

I fucking hated listening to him talking to her, knowing that Noelle was hearing it all.

She didn't react, or at least, not that I could tell.

I know we agreed that what we had at the cabin was just a few days of no-strings fun, but even still, it can't feel good hearing someone plan your replacement.

"I love you," I whisper softly before lifting her hand and pressing a kiss to the back of her knuckles.

"I love you too," she says, a genuine smile lighting up her face. "I can't wait to get home."

"Hmm, me too. Something tells me you're going to have a boy in your room tonight."

Her chin drops as she puts on a fake shocked face as her free hand covers her heart.

"How dare you," she mocks. "Good girls like me don't have boys in our rooms at night."

Wilder scoffs from the backseat, proving that while his eyes might be closed, he's very much awake.

Of course he is. Asshole probably just wanted to get out of driving.

Noelle rolls her eyes but doesn't comment on his reaction.

"You might be a good girl on the streets, but in the sheets..." I taunt, but I don't finish my sentence. Just thinking the words makes me cringe.

"I'll be whatever you want me to be, baby," Noelle says sweetly.

This time, Wilder gags.

"Shut up or get out," I bark, fed up with his attitude.

He's been the same since Noelle and I emerged from the bedroom this morning.

He immediately started grabbing all his shit and loading it in the car.

We had a long drive ahead of us. I wanted to get on the road as well, but I wasn't rude about it.

I guess his time in the middle of nowhere with minimal partying opportunities was finally done.

I get it. Our vacation—sex aside—was about as far away from Wilder's ideal trip as we could get.

Only a few hours ago, he was telling us how glad he was that he joined us.

I've no idea what changed, but it did, and it was about the time I allowed him to give Noelle what she asked for last night.

Did I want him to push inside her ass and take her at the same time as me?

Honestly... I'm not sure.

There's a huge part of me that knew it would be hot as hell. But there was another part that wanted to be the one to have that first from her as well.

If he took her there, she'd never forget it.

I mean, she's not likely to forget him or our vacation. But it would be a bigger reason to remember it all vividly.

I let out a sigh.

"You okay?" Noelle asks, ignoring our passenger.

"Yeah, just want to be home with you all to myself."

"Same," she agrees while Wilder groans again.

Reaching forward, she turns the music up to drown him out.

The last hour of the drive seems to take longer than the previous twelve combined, and when we finally pull up in front of the football team's house, I'm about ready to physically drag Wilder out of the car.

Thankfully, he's more than ready to put an end to our time together, and he throws the door open the second the car slows to a stop.

"Well, this has been fun and all, but I've got a blonde with no panties waiting on me," he announces like the jerk he is.

"Lovely. Make sure you wrap it. You've no idea what you'll catch," Noelle quips back.

"You sure are mouthy now you've had a dick inside you."

Red-hot fury shoots through me, and I'm out of the car in a flash.

"Don't fucking talk to her like that," I seethe, getting right in his face. My heart pounds against my ribs, and my fists curl, ready to physically fight for my girl.

It's been a while since we really got into it. But I'm more than willing to end our dry spell if he's going to disrespect her like that.

"Hendrix, leave it," Noelle begs from inside the car.

My nostrils flare as I fight to drag in the air I need as I continue glaring at Wilder.

"Go on, listen to your woman. You've given her your balls now, after all."

Lifting my hands, I shove him back and out of my space.

"Fucking pussy," he taunts.

"Go and find your whore to take your attitude out on. We're not fucking interested in your little tantrum."

His lips curl into a snarl, but I refuse to back down.

In the past, I would have. But now, I've got something—someone—to really fight for.

He can say anything he wants about anyone in the world. But not her.

Especially not after the week we've had.

"I will. She'll be better than anything else I've had recently, that's for sure."

My arm is moving before I've processed the thought, and my fist lands on Wilder's cheek a beat later.

The front door to the house slams, and someone comes running over to us at the same time Noelle screams my name.

"That's enough," Benny, one of Wilder's teammates, barks as he steps between us.

"We're done anyway," Wilder says, his shoulders relaxing as he swipes his bag from where it fell on the ground.

"Are you okay?" Noelle asks, lifting my hand to inspect the damage.

It hurts. Fuck, does it hurt. But it was worth it. And I'd do it a million times over if he's going to spew shit like that.

"Yeah, never better," I lie.

"Come on, let's go home," Noelle says, taking my hand and leading me back to the car.

I keep my focus on Noelle and the road ahead as I pull

my seatbelt back on. My hands are still trembling with the anger simmering just beneath the surface.

I tell myself not to look back.

He's an asshole, and he doesn't deserve it. But right before I pull away, my head twists around of its own accord.

I find him immediately—twin intuition or some shit—and the second our eyes collide, my heart sinks.

He's standing at the kitchen window watching us, and he no longer looks angry.

He just looks sad.

Noelle reaches over and squeezes my thigh, dragging me from any concerns I might have.

Wilder is big enough to look after himself now. The person who deserves my full attention is sitting beside me.

"Ready to show me your bedroom?" I tease.

"I might have to tidy up first. I've probably got panties all over my floor," she laughs.

"Doesn't matter. We can add another pair," I retort before pressing my foot to the gas and speeding away.

"**H**ome sweet home," I announce as Noelle opens our front door and I haul our luggage inside.

Sucking in a deep breath, I revel in the feeling of contentment that having a safe and secure home brings. I hope it's something I never take for granted.

The door closes behind me, and the lock is twisted into place.

"Alone at last..." she muses as she walks around in front of me, her finger tracing a line around my shoulder and then down the center of my chest. She doesn't stop until it hits my waistband.

I'm exhausted. My eyes hurt from focusing on driving

for so long, but it doesn't stop my cock stirring to life. It's been far too long since I've been inside her.

"So... where should we start?"

Grabbing her hand, I lift her finger to my mouth and bite it gently.

Her teeth sink into her bottom lip before she takes a teasing step back.

I release her finger, too intrigued to find out what she's thinking.

She reaches for the bottom of her hoodie before peeling it up her body, leaving her standing in her thin tank.

My mouth waters, and my eyes follow her hands as they go for the waistband of her sweats.

They drop to her ankles, and after kicking her Crocs off, she tugs the fabric from her feet.

"Wanna play a game?" she asks, her voice all low and raspy. Sexy as hell.

"As long as it involves you losing more clothes."

She smirks. "What? These?" she asks, tugging at the front of her tank enough to give me a shot of her braless breasts beneath.

"Yeah, those."

"Right, well... you can take them off me..." She takes a step back. "If you can catch me."

Her laughter fills the air as she takes off running toward the stairs.

The sound of it makes my heart swell like I've never felt before.

That's happiness.

True fucking happiness.

It's what I've wanted for her for so long.

Kicking my sneakers off, I abandon the luggage and take off behind her.

She might have got a head start, but my legs are longer and I'm faster.

The second I find her tank abandoned on the stairs, I rip my own hoodie from my body, leaving it behind me.

Her bedroom door slams as I hit the top step, and I lose my t-shirt as I continue my chase.

"Coming, ready or not," I shout just like we did as kids playing hide and seek around the trailer park.

Oh, how far we've come.

My entire body is vibrating with anticipation. By the time I get to her door, it takes every ounce of restraint I possess not to just throw it open and dive on her.

Thankfully, the sight of a small scrap of fabric at my feet distracts me.

Reaching down, I pick it up and smirk.

My dirty girl.

Balling them in my hand, I lift them to my nose before stuffing her them in my pocket and throwing the door open.

The sight that greets me makes my breath catch and my lungs cease.

"You are everything I've ever fucking wanted rolled up into one incredibly sexy package," I explain, stalking closer.

She's laid out in the middle of her bed with her legs spread and her fingers exactly where I want mine to be.

It's the best kind of porn I've ever seen.

But as much as I want to stand here and watch, my need to get involved is stronger.

My final items of clothing hit the floor before I crawl onto the bed and straight between her thighs.

"Hendrix," she cries as I suck on her clit. "I love you."

"I love you too," I say against her. "Now lie back and take it. I'm gonna treat you like the queen you are."

And I do. Over and over again.

36

NOELLE

The past few days have been incredible.

Hendrix moved into my room the morning after we returned home, and we've pretty much been in that one room ever since.

In fact, we've barely left the house.

We've had all our food delivered, and there have been days where we haven't even gotten dressed.

It's been heaven.

Just me and my boy.

He makes me so happy. I've never laughed so much in my life.

I didn't realize how much we were both holding back by keeping our feelings for each other a secret, but now we're crossed that line, everything is just... so much more.

We're closer than we've ever been, and I love it.

I love him.

I love who I am when I'm with him.

He brings out a side of me that I didn't know existed.

I've always been the quiet book girl. But with him, I can tap into something else.

I can be the kind of wild girl I read about in my books. And not only that, but he's the perfect boyfriend.

He's everything I always knew him to be, but now, so much more as well.

He's so gentle and yet... also not.

He can make love to me in a way that brings tears to my eyes, but he can also fuck me until my throat is sore from screaming.

Any fleeting concern I may have had that Hendrix wouldn't be enough on his own was obliterated that first night.

He is everything.

More than everything.

But that being said, it doesn't stop my mind from wandering.

We haven't heard from Wilder since the incident outside the team's house.

I've tried to prompt Hendrix to message him, but he's still pissed at him for what he said about me.

I get it. I'm mad too, but I think there's more to it than Wilder just being an asshole.

He was hurting while we were away, that much was obvious. At least to me. He opened up, even if it was just a little bit.

Us returning home affected him in a way that I don't think Hendrix understands.

Hell, I'm not entirely sure I understand either. But I do enough to let go of the anger.

Wilder is... complex. He hides his feelings behind his humor and partying. Everyone thinks he's a gives-no-shits kind of guy, but that's far from the truth.

He's a little bit broken by the past, just like Hendrix and me.

We get it. We lived the same bullshit lives. But Hendrix and I have each other.

Sure, Wilder has us. He has his twin.

But it's not the same. Not when he drowns his feelings and issues with alcohol and loses himself with jersey chasers.

Something bitter sloshes in my stomach as I think about him being with someone else.

But it's something that I'm going to need to get used to.

If Instagram is anything to go by—yes, I've looked—then he went straight back to his old ways.

For the briefest of moments, I wondered if he'd slow down. But it was a silly thought.

He's spent more than enough time taking it slow with us.

Heavy footsteps head my way, dragging my head away from his twin in favor of focusing solely on him.

"Everything okay?" Hendrix asks when he finds me sitting on my bed with my book in my lap, obviously abandoned.

Thankfully, I finished the one I was reading at Christmas before we left. I'm not sure I'd have been able to carry on with it now.

I'm pretty sure I'm going to be off why-choose books for a while, if I'm being honest.

"It's New Year's Eve, and I'm spending it with my favorite person in the world. What could possibly be wrong?" I ask, smiling up at Hendrix.

"Well, when you put it like that..." he says with a smirk playing on his lips.

He stalks closer, passing me the mug he's carrying.

"Where's yours?" I ask, eagerly taking it. My mouth waters at the sight of the whipped cream and melting marshmallows before me.

"I don't have one. I'm too busy."

I raise a brow. "Doing what, exactly?"

He stands a little taller. "It's a surprise." He grins so wide it hits his eyes.

"Oh?"

"Yep. Enjoy that, I'll be back in ten minutes with the first part," he instructs.

"It's got more than one part?"

"Of course," he says before dropping a kiss on my lips and backing away once again. "Relax. I'll be back."

And then he's gone again.

Lifting the mug to my face, I breathe in the scent of rich chocolate.

He's used my favorite.

I don't know why I'm surprised; Hendrix always pays attention to the things I like.

I take a sip, but the silence allows me to drift off into my thoughts again.

My cell sits on my nightstand, taunting me.

Lori and I exchanged a handful of messages earlier.

I tried to play everything off and not cause her any more stress than necessary when it comes to Wilder, but I'm not sure she really bought it.

She said she hadn't really spoken to him. He's been too busy, apparently.

I bet he has...

She and Kian only have a few more days of their vacation, and I dread her turning up here so that we can talk properly.

She's going to dig deeper than anyone else would. And she knows me well enough to know exactly which buttons to press to get the truth.

What is the truth?

I release a heavy sigh that doesn't relieve any of the tension pulling at my muscles.

I'm so incredibly happy right now. Hendrix is everything I've ever wanted. Our relationship is so much more than I ever could have dreamed of.

But...

I don't want to say something is missing, because then that would sound like Hendrix isn't enough, and he is.

I just...

The sound of water running gives me a hint as to what Hendrix is doing.

Excitement stirs in my stomach as I think about what he's planned for tonight.

We've spent New Year's Eve together for years. But this one is different.

This year, we're celebrating the start of a new chapter of our lives.

I'm so excited to find out where the next year will take us and where we'll be a year from now.

The only thing I know without a doubt is that we'll be together.

Hendrix and I are the real thing. Soulmates.

"Finished?" Hendrix asks a few seconds later when he pokes his head around the corner.

"I've barely started," I confess, lifting my mug for a sip.

A quiet moan rumbles in my throat as the rich, sweet hot chocolate hits my tongue.

He waits until I've finished, then he pulls me to my feet and tugs me toward the main bathroom.

Inside, I find exactly what I was expecting: a bathtub full of fluffy white bubbles.

Spinning around, I wrap my arms around his shoulders and stretch up to kiss him.

"Thank you," I whisper, already eager to sink into the hot water.

Reaching for the bottom of his hoodie, I attempt to pull it up his body, but he stops me.

"Hey," I complain with a pout.

"This one is just for you," he explains, making me pout more.

"But—"

He cups my face, staring down into my eyes as if I'm the most precious thing in the world. It makes my heart beat even faster.

"I've still got a surprise to finish off for you." His eyes twinkle happily, and it makes my stomach flutter.

I want to argue, but I can't. He's so excited by whatever he's doing that I can't stop him.

"Okay, but as soon as you're done, I want you up here," I tell him.

"As if I could refuse an offer like that. Keep the water warm for me."

"You got it."

He doesn't leave straight away. Instead, he helps get me naked—which doesn't take all that long, seeing as I'm only wearing his hoodie and nothing else. Once I'm settled, he backs away from me.

He might be choosing not to join me, but I can see the longing in his eyes. It makes the whole situation a little better to know that he'd rather be lying right here with me.

"I won't be long," he says from the door. His fingers are wrapped around the doorframe as if physically holding himself back.

"Are you sure?" I taunt, lifting my leg from the water and resting it on the edge. I make a show of sliding my hand down my body, and his eyes follow with more than a little interest.

He clears his throat. "I won't be long," he repeats before disappearing from my sight.

I can't help but laugh when his groan of frustration rumbles through the air.

"I love you," I call out.

"I love you too."

Hendrix was gone for less than thirty minutes. Apparently, the lure of my naked, wet body was too much, and he hurried through whatever he was doing so he could get back up to me.

I happily pointed out that it was his own fault. The bath was his idea.

He was aware, and he punished me for my sass by sliding beneath me and then impaling me on his cock.

Pretty sweet punishment, if you ask me.

Once the water is cold, and mostly on the bathroom floor, he lifts me out, wraps me in a fluffy towel, and then sets about getting me ready for our New Year' celebrations.

We'd already agreed to stay in, not that there needed to be any kind of discussion about that, so I'm not surprised when he pulls one of his hoodies over my head and leaves it at that.

Perfect evening in, if you ask me.

Being the amazing boyfriend that he is, he even brushes and blow-dries my hair before taking my hand and leading me downstairs.

It's mostly in darkness, but the flickering light from the living room gives me a clue about what I'm going to find.

But I soon find that my imagination pales in comparison when he guides me into the room.

"Wow," I breathe, taking in all the candles and the couch that he's transformed into a huge bed.

It's covered in pillows and blankets, and there's a tray of snacks waiting for us.

"Do you like it?" he asks a little nervously.

"I love it. It's the perfect way to ring in a new year."

"I've ordered your favorite. It'll be here soon. All we've got to do is select the movies."

I let out a contented sigh and lean back against his hard body.

His arms wrap around me and I close my eyes.

I always wondered what it would be like if we got together. But I never could have imagined something this perfect.

As promised, all of my favorite Chinese dishes arrive just over thirty minutes later, and we eat on our makeshift bed with the movie playing in the background.

Much to Hendrix's delight, I've moved on from the cute Hallmark Christmas movies in favor of something with a little more action and less cheese. Not that he'd ever complain about my choices.

With all the food eaten, Hendrix abandons the containers in the kitchen and we snuggle down together to enjoy the rest of our night.

We watch two more movies before we begin glancing at the clock.

Midnight is coming, and there is only one person I want to be kissing when the clock strikes twelve.

Our movie ends with just over five minutes to go, and Hendrix finds a TV channel that will count down to the big event before turning to me and pulling me tighter into his body.

"This is how I want to spend every New Year from here on out."

"I think I could get on board with that idea," I tease.

His lips find mine, and whatever is happening around us fades into nothing as we lose ourselves in each other. At least, until the front door slams back against the hallway wall and heavy footsteps pound our way.

We jump apart before Hendrix dives in front of me, ready to protect me from whoever just stormed inside our house.

But it's not necessary. I already know who it is.

There is only one other person with the key.

And not three seconds later, I'm proved right when a harassed-looking Wilder appears in the doorway.

His hair is a mess, his eyes are wild, and his chest is heaving as if he just ran here from the team house.

"I'm sorry," he blurts. "I'm really fucking sorry."

37

WILDER

I hate this.

Since moving to South Carolina and embarking on life at Trinity Royal College, I've felt like I've found my true home.

The team house was my haven. A place where I could hang out with my boys. A place to party, a place to let go, to celebrate the wins, commiserate the losses, and most importantly, hook up with every and any willing girl.

God, that makes me sound like a whore.

Fuck. I am a whore.

Or... I was.

Since being back, I haven't been short of offers.

Lacey—aka blonde with no panties—has been lingering like a bad rash. She rubs herself up against me and ensures I know that she's still missing her underwear at any possible opportunity.

Old me would have been all over it.

New me... not so much.

I sink lower in my seat, internally groaning that I've resorted to giving myself two distinct personas.

The heavy beat of the music filling the entire ground floor of the house should inspire me. It should fire me up to party long into the night, celebrating the birth of a new year. A new chapter in all our lives.

We're on fire this season; we're right on the cusp of having the Titans' best season in years.

I should be ready for it. I should be eager to get back to training, to kill our final games, and to end with a championship under our belt.

But I'm not. Or at least, not as much as I should be.

My head isn't set on the future and all the challenges that lie ahead.

It's stuck in the past.

Six very specific days in the past.

"Hey Wilder," Lacey purrs before taking it upon herself to climb on my lap.

She straddles my thighs, having no shame that her already obscenely short skirt rises even higher, letting me see... you guessed it.

I stare at her blankly.

I hate to be stereotypical, but she really is being blonde.

I've given her no sign that I'm interested since returning to the house. Sure, in the past I may have. Even as recently in the car on the way home, something I'm now really regretting. But I couldn't help myself. My need to get a reaction out of Noelle was unignorable.

I got to her the morning we left Canada. Worse than that. I hurt her.

I didn't mean to. I was angry. I was...

I was scared.

Fuck. I hate admitting that. Even to myself.

I was scared about leaving that place.

I thought I had the most perfect life here. It was everything I ever dreamed of.

And then this Christmas happened.

It changed something in me. Something I didn't want to change. Something I didn't allow to be changed. But something that changed nonetheless.

Seeing Noelle and Hendrix together... Being with Noelle and Hendrix...

It opened my eyes, and sadly, my heart and vulnerabilities.

And... I miss them.

I miss being with them. I miss being myself—my true self—not the version I allow everyone else to see.

I put on a mask with everyone else. I hide my pain, my insecurities, and I make out I'm something I'm not. The guy everyone here knows is an arrogant jerk. Even I can admit that. I didn't realize how exhausting it is to constantly be that version of me.

"What's wrong?" Lacey whines. "I thought you'd be ready to party tonight."

Yeah, me too.

"I'm not in the mood," I mutter, unwilling to indulge her.

She shifts on my lap, shamelessly trying to drag up some interest.

Sadly, there is none. My body doesn't react to her in any way.

No, that's not true. It reacts, just not in the way it should, or at least in the way it used to.

I'm broken.

Noelle broke me.

And for some reason, I've no interest in getting fixed anytime soon.

"Aw, I'm sure I can change that. How about we go somewhere a little quieter and celebrate the new year, just the two of us?"

Lifting my eyes, I glance at the clock on the other side of the room and my stomach bottoms out.

The new year is approaching, and I'm sitting here wishing that I were somewhere else.

Wrapping my hands around Lacey's waist, I lift her from my lap.

"I thought that might get your interest," she purrs, wrapping her arms around my shoulders as if I'm about to carry her up to my room and spend the night fucking her into next year—literally. "What the fuck?" she squeals as I throw her down on the couch.

She bounces, her skirt riding up over her ass and causing a few of the guys in the room to holler and whistle. But while they might be interested in what she has to offer, I couldn't give a fuck. Without looking more than necessary, I spin on my heels and take off through the house.

A few of the guys try to talk to me, but most give me a wide berth. They've already experienced my shitty attitude in the past few days; they're more than happy not to be on the wrong end of it again.

I stumble out of the front door, the fresh air immediately mixing with the alcohol I've consumed in the hope of drowning everything out.

I've tried since almost the moment I walked back into this house, but as of yet, the only thing it's successfully delivered are killer hangovers.

We've been planning tonight for months. It was billed to be the football party of all parties. I mean, I'm sure it is. I'm just blind to it.

I check my watch as I take off down the driveway.

It's lined with cars and people who are still arriving to celebrate the new year with the team.

"Wilder," someone calls, but I don't so much as bother looking over.

I have somewhere else I need to be, and if I don't hurry, I'm going to miss the deadline.

I don't want to celebrate the new year with these guys. Sure, they're my teammates. They're important to me. But not important enough.

I take off running. The house is two miles away, right on the other side of campus, and midnight is closing in.

Unless I go at full speed, there's a chance I won't make it.

That's not a possibility.

I have to get there.

I have to say the words I've been holding back all week.

I have to bring in the new year with the two most important people in my life.

I have to apologize.

My legs and lungs burn, but the house is in my sights. I'm feet away, and I've still got seven minutes.

Putting everything I've got into the final stretch, I push harder, knowing that the end is in sight.

As I race up the driveway, I pull my keys from my pocket. I can't ring the bell. The second they see it's me, they'll probably put the deadlocks on and refuse to let me in. It would be understandable if they did.

My hand trembles with anticipation and exhaustion as I push the key into the lock, but my adrenaline is still pumping, and the second the door is unlocked, I throw it open, sending it crashing back against the wall, fucking up any chance I had at a calm entrance.

I don't know where they are. Chances are good that they're in bed fucking. Couldn't blame them if they are, but

I'd quite like to get their full attention as I gate-crash their night.

Thankfully, as I rush into the house, I find light coming from the living room, along with the sound of the TV.

I grind to a halt in the doorway just as Hendrix jumps over Noelle as if they're being raided by an armed madman.

I want to say that it's only me and she doesn't need protecting, but I'm not entirely sure that's true. I've already hurt her, and something tells me that I'll probably do it again, even if it is unintentional.

Their eyes are wide as they stare at me, but thankfully, they do relax a little.

Hendrix's mouth opens to say something, probably to demand I get the fuck out of their house, but in a rush, I beat him to it.

"I'm sorry," I blurt. "I'm really fucking sorry."

It's not enough. It's nowhere near e-fucking-nough. But it's all I've got right now.

Neither of them says anything as the guy on the TV announces that there are three minutes to go.

Please don't send me away.

Please.

My heart races and every muscle in my body is pulled tight.

If they send me away then... then I'm going to spend the new year alone and out in the cold.

That isn't the kind of start to the year anyone wants.

I deserve it. I really fucking do.

But... I don't want it.

I want them.

"Wilder," Noelle finally sighs. The sound of her voice instantly makes something within me relax.

Hendrix, though, isn't going to be so easy to break.

"Shouldn't you be at a party with five girls hanging off you right now?" he snaps.

"I left," I explain. "I didn't want to be there. I don't want to be there. They're my teammates, sure. But... they're not you two."

Noelle's expression softens more, but Hendrix isn't willing to budge.

"Well, maybe you should have thought about that before acting the way you did."

"I'm sorry. I was hurt, and it was a stupid thing to do.

"Last week... Last week was everything. Spending time with you both like we did. Noelle," I say, focusing on her, "getting to know that other side of you... I didn't want to come back to my life here and the way I was before."

"But you did," she argues. Her cheeks redden before a confession bursts free. "The photos on Instagram... all you've done all week is party and hook up."

"All I've done all week is be miserable.

"I thought I wanted that. The wild nights, the parties, the girls. But I don't. I want that," I say pointing at their little love nest.

"I want quiet but wild nights with you guys. I want to be where I can be me.

"I want to be the version of myself that I was with you both last week."

Despite the fact I've been thinking these words all week, they still sound foreign coming out of my mouth.

For years, I've dreamed of what college life might be like. I've imagined the parties, the girls, the fun. And yeah, it has been great, don't get me wrong. But it's taken me away from my family, from the people who mean the most to me.

The two people who mean everything to me.

"One minute to go," the guy on the TV announces.

"Grab your drink and shimmy close to the one you want to kiss at midnight."

Fuck. My heart jumps into my throat.

This is it. Now or never.

"I know it's crazy. I know it's weird. I know you two have just got together, and I'm so fucking happy for you, but—"

"Thirty seconds."

"Noelle, I want you too," I say in a rush. "I want what we had last week. Please, I know it's crazy, but... but will you consider it?"

Silence.

"Ten, nine, eight, seven, six..."

She's going to say no.

They're going to say no.

Emotion burns up the back of my throat, and fuck if my nose doesn't itch with impending tears.

Don't cry. Do not fucking cry.

"I'm sorry, Noelle. I didn't mean a word of—"

"Three, two..."

Everything happens so fast. Both of them move as the final countdown continues until they're standing right before me.

"One."

Hendrix wraps his hand around the back of Noelle's neck, whispers "Happy new year," and then slams his lips down on hers.

Pain slices through my chest.

38

NOELLE

The wrecked expression on Wilder's face as he stood before us and tried to explain how he was feeling, and what he wanted, is one I'm not going to forget for a while.

His usual confidence was gone. There was no sight of the arrogant player who struts around Trinity Royal as if he owns the place.

Standing before us was the real Wilder Kemp. The one with feelings, vulnerabilities, and insecurities. A guy who was willing to admit that he was wrong, that he was sucked in by the allure of college life and everything that comes with being a Titan.

Is he saying that he's going to stop partying with the team? No. I don't for a second expect him to. The team, parties, they're all a huge part of his life. But maybe... just maybe, they're not the biggest part.

Family is important to us. We are all each other had for a very long time. We are family. As fireworks explode on the TV and Hendrix's tongue pushes past my lips, I reach out.

Wilder startles at my touch, his entire body flinching as if he weren't expecting it.

I drag my hand down his bare forearm until I find his fingers.

I'm still mad at him for his attitude on our last morning and the things he said when we dropped him off, but I do also understand where it was coming from.

Is he off the hook? No, absolutely not. But has he made a good start to apologizing and making it up to us? Yeah, he's doing okay.

Hendrix pulls back and rests his head against mine.

There's a silent question in his eyes that I can't help but agree to.

"I love you," I whisper before turning to Wilder. "Happy new year, Wild Child," I breathe before grabbing the back of his neck and kissing him just like I did in the cabin.

The second our lips collide, he noticeably relaxes, and the piece of my puzzle that's been missing all week slots back into place.

Our kiss is over almost as soon as it starts.

"Are you sure?" Wilder asks nervously, his eyes darting between the two of us.

"It's New Year's," Hendrix says, taking my hand and tugging me back toward the couch. "I'd planned a relaxed night of movies, so that's what we're going to have."

The two of us crawl back into our previous positions, leaving Wilder loitering at the edge.

"Are you joining us or what?" Hendrix barks after a few seconds of scrolling through the movies on offer.

"Uh..."

"Don't tell us you've changed your mind already?" he asks as if none of this is a big deal.

"No chance," he mutters before toeing off his shoes and reaching for the waistband of his jeans.

"Did you run all the way here?" I ask, watching him closely.

"Yeah. I should go shower," he says hesitantly, taking a step back.

"Tomorrow," I breathe. "We'll deal with everything tomorrow. Tonight, we'll just... be."

Still uncertain, Wilder watches me for a moment.

"Come on, before we change our minds."

That gets him moving. In a heartbeat, he's down to his t-shirt and boxers and diving onto our makeshift bed behind me.

"Missed this," he muses, pinning himself against me under the blanket.

"Wish I could say the same," Hendrix deadpans.

"Oh, come on, Bro. You totally missed me. It's okay to admit it," Wilder taunts.

"Pfft, as if. I had my girl to keep me nice and distracted."

"I bet you did," Wilder mutters as his hand skims down my body. He grabs my hip and grinds himself against me, letting me know just how much he missed me. "Did he treat you well, little rebel?"

"So well I almost didn't notice that someone was missing."

Wilder tenses at my words.

"Ouch," he gasps while Hendrix laughs. "Don't think I didn't notice what you were missing when you crawled onto this couch," he warns.

"She did that for me," Hendrix points out. "For our nice and romantic New Year's celebrations."

"I'm sure she did. But I'm here now too, and I'm feeling pretty fucking desperate, I've got to say."

"I'm sure you can wait a while longer. This one?"

Hendrix asks, having stopped on what looks like a war movie.

"Oh, so romantic," Wilder deadpans.

Hendrix cuts his brother with a look.

"It looks great. Please continue. I can't wait to try to ignore the fact Noelle is lying here panty-less while watching some dudes shoot each other."

"It'll be hard, but I'm sure you can cope."

"Hard. Yeah, that's about fucking right."

I can't help but laugh as happiness bubbles up inside me.

There was never a point this week where I felt like Hendrix wasn't enough.

He is. He's everything.

But now that Wilder is here, I feel complete. And I can tell just by Hendrix's body language that he feels the same too.

He wasn't fully himself this week. Not having Wilder in his life hurt him. They need each other, and apparently, I need them both as well.

Reaching for their hands, I lift them to my lips, kissing Hendrix's knuckles and then Wilder's.

My heart flutters in my chest as I swallow down all the things I want to say.

There will be time for them tomorrow. Right now, I just want to enjoy the moment with them.

Entwined with both of them, I let out a long, slow breath as the movie starts.

This is it. The perfect New Year's.

We're an hour into the movie when Hendrix's snores begin to fill the living room.

"Fucking pussy," Wilder teases.

"Aw, be nice. I think I've worn him out."

"Why doesn't that surprise me, little rebel?"

Ignoring the movie that I wasn't entirely following, I turn to face Wilder.

His hair is still a mess, and frown lines still mar his forehead, but he looks much more relaxed than he did when he first arrived.

Reaching out, I gently drag my thumb between his brows, trying to smooth out the worry lines.

"Are you okay?" I ask quietly.

I know that Wilder doesn't like to talk about the hard things. He'd rather drown them in alcohol or fuck them away. But he started opening up to me while we were away, and after his confession earlier, I can't help but hope we might be turning a corner.

"I am now," he says softly. Honesty shines brightly in his eyes as they bounce between mine.

"Talk to me," I beg. "Tell me what's been going on for you."

He's silent for the longest time, I can only assume battling with himself on whether he's willing to open up or not.

I start to fear that he's not. I hate it. I want to be that safe place for him to be able to say whatever's on his mind. I know that in time, he'll get there, but impatiently, I want that to be now.

"I'm sorry I hurt you," he finally says. His voice is low and laced with emotion.

Reaching out, I cup his jaw. "I know you are," I assure him.

"I was freaking out. To start with, all I wanted to do was

go home and return to my normal life. But as the days, and nights, went on, I was becoming more and more invested in what we had going on.

"You..." He looks down, severing our eye contact before swallowing thickly. "You very quickly became something very important to me. I mean, you've always been important. You're Noelle, our sister from another mister and all that shit. But something changed while we were away.

"You became so much more than Hendrix's best friend —girlfriend," he corrects. "You became... I wanted you too."

"I want you too. More than I've ever wanted anything in my entire life."

My breath catches at his confession.

"My time with you while we were away wasn't enough. Hell, our time together at the Halloween party wasn't enough, but back then, I'd only had a small taste. I didn't know how fucking awesome you really were.

"I was seeing you in a whole new light. Maybe the same light that Hendrix has seen you in all this time.

"For the first time, I got it. I got his fascination with you.

"That final night when you asked to have both of us, I freaked out.

"I knew that if I pushed inside you, I'd be completely fucked. Having you on your knees for me was bad enough, but if I took more... Shit, Rebel.

"I've never wanted a woman like I want you. And just my fucking luck... I can't really have you."

"But you do have me," I argue.

He shakes his head and closes his eyes for a beat.

"No. Hendrix let me join. He let me have a taste, knowing you wanted it."

"It was more than that, and you know it."

"Was it?" he asks, his eyes finding mine again. This time, there's a little hope sparking within them.

"Hendrix wouldn't have allowed that to happen with anyone else. Just you, Wild. He might have held off with me for a long time, but I think he was the first one to figure out what was really going on here."

"No, I'm pretty sure he was as blindsided by all of this as we were."

"Maybe, but he understood and embraced it faster."

He quirks a brow. "Faster than you wanting both our dicks?"

"Oh shush," I laugh.

"Deny it all you like; I know you're thinking about it right now."

I smirk, my temperature spiking. "Well, I never did get my full Christmas wish, did I?"

"Dirty girl," he teases.

"What have you done this week?"

"You mean, other than what you've seen by stalking my socials?"

I want to cringe, but I refuse.

"I was worried about you," I confess. "Your outburst before we parted ways... I knew it was coming from a place of hurt. You might think you hide your true feelings from the world, but I see more than most," I inform him.

"Great," he deadpans. "I really am sorry, though. I didn't mean it. Everything you did blew my mind. You were amazing," he says, reaching out and tracing my bottom lip with his pointer finger. His eyes follow the movement as he sucks his own bottom lip into his mouth.

"So were you."

"Where do we go from here?" he asks, doing a U-turn in the conversation.

I shrug the shoulder I'm not lying on.

"Wherever we want. But we probably shouldn't make any plans while one of us is snoring."

"What should we do instead?"

The speed at which he flips between vulnerable and arrogant gives me whiplash, but I let it go.

He's trying here, but he's also fighting the persona he's worn like armor for years.

"I can think of a few things. You still have some making up to do, after all."

He shifts closer, ensuring that every inch of our bodies is pressed together.

Desire washes through me. Hendrix has kept me more than satisfied this week, but that doesn't mean I'm not ready for more.

"Noelle," Wilder whispers so quietly I almost miss it. "I think I'm falling in love with you."

His lips find mine the moment that confession is out of his mouth, stopping me from responding.

I'm glad he does, because I have no idea how I'm supposed to respond to that.

He kisses me so deeply, it brings tears to my eyes and ensures my heart continues to slam against my ribs.

But despite him being ready for more, he never pushes it further than a kiss.

He's the perfect gentleman while Hendrix is sleeping, and as impressed as I am with his restraint, I'm also a little bit disappointed.

I have no idea how long we make out for, but eventually, we give up and drift off with our bodies tangled together.

I sleep deeper and longer than I have in a very, very long time.

39

HENDRIX

To my surprise, when I wake up the next morning, Noelle is still sleeping soundly beside me.

I can't remember the last time she slept later than me.

The other side of the bed is empty.

The memory of Wilder crashing in here looking haunted hasn't left me all night. I woke a couple of times and looked over, but each time he was fast asleep with Noelle in his arms.

Sure, I was a little jealous. I wanted that hot little body against me, but he needed her more than me.

I've never seen him looking so lost.

Okay, that's a lie. I saw it when I drove away from the house after we got into it the other night.

As gently as I can, I roll out of bed, leaving Noelle to get the sleep she needs, and silently slip from the room.

The scent of coffee gets stronger as I move toward the kitchen, giving me a clue as to where I might find my brother.

When I enter, he's sitting at the island with his

attention zeroed in on my mug. Usually, he only gives his cell that kind of undivided attention.

I move across the room, but he doesn't even notice, which is concerning. He's usually much more aware of his surroundings. We all are, after the way we grew up. If were weren't, anything could have happened.

It's not until I've grabbed a mug and placed it on the coffee machine that he finally looks up.

"Oh, hey," he says, his voice about as rough as he looks. His hair is still messy, his eyes are bloodshot, and the circles around them are dark. If I hadn't seen him sleeping last night I wouldn't believe he'd got any. "Noelle still sleeping?"

"Yeah," I muse, pressing the button to start my drink. "Not sure what you did to wear her out, but she hasn't slept this late in years."

Wilder chuckles. "I didn't do anything, not really. Not with you sleeping right next to us."

"You could have." The words are out of my mouth before I have a chance to stop them.

He stares at me, his mouth opening and closing as if he has a million things he wants to say but isn't brave enough.

He remains silent, battling with his own thoughts as I grab my mug and move to sit beside him.

"I know I'm fucking all this up for you, and I'm sorry. I know I'm being a selfish cunt by wanting what's yours, but I can't help it. She's—"

"Ours?" I finish for him.

The thought makes my heart race, but after a week away and then almost another back at home without him, it's the outcome that makes the most sense.

Noelle and I have had a fantastic few days, but something was missing.

But he's back, and the final bit of lightness returned to her eyes last night.

Sure, I might want Noelle all to myself, but I'm not selfish enough to stop Wilder from needing her too.

It's been the three of us against the world for as long as I can remember; why should it change now we're grown up?

Maybe it was always meant to be that way. Maybe that's why I'm accepting it so easily... because it's right.

We're meant to be.

"How are you okay with this?" Wilder asks me, studying me closely, no doubt looking for lies.

"Because it's us. Me, you, and Noelle. I've loved her for as long as I can remember, and I know you've always cared deeply for her too."

"But this is your chance, your time with her. You should be keeping me as far away from her as possible right now."

"And what would that achieve?" I ask.

I've already considered all the outcomes if I were to do that, and I don't like any of them.

Ultimately, I'd end up losing either one of them, or both.

I can't do that.

I need them.

"You're my brother. I love you," I say, achingly aware that I don't tell him enough. "And she's my girl. I love her too. In a different kind of way," I add when he screws his face up like he's about to mock me.

His shoulders relax and he lets out a long breath.

"I think I do too," he whispers.

I can't help but smile.

"Good," I state.

"W-what?"

"Good. I'm glad you do. It means you might just stand a chance of treating her right."

He glares at me.

"She's not like the others."

"Too fucking right, she's not. She's worth a million of all the girls you've previously hooked up with."

A bitter laugh spills from his lips.

"You don't need to tell me that," he says confidently. "I knew it from the very first time I touched her."

"But you didn't know it was her," I point out.

"No, but I knew she was different. It made all kind of sense when I discovered who she was."

"You know, there might always be a small part of me that hates you for what you did that night."

"Then you're in good company. I never should ha—"

"I know," I assure him.

"I also wouldn't be here right now if I had any doubts about my feelings, about what I want. The last thing I want to do is hurt either of you. But... I'm also a selfish prick, and I need to be here too. I need to be a part of this. I need more of last week."

"So does she," I confess.

"And you?" Wilder asks, forcing me to focus on what I want for once. "If we do this..." He waves his arm around, silently gesturing to each of us. "This relationship, then people are going to talk. Without sounding like an arrogant dick, people know who I am. They'll soon discover what we're doing and—"

"Does that bother you?" I ask, aware that he's the one who'll be truly under the spotlight with this.

Sure, the media who follow the Titans around will be interested in me, but their focus will be Wilder and Noelle.

My stomach knots for her. She'll hate it.

Noelle and I have been there through every win and loss of Wilder's football career so far, but we've always done it from a distance.

At school, neither of us wanted to be a part of that crowd. So we let Wilder do his thing with his team and his friends, and then we celebrated or commiserated at home, away from all that.

If we embark on this, there will be no distance with our support. We're going to be dragged right into the middle of Wilder's life.

Will Noelle cope with that?

"Not if I have her."

All the air comes rushing from my lungs.

Shit. He really wants this.

"And what about the jersey chasers, the parties?"

"What about them?" he snaps as if he's offended by the question.

"I just mean, that life is still going to be there. The girls… they'll still want you."

He smirks.

"Oh, wipe that smug look from your face," I mutter.

"They can want me all they like. They're not going to have me. If I wanted them, I could have had them this week. It's not like they haven't been trying."

"Have you? Slept with any of them this week?"

"Is that a serious question?" he asks, his lips pursed in frustration.

"What? I know you, Wilder. I know what you're like."

"No," he states. "I haven't slept with any of them. I don't want to. The only girl I want is sleeping in the living room."

"You could have had her. Why haven't you?"

"Because I knew that if I did, and then you both told me that we were done, it would wreck me.

"Look, just fucking look at me. This week… it's been fucking hell.

"How the fuck we won that game, fuck only knows. I

wasn't focused. My head was still back in that cabin with you. She's the only thing I've been able to think about.

"I want her. I need her. I fucking love her."

Soft footsteps follow his passionate confession, and we both turn to the doorway to find the girl in question walking toward us.

She's only just woken up, that much is obvious, but the smile on her face takes my breath away.

She studies Wilder for a beat before turning her eyes on me.

"The entire college is going to have an opinion about this, let alone the entire football conference."

"Does that put you off?" Wilder asks.

"Does it you?" she shoots back.

"Fuck no. People will always talk. Might as well give them something to talk about."

"Okay," Noelle agrees. "Rix?"

"I think you already know that I want whatever is going to make you happy."

Noelle smiles. "I do. But this affects you as well. If you don't agree, then—" I take a step forward and wrap my arms around her waist, ducking my head low so my lips brush hers.

"I agree. Nothing about our lives has been normal; why start now?"

Her breath catches when I roughly tug on her hair, pulling her head back exactly where I want it so I can crash my lips on hers.

I kiss her passionately, knowing that Wilder is watching, knowing that he wants her too.

"Go and get dressed," I demand once I release her.

"Why?" she breathes.

"We're going for breakfast. We've got a lot to talk about."

"U-uh... okay."

She takes a step back, ready to do as she's told, but Wilder calls her name, making her pause.

"Come here," he demands, and like the good girl she is, she walks straight over to him.

Spreading his thighs wider, she steps between them with ease.

His hands land on her thighs, and he slowly slides them up, taking my hoodie with him at the same time until he's revealed her bare ass.

Damn, it's fine.

"You like that, Bro?" Wilder asks, aware that I'm watching.

"You know I do."

"Me too," he agrees before spanking one of her ass cheeks and making her squeal as his handprint blooms on her pale skin.

"Make sure you eat plenty, little rebel. Hendrix and I have plans for you later."

"Oh god," she breathes as her knees buckle. If Wilder weren't holding her, I'm pretty sure she would have stacked it.

"That's what you want, isn't it? Both of us at the same time."

Her lips are parted and her chest is heaving as she nods.

"Dirty girl," he muses before moving one hand from her ass.

He kicks her legs apart and drags his fingers through her folds.

"Wilder," she gasps.

"She's so fucking wet for us, Bro," Wilder informs me before lifting his fingers to his lips and sucking them clean. "Damn, I've missed you, Rebel."

40

NOELLE

I squirm in my seat, desperate to get home and find out exactly what Hendrix and Wilder have planned for me.

This whole thing is insane. I get that. But also, it feels so right.

Hendrix hasn't totally forgiven Wilder for the things he said the other day; I can see that clearly every time he looks at his brother.

I haven't either, but I'm softening fast.

Hearing Wilder confess his growing feelings for me sure helps.

He's never come anywhere close to falling for a girl before. So hearing him saying that he's falling for me... Well, it's a heady feeling.

"You okay, Rebel?" Wilder asks, watching me with an amused smirk playing on his lips.

"Perfect," I force through gritted teeth.

Reaching out, he tucks a lock of loose hair behind my ear. The second his finger touches my skin, I visibly shudder.

"You really kept this side of you hidden before, didn't you?"

"It's your fault. You unlocked it."

"That's something I'm more than willing to take the blame for."

"Don't sit there and act innocent when we know the reason you chose to wear that skirt."

I lift my hand over my chest in faux innocence. "I've no idea what you're talking about."

"Is that right?" Wilder deadpans before commanding Hendrix into action.

We're sitting in a diner we found on the outskirts of town.

It's rare to find students here like the ones closer to home. It's what we needed today.

We may have agreed to embark on this thing that's building between us, but we're not ready to let the world know yet. We have a lot of things to figure out before others make their opinions known.

Sure, there will be a few people in here who know Wilder. He's a Titan; he's practically a celebrity around here. But we're granted some kind of anonymity. Clearly, Wilder thinks it's enough that we're able to start playing games.

"Hendrix," I warn, although it's light at best.

I knew what I was doing when I chose this skirt and 'accidentally' forgot to put my underwear on.

Maybe Wilder had a point the other day. I am just like the jersey chasers.

Easy and desperate for his touch.

For their touch.

I flinch when Hendrix's hot hand lands on my thigh and begins to slide up.

You knew you were playing with fire...

I just couldn't help myself.

They've unlocked a side of me that I never want to hide again.

It's too much fun. Too pleasurable.

"Hendrix," I gasp, my hand wrapping around his wrist as he gets higher.

"Spread those thighs for us, Rebel."

"We're in a busy diner."

"Exactly. It's busy. No one will notice."

I've never done anything like this before.

It's... it's wild.

Wilder reaches over and threads his fingers through mine, lifting them to his mouth and nipping my fingertips. Each bite of pain sends a bolt of pleasure straight through me.

My clit pounds, and any second, Hendrix is going to discover just how much I'm enjoying this little bit of exhibitionism we're embarking on.

Having one of them watch me with the other is one thing, but taking it out in public... holy hell am I turned on right now.

"Wider," Hendrix demands, his fingers dangerously close.

The situation alone already has me riding on a knife's edge. I can only imagine what'll happen when he touches me.

Shamelessly, I expose myself to anyone in the diner who cares to look, and not a second later, Hendrix's fingers are right there.

"Oh shit," I gasp, my grip on his wrist tightening, my nails digging into his skin.

"Quiet, Rebel. Unless you want everyone watching you?"

As tempting as that might be, I slam my lips closer and

bite down on the inside of them as Hendrix begins rubbing circles around my clit.

"Fuck, you look so hot right now."

"She's dripping, Bro."

"I know. I can smell it." Wilder can't see, but that doesn't stop his eyes drilling into the table as if he's hoping it'll become transparent. "Love watching you come, little rebel."

"It's a real shame she's not going to then, isn't it?" Hendrix mutters.

"What?" I gasp.

He leans closer, letting his lips ghost along my jaw, all the way to my ear.

"You're not coming until we get you home, Noelle. Until we can both get our hands on you."

His fingers slip lower and my hips lift as he pushes them inside me.

A cry almost slips from my lips just as our server returns with our check.

Oh, holy fuck.

Hendrix stills as she thanks us and wishes us a good rest of the day.

Wilder pulls his wallet out and places enough bills on the table to cover our food and the tip.

"I'm going to kill you," I seethe, desperately trying not to ride Hendrix's fingers.

"No, you won't," Wilder announces confidently. "You need us too much. Rix, clean up. We're heading out."

Pushing from the booth we're seated in, Wilder makes no attempt to hide the fact he's rearranging his boner before holding his hand out for me.

"Rix, you're driving home. I think Noelle and I will take the backseat."

"Fuck off," Hendrix barks from behind us. "She's sitting in the passenger seat."

"I think she'd prefer my idea of laying her out and eating her all the way home."

Every muscle south of my waist clenches with excitement.

"She's not coming until we get back," he says louder this time, seeing as we've made it to the parking lot.

"Did I say I was going to let her come?"

"Do I get a say in this?" I ask curiously.

"Nah, because then you'd choose one of us to ride in the back all the way home, and that'll result in someone being left out."

"And you getting to eat her all the way home doesn't result in that?" Hendrix deadpans.

He pulls his keys from his pocket as we approach his car, and I quickly reach out and snatch them from him.

"I'm driving. You two drive like grannies anyway."

"What?" Rix gasps.

"Oh burn, Bro," Wilder laughs before shouting, "Shotgun."

"Oh no, you won't be able to keep your hands to yourself and we'll all die."

"Nope. No one is dying today," he states before pulling the passenger door open and dropping into the seat before Hendrix gets a chance.

"Asshole," he mutters, joining us.

"What? You had easy access all the way home from Canada. Not my fault you let it pass you by."

"You were being a miserable fuck," Hendrix points out.

"Didn't have to stop you though, did it?"

"Will you two quit?" I ask, attempting to sound exasperated. But honestly, I'm just relieved they've put the other day behind them and are back to their usual annoying banter.

"Holy shit," Wilder laughs as I floor the gas and almost wheelspin out of the parking lot. "Our girl is horny."

Our girl.

Fuck. That sounds good.

I get us home in record time and no sooner have I pulled up on our driveway than I kill the engine and run for the house.

Do I look desperate? Yes.

Do I care? Not a chance.

They've done this. All morning they've been building me up and then leaving me hanging.

Sure, I'm just as guilty. The skirt was a dirty move. But I'm willing to give as good as I get here. Pun most certainly intended.

I leave them in my dust as I rush into the house, abandon my purse on the sideboard, and come to a stop in the kitchen, in front of the counter where I bend over

Shameless. Little. Whore.

My already short pleated skirt rides up and a cool rush of air teases my aching pussy.

Then I wait.

They're both as desperate as I am, so I know they won't be long.

"Oh fuck, would you look at that?" Wilder barks the second they step into the room.

"I'm suddenly ravenous," Hendrix adds.

They move closer and my heart rate picks up.

Sticking my ass out even more, I look back over my shoulder.

And what a sight it is.

The Kemp twins look delectable. And their entire focus is on me.

I could get used to this. Although, I hope I never do.

My skin tingles, my blood boiling as they close in on me.

Wilder reaches out and flips my skirt over my ass, fully exposing me to them before his palm collides.

"I think you look better with my print across your ass. Let everyone know who you belong to."

"Then you need two."

I howl as Hendrix spanks me too, leaving my ass burning.

"Pretty," Wilder muses before dragging his fingers through my folds. "You love belonging to us, don't you, little rebel?"

"Yes. Please. Please," I whimper.

His large hand presses between my shoulder blades and my arms give out, forcing me to fall onto the countertop. Wrapping the length of my hair around his fist, he turns me to look at him before pushing the two fingers he just dragged through my pussy into my mouth.

I moan as my taste explodes on my tongue.

"Good girl," he muses as a thud hits my ears a beat before Hendrix's hot breath covers my core.

Oh god.

His hands grip the back of my thighs, and he spreads my legs.

"You want Hendrix's mouth on you?" he asks.

"Yes, yes, please. Oh GOOOOOD," I scream when Hendrix latches onto my clit and sucks hard.

I thrash against the counter as Wilder drags my sweater from my body and throws it over his shoulder.

"Look at you, Rebel," he muses as he unhooks my bra.

"Just think how hot you'll look laid out up here with your legs spread for us."

I whimper as Hendrix tongues me, my release surging forward already.

"Rix," Wilder barks, commanding him with nothing more than his nickname.

"No," I cry when Hendrix sits back.

Wilder's hands circle my waist and he lifts my feet from the floor and flips me onto my back.

My legs fall open as Wilder pulls my bra from my arms.

I lie there with only my skirt around my waist, loving everything about my life.

Without any words or plans, both of them move to my feet. Their lips collide with my skin and they kiss down my ankle, my calf, and then up my thighs until there's no longer space for both of them.

Hendrix holds still, his hand sliding up my stomach to pinch my nipple as Wilder lowers to my pussy.

My back arches as he licks me teasingly.

He builds me up until my release is right there, and then he pulls back.

The smirk on his glistening face is pure evil, but I don't get a chance to chastise him before Hendrix takes over again.

"Oh my god," I cry, both loving and hating the change of pressure and speed.

They continue alternating until I'm sweating and trembling with my need for release.

"You said when we got home that I could come," I whine.

"We didn't say right away," Wilder mocks.

"Please," I beg, tugging on Hendrix's hair in the hope he'll take pity on me.

"Not yet," he says, pulling back with a smirk that rivals Wilder's.

"Nothing has ever tasted better in this kitchen," Hendrix confesses as he stands, grabs my hands, and pulls me so I'm sitting.

"What are you saying about my cooking?" I quip.

"Nothing. You just taste better. See," he says before slamming his lips on mine.

As he kisses me, he slides me from the counter.

Wrapping my arms and legs around his body, I allow him to carry me out of the room.

"Where's Wilder?" I ask, breaking our kiss.

"Don't worry, he won't be leaving anytime soon," he assures me as we begin climbing the stairs.

Yes. Take me to a bed.

As we step into my bedroom, I discover he was right. Wilder hasn't gone anywhere. Instead, he's just been getting ready.

He's standing in only a pair of pointless boxers, watching as Hendrix places me on my feet at the end of the bed.

"Does your previous request still stand?" Hendrix asks, forcing my eyes back to him.

"Y-yes."

Something hits the bed, and when I look over, I find a bottle of lube ready for us.

My stomach knots with a mixture of excitement and anticipation.

It never even occurred to me that we might not have been prepared last time I made this request.

Wilder was right to hold back that night.

"Then I'm going to need to be naked," Hendrix says, dragging my attention back.

He holds his arms out, allowing me to indulge.

Eagerly, I push his shirt up his torso, grateful for his help when he pulls it over his head. Wilder steps up behind me and unzips my skirt, letting it fall to the floor before his hands slip around my sides, cupping my breasts.

But as good as that feels, I need more.

Dropping my hands to Hendrix's waistband, I make quick work of undoing them and dragging his jeans and boxers down his thighs.

His cock springs free, and I can't help myself—I lean forward and suck him into my mouth.

"Jesus, Noelle," he barks as his hips punch forward.

But as much as he might enjoy me sucking him off, apparently now isn't the time, because after kicking off his clothes, I'm pulled up and then the two of us fall onto the bed, leaving Wilder standing at our feet.

"Put me inside you," Hendrix demands as I crawl up his body.

Not needing any more encouragement, I reach for him and then sink down on his dick.

Both of our groans fill the room as he stretches me open.

"Fuck," Wilder grunts, and when I look back, he's lost his boxers and is stroking his cock.

"Get over here," I demand, holding my hand out for him.

"Are you sure?" he asks as he crawls onto the bed.

"So sure."

"I'll take it slow. And if you need me to stop—"

"I won't," I assure him. I want this. I want this so badly.

Excitement shoots through me when he flips the lid of the lube open.

He shuffles closer, the heat of his body burning down my back before his cool fingers press against my ass.

His free hand snakes around my body, cupping my

breasts and pinching my nipples as Hendrix slowly fucks me.

"So good," I moan as Wilder's finger pushes just inside me.

"Shit, she just gushed," Hendrix informs him.

"Dirty girl," Wilder rasps, letting his breath race over my neck.

My skin erupts in goosebumps as he pushes a little deeper.

"Kiss me," he demands.

Twisting around, I find his lips as I continue to grind on Hendrix's dick.

This is everything.

Every-fucking-thing.

While Wilder teases one of my breasts, Hendrix reaches for the other, both of them building me higher and higher.

"Not yet," Wilder commands.

"Yes, please," I beg.

"I thought you wanted both of us," Hendrix rasps through gritted teeth.

"I do. I do," I pant. "Wilder?"

"I want to make sure you're ready."

"Please. I need you."

Releasing my breast, Wilder presses a hand between my shoulder blades and gently pushes me forward onto Hendrix's chest.

"Hey," Hendrix whispers before taking my lips as Wilder pushes his fingers deeper.

It's an alien feeling. It's intense in a way I've never felt before, but I want more. I need it.

Pushing my hips back, I take both Hendrix's dick and Wilder's fingers deeper.

"Greedy girl wants both of our dicks."

"Give it to her," Hendrix demands, breaking our kiss.

I cry out when Wilder pulls his fingers from me, and I can't help but look over my shoulder, searching for him as my muscles continue to clench around nothing.

I watch as he rips open a condom packet and smears himself with lube.

"I'll get tested," he tells me when our eyes collide. "I don't want anything between us. But I won't ever put you at risk like that."

Thankfully, the sentiment behind his statement helps to squash the bitterness that bubbles up from him referencing his manwhoring ways.

I don't get a chance to say anything because he's right there, the head of his cock pressing against my entrance.

"Relax, Rebel, or this is going to hurt."

Hendrix's fingers twist in the hair at the nape of my neck and he kisses me as deeply as he can. Wilder's hands roam around my body, and with his increased breath in my ear, I manage to relax a little.

"That's it. We're going to make you feel so good, Rebel," he tells me as he pushes inside. "Fuck, you're so tight," he groans as if he's in pain.

He's not wrong. It is tight, painfully so. But I refuse to back down now because of a little pain. I need them both too badly.

"More," I groan into Hendrix's kiss.

"Damn, Noelle. You're ruining me for anyone else," Wilder barks.

"Good. You're mine. Both of you. You're all mine."

41

WILDER

"Fuuuuck," I groan as Noelle ripples around me.

She's so fucking tight, it's insane.

Gritting my teeth, I keep the steady pace of my hips, hoping that I can stave off my release long enough to get her and Rix there too.

"I can feel you," Rix says through gritted teeth.

"Same," I force out.

"Oh god," Noelle gasps, her body trembling.

"We're going to make you come for us, Rebel. You're going to come over both our dicks."

She nods, unable to form words as she takes us both.

Sliding my hand down her stomach, I find her clit.

She cries out, her hips bucking against us, forcing us deeper.

"Not gonna last," Hendrix grunts.

"She's close," I tell him.

Wrapping her hair around my free hand, I drag her up.

"Wilder," she whimpers at the position change. Twisting her head around, I find her lips as Hendrix watches.

"Is this what you wanted, Rebel? Both of us stretching you open? Both of us fucking you?"

"Yes, yes," she breathes.

Hendrix reaches up for her tits as I pinch her clit, and with both of us buried inside her, she shatters.

It. Is. Fucking. Beautiful.

Both of our names fall from her lips as a plea, and I swear my heart explodes then and there as she drags me over the edge with her.

Hendrix goes too, and a few seconds later, the three of us fall limp in a mess of sweaty limbs in the middle of Noelle's bed.

Nothing but our heaving breaths can be heard as we come down from our highs

"That was—" Hendrix starts.

"Epic," I finish.

"Everything," Noelle says breathlessly.

"Everything you wanted?" Hendrix asks.

"And so much more. Thank you," she says, turning to kiss me. It's way too short for what I really want, but I can't argue when she turns to Hendrix. "I love you."

"So that's it, then? We're officially a throuple?" I ask.

Noelle bursts out laughing.

"That's an awful title. We're... us. No other title is needed."

"Fuck buddies?" I offer.

"Dude, that's even worse. And anyway, there are no buddies here. We're endgame, baby."

"Ugh, don't use football puns. They don't suit you."

"Speaking of football," Noelle pipes up. "The game is about to start."

My heart sinks like it has done every time I think about the playoffs.

We were so close. So fucking close.

Playing college football was always my dream, but making the playoffs in my first year was a fantasy. One I almost managed to achieve.

Clearly, it wasn't meant to be.

"It's okay. I don't need to watch."

"Wilder," Noelle sighs, curling into my side and sliding her hand up my stomach before resting it on my chest. "It's important to you, so it's important to us."

"Yeah, man. You need to watch because next year, you're going to be there. We all will be."

A little hope blooms inside me.

"Yeah," I say, a smile twitching at the corners of my mouth. "Next year."

"Come on," Noelle says, suddenly jumping up and off the bed. "You two got me all dirty. I suggest you clean me up." Before we get a chance to comment, she's gone, racing toward the bathroom.

"Well, what the fuck are we waiting for?" Hendrix asks, hopping up almost as quickly to give chase.

Throwing my legs off the edge of the bed, I stop and take a breath as Noelle's laughter fills the air.

This is not where I expected to begin the new year. The past two weeks have been... a surprise, but in the best possible way.

I've had time to stop and think. I've been able to have heart-to-heart with people who don't even consider judging. I've been vulnerable and open, and... I've fallen in love.

I mean, maybe I always have been; I've just been too busy teasing Hendrix about his crush on his best friend to notice that I wanted her too.

Whatever it was, it's over, because I want her in a way I've never wanted anyone.

She's given me so much more than I could ever attempt to explain, but most importantly, acceptance.

She accepts me for who I am, and in turn, she's teaching me to do the same.

I don't need to put on an act and behave in a certain way. I can be exactly who I am and still be a good person and a fantastic football player—maybe even a half-decent boyfriend, too.

Shit. I'm a boyfriend.

A laugh bubbles out of me.

I might be a boyfriend, but Noelle has two.

I shake my head. She is one brave woman.

A squeal of delight rips through the air, and I'm on my feet in a flash. I don't want to miss anything.

The bathroom is already full of steam when I get there, but it doesn't stop me from seeing her. I'm not sure anything ever will.

"I'm running to the store for beer," Hendrix says as I sit back in the couch, ESPN playing on the TV before me.

"It's a full day of football, and you don't have beer?" I gasp in horror.

"We only watch when you're playing. You know that."

"And it warms my heart to know that you are."

Hendrix rolls his eyes.

"Be good while I'm gone."

"Pfft, when am I ever good? You know I'm the naughty one. That's why Noelle likes me more."

"As if. She's always been more of a fan of the nice guy."

"Whatever. It took you eighteen years to fuck her."

He raises a brow. "Because you've been doing it for years?"

My mouth opens to bark back a response, but I don't have one.

"Well, we both figured it out in the end, I guess."

"We did," I agree. "Is everything okay?" I ask when he continues to linger.

"Yeah. It's just..." A frown appears between his brows, and for a moment, I think he's going to tell me that he's changed his mind. Thankfully, those aren't the words that come out of his mouth. "I know people will think it's weird, but... it just kinda feels right, doesn't it?"

"Most natural thing I've ever done. I always thought falling in love would be scary but... it's not."

He shrugs. "It's Noelle," he says as if it explains everything. Then without another word, he takes off, leaving us alone.

The temptation to go in search of her is strong, but I resist. She'll be down when she's ready.

Thankfully, the game starts and I lose myself in the first quarter.

There are only thirty seconds left on the clock when I finally hear her footsteps on the stairs. My eyes remain locked on the screen, needing to see if the Maddison Kings Panthers manage to hit the end zone before time runs out, but just as they make their last pass, Noelle appears in my peripheral vision.

Her steel and black outfit steals my attention, and when I finally look over, the full sight of her takes my breath away.

"That's... that's my number," I blurt like an idiot.

She smiles at me before looking down at her Titan jersey.

"Oh, is it?" she asks innocently before glancing back at me through her lashes. "I didn't realize."

"You're bad, Rebel. So freaking bad." Her smile grows.

I fucking love this mischievous side of her. Sure, I'd seen snippets of it in the past, but nothing like I am now.

"So, you think it suits me?"

"I think it looks a whole lot better on you than it does me."

She saunters closer. "Hendrix has gone to the store."

"So I heard," I murmur, my eyes dropping to her exposed legs.

I wonder if she has panties under there...

"We've got the house to ourselves."

"We do."

"And..." She glances back at the screen. "We've got two minutes without play What should we do?"

Scooting forward, I wrap my hands around her waist and pull her onto the couch with me. It's still made up as a little love nest from last night. Perfect.

"Shame it isn't halftime," she muses.

"Don't worry, Rebel. I can do a lot in two minutes."

"I'll believe it when I see it," she counters before I flip us, pinning both her wrists above her head, allowing her jersey to ride up enough to get the answer I needed.

"You seem to have forgotten something again," I muse as her legs wrap around my waist, dragging me closer.

"I haven't forgotten anything. You have, though, because you should be kissing me right now."

"My girl sure is demanding," I tease, nudging her nose with mine.

"Your girl," she breathes.

"Well, you are wearing my number. No other girl has ever been given permission."

"Oh, I'm special," she says, wiggling her hot little body against mine.

"Little rebel, you have no idea," I confess before diving for her lips.

I'm vaguely aware of the game starting again behind me, but I don't care. Not when I've got Noelle all to myself, and it seems she's wrapped in nothing but my number.

"Obsessed with you," I confess as I push her jersey up, revealing her tits. "Can't get enough."

"Same," she gasps as I suck her.

I'm not going to go all the way. She needs a rest after what we did earlier, but... I can't help myself. I need her. Always.

And this is the first time we've had this kind of time together. I want to make the most of all of it.

"You're mine now, Rebel. And I'm yours. I need you to know that. It doesn't matter what any jersey chaser says, or what rumors go around. The only girl I see is you. You got that?" I ask, lifting back up so I can look into her eyes. "I love you, Noelle."

Her breath catches at the honesty in my words.

"No one else compares to you. They never will. Promise me, no matter what happens, that you'll stick with me, that you'll fight for me."

She nods, her eyes filling with tears. "To the end," she agrees.

"Fuck." My chest tightens, stopping me from sucking the air in that I need.

"I love you too, Wild Child."

I miss all of the second quarter, halftime and almost all of the third quarter. By the time I look up at the screen, the Panthers are winning twenty-nine to three.

"You're the best kind of distraction," I muse as we get comfortable to actually watch some football.

"Sorry," Noelle laughs.

"Never apologize for that," I say, pulling her close. "I can't wait to have you cheering for me at my next game."

"I've been doing that for years," she points out.

"Yeah, but it's different now. I know you mean it."

"I've always meant it. I've only ever wanted the best for you."

"Well, now I've got it," I say kissing her head.

"We won't tell anyone that you've turned into a sap," a deep voice rumbles from the doorway, making Noelle jump.

"What happens in our house stays in our house."

"I thought that was the cabin," Noelle argues.

"It can be anywhere we do naughty stuff," I tease, lifting her jersey so Hendrix can see her bare ass.

"So that would be everywhere, then," he says absently.

"Oh, this is going to be fun," Noelle laughs.

After putting the beer away, Hendrix joins us on the couch for the last quarter.

"What have I missed?"

Noelle's eyes lock with mine before she begins giggling.

"Oh, it's been a really good game," I lie. Well, I don't entirely lie; the score says it's been a good game. We just... haven't seen it.

"Really?" Hendrix deadpans, his eyes dropping to Noelle's neck. "The hickies would suggest you weren't paying attention."

"I could see the screen when I gave her those. The others not so much."

"I told you to be good," Hendrix mock chastises.

"Oh, we were very good..." Noelle agrees. "Let me show you just how much..."

She rolls on top of him and drags his hands up her thighs.

"Good?" she asks, continuing to lift them higher.

"Better," he groans once he has two handfuls of her breasts. "Is there a game on?" he asks.

"No idea, Bro. No fucking idea."

42

NOELLE

We've been back at school for two weeks, and it's been pretty quiet in terms of gossip.

Wilder's teammates, or at least those he's close to, know what's going on. I mean, it was pretty obvious when he all but moved out of the team's house and in with us.

Then he invited Benny and a couple of others over for drinks to watch the semifinal playoff games.

It was a great night with the games streaming on two different screens so they could keep up with the action.

To begin with, I expected Wilder to keep his hands to himself. We hadn't discussed how we'd act with guests in the house, but from almost the moment they arrived, it became clear that nothing was different for him.

He continued touching and kissing me just as he would if the three of us were home alone, and Hendrix wasn't any different.

If Wilder's friends were confused by how our setup was working, then they certainly got a front-row seat to understand it.

They were awesome. Told us not to worry about anyone else and just to live our lives in a way that makes us happy. Having their support meant everything to Wilder, and in turn to me and Hendrix.

And it seems that the Titans are a tight-knit team who look after their own because, since that day, others have both waved and smiled at me from a distance. Others stop and talk when we pass in the hallways.

I feel like I've been welcomed into a whole new family. It's nice.

Speaking of family... Lori and Kian turned up at our front door—as expected—almost as soon as they touched down from their vacation.

While the guys hadn't filled their sister in on what was happening between us all, I had, and she turned up with the biggest smile on her face and huge hugs for everyone.

As our stand-in mom, she could see the difference in all of us. She knew we were happy and that the dynamic we'd found was working. That's all she wants. They stayed for two days before they had to return to Chicago for work. They had a fantastic vacation—as did we—but we've all agreed that next year, we're going to be together, whether it be at home or away. It was just too weird being separated.

Hitching my bag higher on my shoulder, I follow the stream of students out of the lecture we just attended.

Wilder has been with the team and Hendrix is in a meeting with his academic advisor.

My plan is to grab a coffee and make a start on the assignment I've just received.

I'm barely out of the door when I discover that plan has been shattered.

"Rebel," Wilder calls.

I search through the crowd in front of me to find him. It's not hard, seeing as he's taller and wider than most.

My eyes find his before dropping to the wide smile on his lips and then the very fitted long-sleeved Titans t-shirt he's wearing.

Warmth spreads through me.

He's mine. All freaking mine.

And it only gets better when I look back up, because he's not alone. Standing beside him is Hendrix.

Damn, it should be illegal for two people to look that good.

Suddenly, I'm very aware of the people around me, but mostly the comments of the girls.

"As if Wilder wasn't hot enough already, there are two of them."

"Hendrix is a little nerdy, but I'd totally go there."

Most of them, I agree with. My boys are hot as hell, but there's another comment that really steals my attention.

"Haven't you heard? They're taken."

"What? Both of them?" another girl asks, sounding disappointed.

"Yep. *By the same girl.*"

"No."

"Yep. She's fucking both of them."

Bitterness bubbles up. I'm not just fucking them. There is so much more to our relationship than that. But of course the jersey chasers of Trinity Royal only think with their vaginas when it comes to the football players.

"Yep. Fuck knows why she's so special, though."

"Her pussy probably isn't as loose as yours," the friend deadpans.

"There is nothing wrong with my pussy. Just ask the team; they'll tell you."

"My point exactly."

"Bitch," she laughs, playfully swatting her friend on the shoulder. "Seriously, though. Do you know who she is?"

"I've seen a photo online."

Online? My heart rate picks up.

I knew this was coming. Honestly, I'm amazed that I haven't been lynched by the jersey chasers already.

But despite knowing it was inevitable, I'm not ready to deal with the backlash of taking one of their favorite players off the market.

"She really isn't anything special. We're both hotter."

My brows shoot up. Modest and a bitch... well, okay then.

"I thought Wilder had better taste than that."

"Well, he did turn you down, Lacey."

Lacey...

My fists curl.

Okay, so it's not her fault that she was propositioning Wilder over Christmas. But it's enough to make me not like her.

"How was I to know she's cast some voodoo spell over him that meant he was only interested in sharing her with his brother?"

"I can't decide if that's hot or gross."

"Hot, definitely hot. But it won't last. She's too... average for Wilder. The other one, sure. But not our Wild."

Finally, the people in front of us disperse and I'm able to move away from the blonde with no panties and her bitchy little friend.

Looking up, I find my boys. My heart yearns to step up to them and claim them as mine publicly, but I'm scared—no, terrified—of what everyone will say. I agreed to this knowing that I was going to be on the receiving end of their jealously, but it seemed okay while I was safely locked inside our house. Now we're here out in the open, I'm not sure I'm ready or strong enough.

But while turning in the opposite direction and running

the hell away is an option, my legs take me to where I belong.

"Noelle, what's wrong?" Hendrix asks the second I'm close enough for him to read my expression.

"Rebel?" Wilder asks as both of them surround me. It's the first time we've been this blatant in public. But now they're with me, I don't second guess it. I can't. Not when I know they'll always protect me.

"Nothing. It's nothing."

Hendrix takes my hand in his warm one as Wilder's possessive side takes center stage. His fingers grip my chin and he forces me to look up at him. He studies me closely before guessing, "Someone said something."

"It was nothing. Just forget it."

His eyes narrow and his nostrils flare before he scans the people around us, looking for the culprit.

His attention locks on someone, and I can only imagine he's found her.

The rejected little jersey chaser who can't cope with being told no.

"You need to ignore them, little rebel. You're worth a million of them."

"It's no big deal. Let's just go," I say, attempting to take a step back, putting an end to our three-man show.

"Nah, I refuse to have anyone gossiping about our girl. If they want to talk, then they need to know all the facts.

"I love you, Noelle, and I want this entire campus to know about it."

Before I can say anything, his lips are on mine and his tongue is in my mouth.

I respond because I'm powerless to do anything else.

There's a part of me that expects Hendrix to step back, to slip into the shadows. It's what the old version of him would have done. But Wilder hasn't been the only one to learn a thing or two about himself recently, and Hendrix is well and truly finding his feet and his confidence. So really, I shouldn't be surprised when he steps up behind me, letting his strong, hard body warm mine. His hand wraps around my throat, and with his thumb and forefinger, he drags me away from Wilder and turns me to him.

"I love you too, and I'm not ashamed of anything."

I'm pretty sure the people around us react, but I'm too lost to my boys to hear any of it.

"If they're going to talk, you may as well give them something good to talk about," Wilder whispers in my ear. "Now, are you ready for your surprise?" he asks, reminding me that they were both meant to be busy.

"Uh..."

"We lied," Hendrix offers. "And now we're taking you out on a date while this lot discuss how fucking awesome your life is."

Both of them take my hands, and without looking back, we walk away with our heads held high.

Together. Just like we always will be.

EPILOGUE

Noelle

Nine months later...

I sit in the stands with Hendrix on one side and Lori and Kian on the other.

The noise from the rest of the Titans fans surrounding us makes the seat beneath me vibrate. I don't need to fuel my nerves. They're already out of control.

I've watched Wilder play a million times before. But I have never been this invested.

Thanks to him and his passion for the sport, I know everything about the Titan roster for this season. I know everyone's strengths and weaknesses. I know the players he thinks are going to make it to the NFL and the ones he doesn't think have it. I know how much he respects his coach, and how much he looks up to Benny and a couple of other teammates who have become close friends to me and Hendrix now as well as Wilder.

I'm no longer just here to support Wilder; I'm here for all of them. For the team, my extended family.

"Are you okay?" Lori asks, squeezing my hand as if that'll help.

"Yeah, of course. Why?"

"You look like you're about to vomit."

Honestly, I might.

I just need to see him. Everything will settle once he comes running out onto the field.

He knows where we're sitting, and something tells me that he'll be searching me out just as much as I do him.

He was disappointed with where they finished last year, so he's feeling the pressure already to ensure that they go all the way this season. And of course, they're starting the season going head-to-head with last year's national champions.

He has this idea that if they can beat them tonight, they've got a one-way ticket to the final next year.

I want it for him so much. I just wish I could do something to help, aside from being his number-one cheerleader.

"They've got this," she says confidently.

"I know," I choke out.

Hendrix reaches over and squeezes my knee. On the outside, he appears to be much calmer, but I know the truth. Beneath his cool facade, he's freaking out too.

I gaze out over purple-filled stands opposite us and try to imagine what it must have been like for them earlier in the year when their team lifted that trophy.

Goosebumps erupt and rush down my arms as I think about just how epic that must be. All those years of hard work, the sacrifices they've made for the game they love and to make it right to the end...

It's going to happen.

Wilder deserves so much good and happiness in his life.

All the bad shit is behind us now. From here on out, our lives are going to be full of laughter and light, and wins. All the freaking wins.

Suddenly, the crowd around us erupts when smoke begins to billow from the Titans' tunnel.

"Oh my god," I breathe as we jump to our feet to watch our boys appear.

Hendrix grabs one of my hands as Lori continues to grip the other, and the second he appears, I scream bloody murder for him.

And just as I predicted, the second he clears the smoke, his eyes lock on my position.

He lifts his hand to his mouth and blows me a kiss.

My heart shatters all over the floor right there and then.

I'm so lost in him that I don't realize that everyone is looking at me until Hendrix points at the jumbotron where a replay of that sweet moment is playing with little hearts on the screen.

My face burns beet red, and I turn to hide in Hendrix's chest.

"Oh no, he's going to want you watching," Hendrix says, pulling me back so I can focus on the field.

When I look back at Wilder, he's laughing.

No one else would be able to tell because he's wearing his helmet, but I know, and so does Hendrix.

"I've never seen him happier than he has been this year."

"I could say the same thing about you," I shoot right back.

"You're all happier than I've ever seen you," Lori says, using her proud mom voice. "You're all good for each other."

Unable to argue with them, I keep my mouth shut and

watch the coin toss. Both teams line up ready to begin, and my nerves quadruple.

"They've got this."

Benny claps Wilder on the shoulder and then everyone stops.

Please, please, please, I silently beg.

But then the ball is snapped and all my fear and nerves drift away as I watch Wilder do what he does best.

It feels like the entire stadium erupts when we get our first touchdown of the game in the third down.

"See," Hendrix says smugly once the volume has reduced. "I told you."

The game continues with the Titans dominating.

At no point do they lose their win, and by the time the final whistle blows, the previously excited sea of purple is looking a little dejected.

I guess it just goes to show that a winning streak never lasts. It's been a long time since their huge championship win. The roster has changed, and many of their senior players last year are now embarking on their rookie year in the NFL.

As the guys celebrate, Wilder looks up at us and rips his helmet off.

The smile and happiness on his face takes my breath away.

It takes every ounce of restraint I possess to keep my feet on the ground and not run to him. All I want to do is jump into his arms and tell him how proud I am.

We sit there long after the players have celebrated and disappeared into their locker room.

I'm still buzzing, and I know that Hendrix and Lori are too.

We're all going out for dinner before Lori and Kian need to fly back out.

We invited them to the team's party tonight, but unsurprisingly they've graciously declined.

Kian might be up for a laugh, but I'm not sure a college football party is really him. His younger brother Kieran would be, though. But then, he is just one of the guys. He'd probably love a throwback to an old-school college party now he's living it up in the NFL.

Once we're confident that Coach will let them out soon, we make our way out of the stadium and around to the locker room exit.

There's a small crowd gathered, many of the players' friends and families, but obviously there are more than a handful of jersey chasers hoping to get in on the celebrating early.

The wait is excruciating, and when the door finally opens, my heart jumps into my throat. But he's not there. Instead, Benny and a few others come running out.

Benny's eyes light up at the sight of someone waiting for him, and when I follow his line of sight, I find a blonde lady holding the cutest little girl.

She squeals and holds her hands out for him. He rushes over, takes her in his arms, and spins her around. The pair of them laugh like no one is watching. It's incredible. And when I look at the lady, she's got tears shining in her eyes.

"That's Benny's sister and niece," a familiar voice whispers in my ear.

My entire world freezes as my brain tries to catch up.

"Wilder," I squeal, spinning around and jumping into his arms.

"Hey, little rebel. Were you waiting for me?" he asks before finding my lips and kissing me as if we're not surrounded by people... and his big sister.

"I'm so proud of you," I whisper as he kisses along my jaw. "You were so awesome."

"I was, wasn't I?"

"Modest too," Hendrix says, clapping him on the shoulder.

Wilder releases me and embraces Lori. "Thank you for coming."

"You know we wouldn't have missed it for the world. Are you hungry?"

The two of them share a look. We all know that Wilder is ravenous after a game.

"Yeah," he says nonchalantly, "I could eat."

"I've found a place that does wings just a few blocks away. Sound good?"

"Sounds good," Wilder says, holding his hand out for Kian.

"Great game. Kieran said to tell you that you smashed it."

Wilder preens at the praise. Kieran tried to get here for Wilder's first game of the season, but he couldn't make it happen. He promised to watch, though, which made Wilder's day.

Together, the five of us head toward our cars and then the restaurant Kian has found with matching smiles on our faces.

"Come and dance with me," Wilder slurs when he finds me hanging out with some of his teammates' girlfriends on the couches in the living room.

The guys have been playing some kind of drinking game in the kitchen, and we decided it was something we didn't need to witness.

The party is raging around us, but despite having been

to a couple of team parties now, I still don't feel entirely comfortable.

I'm just not a party girl. Although, I'll do anything for my boys.

"Aw, you're not going to deny that face, are you?" one of the girls asks with a laugh.

Wilder puts on his best puppy dog face and holds his hand out for me.

Unable to do anything but comply with his demands, I slide my palm against his.

"Good girl," he whispers in my ear once I'm on my feet.

"If you'd have lost tonight, you might have received a different response," I tease. We both know it's a lie. I can't deny my men anything.

He tugs me through the room, out into the hallway and then to what should be the dining room. But seeing as this is a full of college football players, it's actually the party room with speakers permanently set up and a makeshift dance floor.

The people who are already here seem to part for us. I guess I shouldn't be surprised; Wilder is a god tonight.

"Now that's more like it," Wilder muses as he pulls me into his hard body. "Missed you, Rebel."

"I haven't been anywhere," I point out.

"I love having you watch me play," he confesses, his lips dropping to my neck.

A shiver of desire races down my spine, zeroing in on my clit.

The song filling the air around us fades to nothing as we move together, his hips locked against mine as his hands and lips roam.

As per his demand, I'm still wearing his jersey. He told me that the only person who's allowed to take it off me tonight is him, and I'm more than happy to comply.

His lips find mine as his hands grasp my ass, hitching his jersey higher.

For the game, I wore pants and sneakers, but for the party, I've gone a little... wild.

His kiss is frantic, almost violent, and I match him move for more.

I'm so proud of him.

"Can't get enough of you," he confesses into our kiss. "You're my everything."

As our kiss and our touch become more and more indecent, my body temperature spikes. It can only mean one thing.

Glancing over my shoulder, I find Hendrix leaning against the door frame, watching us with heated eyes.

Oh god.

Over the past few months, the three of us have found a good rhythm, and the guys are getting pretty good at sharing.

Most nights, the three of us end up crashing in my room. We upgraded the bed early in the new year, so there's space for all of us to sleep comfortably. But every now and then, I'll spend a night with each of them alone. Being together as a group is fun, but there is something so intimate and special about being one-on-one with them.

"I think we should take this upstairs, don't you, Rebel?"

"But it's your party," I argue, albeit lightly.

"Trust me, the only place I really want to celebrate is upstairs with you."

He sucks on the sweet spot beneath my ear and I cave, obviously.

"Okay. Take me to bed, Wilder Kemp."

"Fuck. I want to hear you say that every day."

I gasp as he picks me up and wraps my legs around his waist.

"Then you'd better keep winning."

"I fully intend to, don't worry."

He walks us through the crowd before slowing at the door.

Hendrix is still watching us, and I expect him to follow as we move past him, but to my surprise, he stops us.

"You've got thirty minutes," he states. "Make the most of her before I come and take my share."

"B-but I won," Wilder pouts. He doesn't mean it. Both of them love our little group activities as much as I do.

"You're wasting your time, hotshot," Hendrix mocks, looking at his watch. "If I were you, I wouldn't be standing here arguing."

"Good point," he mutters, taking off again. He runs us up the stairs and in only seconds, we're in his room.

The door slams behind us and my back crashes against it.

Wilder is... well... wild. His hands frantically roam over my body, pinching and squeezing in all the right places as he kisses me into a frenzy.

In only minutes, I'm panting and grinding myself against him, desperate for more. And just when I think the friction from his jean-covered erection will be enough, he takes a step back.

"Take your panties off," he demands as he drags his shirt over his head.

My eyes drop to his body. He's worked harder than ever in preparation for this season, and it shows.

"But leave the shoes and the jersey," he adds.

Tucking my thumbs into the sides of my panties, I shimmy them down my legs before kicking them off.

I don't mean to send them flying, but Wilder catches them with ease and lifts them to his face.

"Now get on your knees and crawl to me. Then I want to watch you suck my dick."

Oh, he is on fire tonight.

With my blood flowing through my veins like lava, I drop to the floor and do as I'm told.

He watches my every move. His jaw ticks and his chest heaves with desire, and his pants... well they're barely containing his excitement.

My mouth waters to get closer and discover just how much he needs me.

"Good girl," he praises when I'm in front of him. "Now get him out."

Without missing a beat, I rip his jeans open and drag both them and his boxers down his legs.

His cock glistens with precum as it bounces free. But Wilder isn't messing about, and he takes himself in hand, threads his fingers through my hair, and drags me forward.

I moan as he pushes past my lips, filling my mouth.

"Arch your back," he demands, making me frown.

Looking up, I don't find him staring down at me like I was expecting. Instead, his eyes are locked on something behind me.

Curious, I pull my head back and turn to look.

Knowing what I'm going to find, he allows the movement, and I gasp when I discover what has him so enthralled.

There's a mirror. And it's giving him an uncompromised view of everything.

Jesus.

"Fucking hot, right? Now I can see how wet your pussy gets when you're sucking me." I stare at our reflection, oddly enthralled by the sight.

"Don't worry, I've got one for home, too," he tells me

before turning me back around and pushing inside me again. "I know how badly you want to watch us fuck you."

A moan rumbles deep in my throat at the thought.

"Our dirty girl," Wilder mutters, his thumb caressing my cheek.

With my eyes locked on his, I suck him as deep as I can.

His lips pop open and a groan spills. It fires me up, knowing that I'm pleasing him.

I work with fervor, wanting to drive him right to the edge, but just as his dick begins to thicken in my mouth, he pulls me back.

"Not tonight, Rebel. I have plans for how this ends, and it's not in your mouth."

Effortlessly, he lifts me onto the bed and then drags me on my hands and knees right to the edge.

"You look hot as fuck," he tells me as he pushes my jersey up to my shoulders, exposing my ass and back to him.

"Wilder," I squeal when he spanks me.

"Mine," he growls possessively.

"Yours. Always yours."

With his hand locked around my hip, he drags his cock through my folds.

"So wet for me," he muses before pushing the head inside.

My muscles clench, desperate to drag him deeper.

"Best celebration ever," he announces before sinking balls deep inside me. "Yes, Rebel."

He fucks me hard and fast, using up some of the adrenaline that's still pumping around his body.

"Wilder," I cry as he hits me so deep over and over.

"Mine," he barks again before twisting his hand in my jersey and pulling me from the bed.

My back presses against his front as his hips continue to move.

His hands slide up my stomach to cup my breasts.

"I love you, Noelle."

"I love you, too," I gasp as he pinches both of my nipples before dropping one hand to my clit. "Oh god."

"I'm not coming until you do, Rebel. And I want it loud enough for Hendrix to hear."

"Yes, yes, yes," I chant as he works me, my release building.

"Do you want us both tonight, Rebel?"

"You know I do," I whimper.

"Good girl. But you're mine right now. All fucking mine," he rasps in my ear. With one hand on my clit, the other lifts to my throat, and he squeezes with just the right amount of pressure that I shatter.

I'm just coming down from my high when he groans and his dick jerks inside me.

"Fuck, Noelle. Fuuuuck."

No sooner has he finished than the bedroom door slams closed.

"Looks like I'm just in time," Hendrix says.

I don't need to turn around to know he's smirking; I can hear it in his voice.

"Well, what are you waiting for? She's ready for you."

Wilder lifts my jersey higher, exposing my tits to Hendrix, who eagerly crawls onto the bed.

He's already lost his shirt and opened his pants. This boy is ready for some action.

"So she is," he muses before his lips find mine and his hands land on my body.

I love being with them individually, it makes me feel closer to them each time, but nothing beats us being together.

Nothing.

Want more from Noelle, Wilder and Hendrix? Grab your
copy of their extended epilogue now!
DOWNLOAD YOUR COPY HERE
https://dl.bookfunnel.com/5se3q9vn9j

Not read Kian and Lori's story? Grab a copy of their book,
By His Rule now!

Want to be the first to know about my books in progress?
You can join my Patreon for sneak peeks, special edition
paperbacks, and more!
SUBSCRIBE NOW
https://www.patreon.com/tracylorraine

<u>Play You</u> #4

<u>Inked</u> (A Rebel Ink/Driven Crossover)

<u>Rosewood High Series</u>

<u>Thorn</u> #1

<u>Paine</u> #2

<u>Savage</u> #3

<u>Fierce</u> #4

<u>Hunter</u> #5

Faze (#6 Prequel)

<u>Fury</u> #6

<u>Legend</u> #7

<u>Maddison Kings University Series</u>

<u>TMYM: Prequel</u>

<u>TRYS</u> #1

<u>TDYW</u> #2

<u>TBYS</u> #3

<u>TVYC</u> #4

<u>TDYD</u> #5

<u>TDYR</u> #6

<u>TRYD</u> #7

<u>Knight's Ridge Empire Series</u>

<u>Wicked Summer Knight</u>: Prequel (Stella & Seb)

<u>Wicked Knight</u> #1 (Stella & Seb)

<u>Wicked Princess</u> #2 (Stella & Seb)

<u>Wicked Empire</u> #3 (Stella & Seb)

Harrow Creek Hawks Series

Lawless #3

Fearless #4

Callahan Billionaires

By His Vow #1

<u>Never Forget Series</u>

<u>Never Forget Him</u> #1

<u>Never Forget Us</u> #2

<u>Everywhere & Nowhere</u> #3

<u>Chasing Series</u>

<u>Chasing Logan</u>

ABOUT THE AUTHOR

Tracy Lorraine is a *USA Today* and *Wall Street Journal* bestselling new adult and contemporary romance author. Tracy has recently turned thirty and lives in a cute Cotswold village in England with her husband, baby girl and lovable but slightly crazy dog. Having always been a bookaholic with her head stuck in her Kindle, Tracy decided to try her hand at a story idea she dreamt up and hasn't looked back since.

Be the first to find out about new releases and offers. Sign up to my newsletter here.

If you want to know what I'm up to and see teasers and snippets of what I'm working on, then you need to be in my Facebook group. Join Tracy's Angels here.

Keep up to date with Tracy's books at
www.tracylorraine.com